A BREEZE ACROSS THE AEGEAN

A BREEZE
ACROSS
THE AEGEAN

ROBERT COLE

Matador
9 Priory Business Park,
Wistow Road, Kibworth Beauchamp,
Leicestershire LE8 0RX
Tel: 0116 279 2299
Email: books@troubador.co.uk
Web: www.troubador.co.uk/matador
Twitter: @matadorbooks

ISBN 978 1 83859 535 7

British Library Cataloguing in Publication Data.
A catalogue record for this book is available from the British Library.

Printed and bound in Great Britain by 4edge Limited
Typeset in 11pt Garamond by Troubador Publishing Ltd, Leicester, UK

Matador is an imprint of Troubador Publishing Ltd

To Jo, Carlaine, Angus, Guy, Wanda and Martin for your patience, advice and encouragement. Many thanks must also go to Belinda for your valuable editorial input.

And of course to Greece and your magical islands for providing such a rich canvas for this story.

Dodecanese Islands

Chapter One

RHODES

Nicholas felt cold, dispirited and alone. Perhaps a final drink in the hotel bar would help. He pushed open the frosted glass door to find Lindsey Buckingham singing "Go Your Own Way" to a cheerless, windowless room. Dimly lit, gilt uplighters did little to improve the atmosphere. Only two others sat in the gloom. Both looked like businessmen. One was slumped in a corner nursing an ouzo; the other tapped tiredly at a laptop.

He opted for a stool at the dark-wood bar with its polished brass countertop and untouched bowls of pistachio nuts. He ordered a large Metaxa, took a sip and thought over his day. Searching the home of a virtual stranger, however necessary, had felt intrusive and alien to him. What was the abandoned apartment trying to tell him? It had looked as though it had not been lived in for some time, but its occupant had clearly intended to return. He ran a weary hand over his face, brushing hair still damp from the evening drizzle from his eyes.

Distracted with his thoughts he didn't notice someone take the stool next to him. Hearing a woman's voice order a red wine in Greek from the barman gave him a start and he glanced at her. She took a couple of measured sips, then turned to him and said, in accented English: "You are Nicholas." It wasn't a question.

Recovering his surprise Nicholas studied her before answering. She was slightly older than his 37 years, dark-haired and dressed immaculately. There was a small birthmark high on her left cheek.

"Yes I am. I'm sorry, do I know you?"

"No, I am afraid you don't."

Was she trying to flirt with him? He wondered how to respond. He would be happy to have some brief company after his unsettling day – and she was attractive, if in a rather formal way. He was shocked out of that notion when her eyes narrowed and, lowering her voice, she said: "I want you to listen to me very carefully. You are getting yourself involved in things that do not concern you. Whatever it is you think you are doing you need to stop. And you need to stop now."

Nicholas felt anger rise. "Who the hell…?" She interrupted him with a raised hand.

"At the moment, Mr Adams, we will leave this as a warning. Go back home to your work and your life in England and nothing further will happen to you." She took a deliberate sip of her wine and, leaving a half-full glass, stood up and put on her coat. Smiling down at him she said quietly "You will not be given a further chance" and walked out of the bar.

Feeling shock, Nicholas stared unseeing at his brandy. He did not think to follow the woman. Her words, and their quiet menace, had stunned him. He had never been threatened before – such things didn't happen in his world. He looked up and tried to focus. Nothing in the bar had changed. The businessmen had not stirred and the barman was now engrossed in polishing glasses. For the first time, he wondered what he had got himself into. Coming back to Rhodes had seemed the right thing to do. He lingered for a time over his drink, trying to take it all in. Fleetwood Mac's "Rumours" played on in the background as he thought back to what had led him to this: the day he had met Alessandra.

—

It was a Friday in mid-October. There was a sweet-scented cooling breeze. It was not unwelcome, as it promised to be another warm day. A dog slumbered in the shade under an old red Fiat parked outside the taverna. Sitting beside the water in the tiny port of Skala Kamirou, Nicholas was savouring a strong black coffee. Fishing boats bobbed and scraped in the swell. The early morning sky was cloudless. A seagull eyed him expectantly from the low wall that enclosed the taverna. There was no sign of the ferry, but it was still early. For the first time, he felt a sense of expectation. He had been alone on this holiday for too long already and, to his surprise, he looked forward to being among people. Apart from enforced interactions with his work colleagues and keeping in touch with his parents, he had avoided social encounters for a long time.

Nicholas had come to Rhodes a week ago, as a last-minute decision. He shook his head in amusement at the very idea that he had acted on a whim. Planning was one of his strengths; spontaneity naturally made him uneasy. He had been to the island once before, many years ago, and lingering memories of sun on his face, rocky coves and welcoming locals had brought him back. He had needed to get away – not just from the autumnal grey of England, but also to escape from the pervasive thoughts that crowded in. He had felt out of sorts for too long.

He had rented a white-fronted villa set on a hillside among olive groves, overlooking the sleepy village of Pylona, just inland of Lindos, on the east coast of the island. Clad in purple and red bougainvillea, with a swimming pool to the rear, the villa was the perfect spot for a romantic getaway, but he was alone.

The name of the villa had intrigued him. Villa Cleobulus, according to the bookings website, was named after a local tyrant king of the sixth-century BC. Paradoxically he was also known as one of the Seven Sages of Greece, a contrast in attributes that had resonated with Nicholas. Rhodes, and the little village he had chosen to stay in, suited his present mood. With only villagers and watchful stray cats as neighbours, he was already feeling more relaxed. He needed time to think. He wanted to go home with at least the beginnings of an answer. He hoped this brief break away might allow him to move on.

As the sun climbed higher, he saw the ferry edge its way across from the headland and through the small harbour entrance. A bus emblazoned with "Aegean Tours" in blue lettering clattered along the dusty streets, then swept past through the square, where straw-coloured weeds lined the kerbside. It stopped below the granite cliff. Passengers emerged, blinking in the morning brightness before huddling on the dock, waiting for the arrival of the morning ferry to Halki. Nicholas looked at his watch. There was forty-five minutes before it was due to leave. The cicadas chorused the rising heat. A woman in a red skirt and white top with the badge of the tour operator flirted with the young ticket seller. Another coach arrived. The largely middle-aged and elderly passengers disembarked carefully.

Nicholas's coffee was long finished when the Nikos Express reversed slowly towards the harbour wall. The gangway was lowered, its rusted chains grinding, amid shouted instructions from the crew. He watched the ferry being loaded with boxes of canned goods, vegetables and large plastic water containers. A crane at the back was hoisting a palette of cement bags. As he looked out over the jetty at the gathering crowd he joined their shared anticipation of visiting a new place. He was happy to be with others. Back home he had become too accustomed to his own company. Now, he felt more positive, almost buoyant.

"Efharisto," Nicholas said with a smile and nod to the elderly grey-faced waiter. He was not a linguist and felt embarrassed by the limitations of his vocabulary. He paid and left the taverna.

By the time he had bought his day-return ticket all the seats downstairs in the cool of the air-conditioned cabin had been taken. He climbed the stairs to the upper level to find shade under a canvas awning, and squeezed in among the excited tourists. The forced jollity, loudly orchestrated by the animated tour leader, made him feel uncomfortable. His British reserve took over as his new optimism receded. Was this trip going to be a nightmare, rather than the pleasant diversion he had hoped for? He opened his guide to Rhodes and the Dodecanese and prepared to bury himself in the section on Halki, but his attention was drawn to the woman to his left. Dressed in a blue, tie-dyed T-shirt, white shorts and sandals, she was young, attractive and tanned. Her long dark hair and vivid blue nail varnish made her stand out. He watched as she rummaged through a shabby green canvas bag at her feet, pulling out a jumble of notebooks and maps, before she freed a bottle of water and took a drink.

The engines' vibration grew stronger, as the ferry headed out to sea. Tourists gathered around the railings to watch the receding harbour. A bulky, older woman, dressed in shapeless khaki trousers and an old greying top, not wanting to miss a photo opportunity, heaved herself awkwardly up from the slatted wooden seats. Clutching her rucksack and phone, she tottered across the deck. A sudden increase in the sea swell sent her staggering across the aisle and she dropped her bag. Nicholas's neighbour leapt up to take the woman's arm and steady her. "Are you all right?" she asked in English, as she guided the woman back to her seat, before retrieving the fallen bag. Once the woman had recovered, her rescuer said: "You sit quietly for a moment. Here let me take that photograph for you."

The woman nodded. "Danke. Thank you. You are very gracious." She sounded shaken.

As the ferry followed the mountainous west coast of Rhodes south, past the sixteenth-century Kritinia Castle overseeing the port, Nicholas turned to his neighbour, holding the water bottle that she had dropped in her haste to help the woman. "That was a really nice thing to do. Are you with any of these tour groups?"

Her eyes crinkled as she squinted into the sun. She regarded him for a moment, then replied: "No, I am actually living here at the moment. This is actually a day off from work. I didn't think it would be so busy today, though," she said, with a grimace. Thanking him for the water bottle she asked "And you?"

"I'm a visitor, I've come to Rhodes for a couple of week's break from work. And, to briefly escape the English weather" he added. "I thought I should visit some of the nearby islands while I'm here. Have you been to Halki before?"

She hesitated momentarily. "No … no I haven't. I have visited most of the islands around Rhodes, but not Halki. My name is Alessandra, by the way."

She spoke good English, but with an appealing hint of a continental accent, which he struggled to place. "It's good to meet you, Alessandra. Mine's Nicholas, Nicholas Adams."

A large barren island had appeared on the right. He searched for signs of habitation. He could just make out an outline of a ruined church or castle high on a hillside. There were no beaches, just a jumble of large grey rocks tumbling into the dark sea. As the ferry edged by, Nicholas saw what he took to be a goat, standing alone on a rock staring out over the water. Alessandra's attention had also been drawn to the island. She looked out over the arid and unwelcoming landscape, seemingly lost in thought.

At the back of the ferry a group of Dutch passengers proudly extracted from their bags sandwiches and fruit wrapped in paper serviettes, clearly the spoils of the hotel breakfast buffet. A gull wheeled noisily over their heads warning others to keep their distance.

Alessandra turned and smiled, focusing her attention back on Nicholas. He told her of his last-minute decision to get away from work and about the villa he had found near Lindos.

"Oh, I love Lindos. Those narrow whitewashed streets that run down from the Acropolis are so pretty, I always feel desperately sorry though for the donkeys that take tourists up to the Acropolis. That hill's so steep. I try to encourage visitors to walk. It's so much better for them – and for the poor donkeys as well. Do you know the Captain's Bar? It is one of my favourite places in Lindos. It's on the way up to the Acropolis. I go there a lot. It's meant to be the oldest building in the town. I love its courtyard – it's a perfect place to have a drink and unwind."

Alessandra's attention was directed entirely on him. Nicholas was not accustomed to such openness, but he found he was enjoying it. "No I don't, but when we get back I will make a point of visiting it. Are you coming back today or are you staying on Halki?"

"No, I am just going over for the day," she replied. "I am meeting an old friend. I'll be on the same return ferry as you, at five o'clock" she said, pointing to his blue ticket. "I work on Saturdays."

"I think we are more than half-way. See the mountainous island over there." She pointed ahead. "That's Halki."

Nicholas turned. Dominating the horizon was a hulking, grey landmass. It was his first sight of the island and there was a slightly ominous look to it. Its brooding outline was unlike any other Greek island he had seen. Nicholas felt a sudden shiver.

Chapter Two

HALKI

SEEING HIM GAZING OUT TOWARDS THE ISLAND AHEAD, Alessandra said: "Did you know that Halki was also known, many hundreds of years ago, as the land of the Titans."

He turned to her again and she said: "So, Mister Nicholas Adams, tell me a bit about yourself. Are you here in Rhodes on your own?"

"Yes I am. I was married but I have been on my own, by and large, for the past couple of years."

"Oh, I am sorry. It really wasn't meant to be a leading question. I didn't mean to pry" Alessandra said apologetically.

"No, you are not prying. I am slowly getting used to travelling on my own again." Nicholas replied.

"So, what do you do when you're not travelling?"

"Sadly, my work is not that fascinating ... but it does pay the bills. I work in marketing for a large pharmaceutical company. I joined them straight from university thirteen years ago and went through their graduate programme before eventually ending up in marketing. Since then I have moved around with the company a bit, spending some time in their Paris and Madrid offices. Sorry, this sounds very much like a CV.

"I've been in pretty much the same job for the past three years. I'm clearly in a rut," he laughed. "And I am increasingly feeling that the time is right for a change.

"And you... what brought you to live on Rhodes – apart from the very obvious attractions?"

"Actually, I was born on Rhodes. My father is Italian, although my mother is English."

So that accounted for her slight accent. And for the sun-drenched Mediterranean look about her.

Alessandra described her early life as a young girl growing up on a Greek island. It all sounded carefree and idyllic, with the freedoms associated with a bygone age.

"I then went to boarding school in England and on to uni in Bath. English and philosophy did not obviously qualify me for anything." She smiled broadly, showing even white teeth. "Even the post-grad work I did on Chaucer and the relevance of the Canterbury Tales in modern story writing didn't provide any particular direction."

"I think I can relate to that. I remember back to when I emerged from the protection of university life and then thinking...and now what?"

Nicholas asked Alessandra whether she would like something from the small bar on the upper deck.

"I'll just have a coffee, thanks." He bought two coffees in plastic cups and carried them back carefully. "Shit," he exclaimed, as the boat pitched and the hot liquid spilled over his hand. Alessandra giggled as elderly heads swiveled in his direction.

"I'm so sorry," he said handing Alessandra her coffee. She continued to beam as he wrung his hand, his embarrassment subsiding.

Alessandra sipped the hot liquid and picked up her story. She had kicked off her sandals. "So, then I moved up to London, as everyone seems to do. I travelled for a bit – to Thailand and Vietnam – and in between did various jobs. I worked as a PA, did some waitressing. I hated that. I worked as an administrator in a legal firm in the City and then this job came up.

"My parents had moved back to the UK six or seven years ago, but I had missed Rhodes. A friend suggested I apply to be a researcher with the Ministry of Culture here on the island."

Nicholas enjoyed listening to her talk. There was something of the free spirit about her. He found it rather disarming.

"A job had just become vacant at the museum in Rhodes town. Despite my background, I had always been interested in archaeology. Perhaps it was being brought up on Rhodes where you are surrounded by ancient history wherever you are. Looking back, I should probably have done archaeology rather than English.

"Anyway, somehow I managed to get the job. I think my complete enthusiasm for the opportunity must have made up for my lack of technical competence. That was last year, and I have been here ever since. I have learnt so much in this time."

Alessandra's warmth and her sheer exuberance was captivating. Her face was alight, her excitement obvious. Nicholas enjoyed watching the changes in her facial expression and her animated hand gestures as she took him through her immersion in the history of Rhodes. Nicholas didn't doubt that she had persuaded her interviewer to take her on. He suddenly felt more alive than he had done in a long time.

"That sounds wonderful. I am envious. Many congratulations for following your dreams." He raised his plastic coffee cup to her.

"That's kind of you. I've decided I'm going to start a course next year here at the university." She leant towards him. "I love the work I do. Even the more repetitive work, the documenting of each artifact that comes into the museum. I can really lose myself in some of the early history of Rhodes and the Eastern Mediterranean. There is something special about the whole area.

"It's very varied and I actually get to go out to some of the sites where excavation work is going on." Her face shone.

"Have you been to Ancient Kamiros?" she asked. "If you came from Lindos you would have passed the signs on the way this morning." Nicholas said that he had visited the ruins the last time he was on Rhodes but suspected he might not recognise it now.

His eyes followed her hand, as Alessandra brushed a strand of hair away from her face, drawing attention to her slightly upturned nose and the small scar high on her right cheek, near the corner of her eye. He wondered how she had acquired that.

"The site probably has changed a lot. A large amount of excavation has been done over the last few years. In fact, I've just finished doing some work there, documenting what we found from the most recent dig. We have all been really excited by a recent find of a marble head of what we now believe to be the god Hermes. It has just been put on display at the museum, which is where I am now working, back in the office."

Nicholas's attention wandered slightly as he tried to estimate her age. She was probably five or six years younger than him. Late twenties? Perhaps thirty? The landscape around them forgotten, they didn't notice that Halki was becoming ever closer as they chatted.

Alessandra told Nicholas that she had made good friends on Rhodes since her return. She already had a few close school friends from when she lived on the island before. When she wished to emphasis a point she placed her hand lightly on his arm. The touch felt good.

Nicholas talked about his interests. He had until fairly recently, played a lot of competitive tennis and cricket. Looking slightly sheepish, he admitted that he had also played bass guitar in an indie rock band at University. "We were not great, but we modeled ourselves on The Strokes. We thought that we sounded just like them, but of course we didn't. We played around the campus and had the occasional gig at local pubs in the area. It was fun but I have not played in many years."

Alessandra surveyed Nicholas critically and then said, smiling "Sorry, I am struggling to see it."

"Ah. I looked slightly different then – much more like your typical impoverished student."

He was an only child and Alessandra said she was too. They shared experiences that were familiar to them both. Nicholas also told her a bit about his parents, who were now retired and lived in the Hampshire village of Chawton – as a literature student, Alessandra knew this as a place of pilgrimage for Jane Austen devotees. Nicholas became aware of how much he had opened up to this fascinating woman. That had not happened in a long while.

Suddenly they noticed that the port on Halki was close.

Alessandra found that she was attracted to this tall, slightly awkward, Englishman. He was not normally her type but she found herself asking "Have you been to the museum on any of your trips to Rhodes town?"

"Not yet, I'm afraid."

"Well, if you are planning another trip into the town, why don't you come by? We are in the Old Town area just across from the main port. It's in the old Knights' Hospital, signposted as the Archaeological Museum.

"Come by and we can go for a drink or even have a bite to eat in the old Knights' Quarter – if you have the time. It is quite atmospheric in the evenings and I can show you some of the interesting areas."

Nicholas had been looking for a way to suggest they meet again. He tried not to sound too eager. Would she be there on Tuesday or Wednesday next week?

"I'll be there on both days. Just ask for Alessandra Bianchi at the desk when you come in."

"OK, I'll do that. It will be nice to see you again. But, of course, you'll be on the ferry home."

The ferry was pulling into the harbour and the first thing Nicholas noticed were the three windmills on the hillside to the left overlooking it. Alessandra pointed out the white, blue and yellow villas, all with their terracotta roofs, framing the crescent-shaped port.

"You find exactly the same Italianate-style houses surrounding the harbour when you come into the port on Symi."

The ferry turned slowly towards the land, revealing cliffs honeycombed with caves, set deep into the limestone around the water line. Some were barred with iron gratings that were concreted into the stone. Nicholas wondered what they might contain.

The small town of Emborio came fully into view, nestling below sunburnt foothills leading up to the craggy mountainous interior. Alessandra picked up her bag and packed away her water bottle. A snorkel fell from the bag and rolled across the aisle. Nicholas sprung up and retrieved it from under the seats opposite. "Thank you kind sir," she said laughing.

"Are you heading for a beach?"

"I thought I might do later. I've arranged to meet my friend at her place in the town. After that we will probably go for a drink. We've some catching up to do." Nicholas thought he could detect a slight anxiety in her voice. "I will see. And you?"

Nicholas hesitated as he consulted his guidebook. "I am here purely as a tourist for the day. I think I am going to explore the port area and then look around the town. I might go to Pondamos beach later – my guide book says it's the main beach and just over the hill. Presumably over there" he pointed.

"If I have time I might come by the beach. I have to resolve a few sensitive things with my friend. I might be in for a difficult day I'm afraid." A frown played fleetingly over her face.

"Will you be all right?"

"Oh, I will be fine. Thank you. If I don't make it to the beach, why don't we meet at the ice cream cafe in the port? It's highly recommended, according to my friend. It should be near where the ferry will dock. We could meet there at, say, four-thirty?"

The ferry made its way through crystal waters to the harbourside. Fish darted amid abandoned fishing pots and barnacled anchors marooned among the rocks. Suddenly everyone was getting to their feet, jostling on the gangways and stairs to reach the lower level. Nicholas helped Alessandra off the gangplank to the quay. She kissed his cheek, saying: "I have really enjoyed meeting you, Nicholas. Enjoy your day." She headed towards the narrow lanes between the stone and ochre-painted shops and houses. Before she turned the corner she called out: "See you later, Mr Adams," and waved.

Chapter Three

HALKI AND RHODES

As ALESSANDRA HEADED AWAY FROM THE PORT, SHE FELT lifted. The meeting to come would be difficult, but the encounter with Nicholas had left her feeling happier ... and more positive. She hadn't enjoyed talking to a man so much for a while and she was glad they had arranged to meet later. The split with her boyfriend, the impact of the breakup on those around her, coupled with her recent concerns about the behavior of her boss at the museum had left her feeling raw and untrusting.

She replayed her conversation with Nicholas, as she made for the narrow street where her friend lived. If she could still trust her instincts, there was a kindness and solidity about him. That she could somehow also sense a vulnerability only made him seem more attractive. There was something there and she wondered what that could be. She smiled to herself. She was looking forward to seeing him later. For now she needed to concentrate on what she had to do.

Alessandra knocked on the white door and, moments later, her friend opened it. "Come in," she said. The two embraced. "It is good to see you." Her friend seemed nervous.

Like all the traditional houses on the island the dark wooden beams made the house seem dark inside. Downstairs was a small living room, with a kitchen to the rear. To one side was a wooden staircase leading up to the next floor. Alessandra sat while her friend disappeared into the kitchen to make coffee. She looked around. Little had changed since the last time she had stayed there. The furnishings were simple and old fashioned, in keeping with the style of the cottage. The only concession to modern living, apart from the air conditioning, was the hi-fi system and the laptop and monitor sitting on a desk in the corner. The smell of percolating coffee started to permeate the room.

Alessandra was surprised at the sound of heavy footsteps coming down the stairs. She turned and was startled to see the last person she expected.

"Hello Alessandra," he said smiling. "It is good to see you."

"What are you doing here?" she gasped, half-standing. She momentarily felt dizzy with the shock and put out her hand to steady herself. Her friend came back into the room carrying a tray with three coffees. She smiled and handed Alessandra a cup. " No milk or sugar," she affirmed.

"What is he doing here?"

"I'm very sorry. He needed to see you. I'd told him you were coming over today."

"What I came over to discuss with you was between us, only" Alessandra replied. "No one else. You told me you could help to sort everything out with him. You knew I have no wish to see or speak to him," she said, nodding her head angrily in his direction.

"Don't be like that," he interrupted. "She is only trying to help us resolve our differences."

"I told you that I never wanted to see you again. I expected you to respect my wishes. We have nothing, nothing at all to

resolve. These were not just differences of opinion. Just leave …
please," she implored.

"I am afraid it is not going to work like that, Alessandra. You
know what I am looking for."

Alessandra turned, angrily, to her friend. "You knew I didn't
want to see this man again, ever. You also knew exactly why. You
said you knew how you could stop him trying to contact me.
That's why I came over to see you."

"I am so sorry," her friend repeated. "You need to just do what
he says. Please give him what he is looking for. He has promised
that if you do he will leave you alone. It's the only thing you can
do."

"You tricked me into coming here. Why have you done this?
I've known you most of my life. You're meant to be my friend."

"She is also my friend," he interrupted quietly.

"What!" exclaimed Alessandra. "What on earth do you mean
by that?" she looked from him to her friend.

"He is now with me," she confessed, quietly, looking away.

"Dear God, when? … How did that happen?"

"I don't think that is important," he interrupted, standing in
front of the door. "Sit Alessandra, please. You don't look well."

"I feel sorry for you," Alessandra said ignoring him and
turning back to her friend. "You know you both probably deserve
each other."

"I am not going to hurt you," he said. "I just need you to
be reasonable and help me find what we were both looking for.
That is all I need. I promise I will then leave you alone. You will
never hear from me again. You can then get on with the rest of
your life."

"You know I can't do that. You see, I now know exactly what
your business is about, and it disgusts me."

She turned to her friend. "I wonder if you actually know what
he really does for a living?"

"Yes I do. I have known for some time."

"Look, this is not getting us anywhere," the man said, getting increasingly impatient. "You are going to tell me where it is and take me there."

Alessandra began to feel frightened. She knew the violence he was capable of. She released her grip on the chair and made to leave. "I feel very sorry for both of you. I want you both out of my life." She moved towards the door, but he blocked her way. He was a good six or seven inches taller than she was.

"Sit down Alessandra."

—

Nicholas watched Alessandra until she disappeared, then looked about him. The village spread out around the bay on both sides. He headed for the church he had seen from the boat and up the steep steps. Inside he sat for a while gazing at the gilded ceiling and the well-preserved dark-blue frescoes above. The cool, calm interior provided a respite from the jumble of his emotions.

Alessandra was certainly very attractive, but it was her nature, her obvious spontaneity and love of life, together with her compassion, that drew him. On the surface she reminded him of the actress Julia Roberts in Pretty Woman. Alessandra had the same tumbling curls and wide appealing smile. There was a similar vivacity, particularly when she laughed.

Nicholas was not the most spontaneous of men, he knew, but he could appreciate that quality in others. She had touched something in him. She had made him laugh. He hadn't laughed in such a long time, nor felt as free. Her vitality had infected him. He replayed their encounter on the ferry in the stillness of the church. There was one thing he had noticed at slight odds with her natural openness. Most of the time Alessandra had been fully engaged with their conversation. Every so often she had seemed distracted, her attention diverted briefly to the stairwell whenever someone came up from below. Had she been expecting someone? Whilst he quickly put the thought out of his mind – he was sure he was making too much of it – he had sensed that she was concerned about the meeting with her friend. He wondered what it was about and hoped it went well for her.

He was looking forward to seeing her later, if not at the beach then at the café in the port. His spirits lifted at the thought.

Emerging from the quiet of the church he turned right, walking back down towards the sea. The small harbour was lined with bars and tavernas, already starting to fill with early-lunchtime customers. He saw a tour group he recognised from the ferry enjoying drinks in the shade of a plane tree and was reminded that he had missed breakfast that morning.

The small town seemed to fan out up the hill behind in a series of terracing, perhaps six or seven houses deep. Most were large neoclassical villas, dating back to the nineteenth century. Some seemed to be holiday rentals. others had been renovated to offer more modest individual rooms to rent.

Small roads snaked around the hillside, one leading steeply up towards a ruined castle, standing alone on the bare mountain two thousand feet above. Nicholas sensed an air of mystery and foreboding about this majestic backdrop to the island, contrasting the tranquility of the harbour scene.

He turned back from the end of the waterfront at a fisherman's house at the water's edge. He walked back along the pedestrianised waterfront, where brightly-coloured fishing boats bobbed in the breeze. Taking out his phone he took a number of photographs of the port, the moored boats alongside, the buildings and restaurants, as well as people going about their normal business. Looking directly away from the sea he also took a number of photos of the skyline behind the town; the palette of painted villas outlined against the stark grey mountains above.

Outside the bars and tavernas, cats sidled around chairs and tables or dozed, still watchful, in the shade. He passed a small "super market"; watermelons piled high on the trestle table outside.

The heat of the day was increasing. A cold beer would taste good. He headed along the cobbled pathway leading away from the port. The winding road passed shuttered villas, closed for the season. The beach further along the road would be his final destination.

He found a taverna at the far end of the bay and ordered the beer he had been looking forward to, a prawn saganaki and Greek salad. The saganaki was good, spicy with a rich chili-based tomato sauce and sprinkled with feta. The taverna at Pondamus Beach fronted the sea. Nicholas had become used to eating alone at restaurants and had become adept at people-watching. He noticed a few of the passengers from the morning ferry at tables along the water's edge.

Nicholas spent the rest of the afternoon on the beach beside the taverna reading, every so often looking up in the hope of seeing Alessandra. He was disappointed. She didn't turn up at the gelateria either.

Nor was she on the boat. He had boarded just before five o'clock and found a seat upstairs, near where they had sat previously. The boat had already filled up. The engines were running, but departure was delayed as the crew and tour guides tried to reconcile the number of blue tickets collected with their lists of returning passengers. There was still time for her to arrive. His gaze was fixed on the stairs.

There was much shrugging and animated discussion among the crew. One, clipboard in hand, the name Nikos Express in yellow letters on the back of his blue jacket, went around the boat counting the passengers. He eventually confirmed what they had initially suspected – they were one short. After further discussion between the captain and the tour guides a decision was reached. The gangway was hoisted. The throb of the engines grew and the ferry left, twenty-five minutes late.

Once out of the bay and with the ferry headed into the lowering sun, Nicholas, his disappointment growing, searched the ferry, scanning the faces of passengers, only to confirm that Alessandra was not sitting in the cabin below or anywhere else on board. He realised then that they had not even exchanged phone numbers.

After a journey that seemed far longer than that going out, the ferry eventually docked in Skala Kamirou. On the hour-and-a-half drive back to his villa in Pylona, Nicholas felt more alone than when he had left the house that morning.

Over the next few days he relived the trip to Halki. He could not get Alessandra out of his mind. He had felt real disappointment that she had not been on the return trip to Rhodes, but knew it was important to see her again. He spent most of his time at the villa. He had received some urgent emails from the office that he needed to catch up on. One day he took himself to Lindos and made the long, dusty trek to the opposite promontory to visit the tomb of Cleobulus. The warm October weather had continued through into the new week.

Nicholas had found a much-read copy of Laurence Durrell's "Reflections on a Marine Venus" in the villa's well-stocked bookcase. Sitting beside the gently lapping water of the swimming pool, he read of the author's time on Rhodes as a British civil servant after the end of the Second World War. He was intrigued to read Durrell's words that "In Rhodes the days drop softly as fruit from trees. Some belong to the dazzling ages of Cleobulus and the tyrants, some to the gloomy Tiberius, some to the Crusaders." He put the book down and gazed across to the dusty hills behind. He was starting to get a feel for the contradictions so intrinsic to the character of this ancient landscape.

That evening he went to one of the many rooftop restaurants that provide a panoramic view over Lindos town and the bay. As the sun slowly dipped below the buildings, he found himself going over his meeting with Alessandra once more. He tried to work out why he had felt such a strong connection. The surfacing of such feelings surprised him. Undoubtedly, he found her attractive and appealing.

She was also refreshing and exciting. But there was so much more. He had felt a bond, a recognition. Perhaps it was simply that, not having known him previously, she was able to respond to him as she found him. He had learnt to keep his emotions well hidden. He was not a great believer in luck, but this felt right. He was sure Alessandra had also felt something. Alone on the rooftop, watching the other diners, he realised how solitary he had become, but was he ready for a new relationship? There was still guilt. Had he healed sufficiently? It had been two years, after all.

A few days later, Nicholas drove into Rhodes town to the museum. He had waited until the Wednesday, so as not to appear too eager. Dressing with more care than usual he was wearing a blue jacket and carefully ironed shirt. He gave himself enough time to park outside the old walls and locate the building. He had spent the past few days waiting to see Alessandra again and wanted to make sure he would get to the museum well before it closed.

At the ticket office inside the airy medieval entrance he asked for Miss Bianchi and was referred to an information counter, inside the cool of the museum.

"Alessandra has not been in to work so far this week. Perhaps she's not well," the efficient middle-aged woman behind the counter told him.

"Has she called you?"

"I'm sorry, I don't know."

"Did she by any chance leave any message for me? My name is Nicholas Adams and I was due to meet her here."

There was no message. The woman suggested he try later in the week. Nicholas asked if he might leave a message for Alessandra, with his mobile phone number. In the note he asked Alessandra to contact him and reminded her he was leaving Rhodes on Friday.

He left, puzzled, and with an unsettling sense of regret and disappointment. He had been so sure that the attraction was mutual. He had had even allowed himself to think that they might have had a future. He had obviously misread the signals from the ferry trip. How had he got it so wrong? He thought he was getting better. He shook his head. He had even had some feelings of guilt that he had such emotions. After eight years of marriage, he was clearly still not ready. Alessandra was colourful and vibrant, with the world ahead of her. So unlike him. What was he thinking?

He did not hear from her again.

Chapter Four

ENGLAND

THE RED AND GREEN NEON REINDEER LEAPT ACROSS THE FRONT lawn. Fairy lights danced along bare branches on each side of the street. Nicholas turned into his road. He felt weary. It had been a day of many meetings, and not much action. The roads had been clogged with pre-Christmas traffic crawling through the dank evening fog. He reached his driveway, parked and turned the key to the front door. In the hallway, he checked the mail – mainly flyers offering carpets, blinds and pizza deliveries.

It felt as cold inside as it was outside. Little had remained to remind him of his wife. He had not been able to bear being among her personal things or those that they had bought together. Her clothing had been the first to go. During the early months the constant reminders of their shared life and dreams had been given away or taken to his local charity shop. Looking around at the sparse and impersonal furnishings, he hardly recognised the house now. He regretted some of his hasty decisions, but he had not been himself. Nicholas looked around the cheerless living room and thought once again of selling up.

It was the same in the kitchen. All Lynda's recipe books and other gadgets had long gone, leaving a utilitarian space. Perhaps a few changes were now needed. He searched the fridge for a ready-meal to microwave.

In the living room he caught his reflection in the mirror above the mantelpiece. He looked tired. There was a hint of grey at the temples of his thick, unruly dark hair. When had that happened? The collar of his shirt had started to fray. He looked washed-out and distracted. Nicholas took off his tie and turned on the imitation-flame gas fire. Lynda had wanted to replace it with a woodburner, but he had argued for practicality. He poured himself a cognac – he would have preferred a gin and tonic, but had forgotten to buy the mixer.

Nicholas slumped onto the sofa and turned on the television. More of the same from the White House. He flicked through the newspaper in front of him, sipping his drink with a slight grimace. The local news came on. There was an item about stores already holding pre-Christmas sales. The next story suddenly caught his attention. A picture of a laughing, dark-haired woman flashed up on the screen. His breath caught. It looked just like Alessandra. He leaned forward, gripping his glass and turned up the volume. The newsreader reported that the search for a local woman, missing on the island of Rhodes, had been called off after Greek police had failed to find any leads. A representative from the British Consulate said that, despite an intensive search, they had no more information on the disappearance of a British subject, Alessandra Bianchi, who had been living on Rhodes but had previously lived in Balham, South London. The report continued with a clip of a frightened and uncomfortable-looking couple in their sixties – her parents – sitting in the living room of their home in Amersham, Buckinghamshire. A local reporter was interviewing them.

"We can't imagine what has happened to our daughter," said the father. "She always seemed so happy living and working in Rhodes."

"Alessandra had always been an independent person and made her own decisions," said her mother, looking overwhelmed by the presence of the reporter. "But when she hadn't returned our calls for a few weeks we became very worried," she glanced towards her husband as if she needed his confirmation of their concerns. Nicholas thought they looked a couple ill at ease with each other.

"We contacted the museum where she worked." Her voice shaky, Mrs Bianchi said that the museum told them that Alessandra had sent them a text message some weeks before, saying she was unwell and would contact them when she was ready to return to work. "We have not spoken to her since. When we told them that she hadn't answered her phone, we were told a work colleague had gone round to her flat, but there was no response. It's very worrying." Mrs Bianchi looked down and fell silent. She was distraught, but the reporter encouraged her to continue.

"We contacted the Consulate and told them it was very unlike Alessandra to make no contact. They alerted the local police, but they had also found no sign of her at the flat.

The reporter said neighbours in the apartment block had not seen her over the past couple of months.

"We think they assumed that she had returned to the UK for a visit," said Mrs Bianchi, her voice was breaking down.

The report ended. The national weather forecast came on. Nicholas turned off the television. He felt shaken and confused. He had thought of Alessandra often over the past months, imagining her going about her work at the museum in Rhodes. He wondered whether she had gone missing on Rhodes, or whether she had disappeared from Halki. He had been so startled he couldn't remember what the report had actually said. Had they mentioned when she had disappeared? A thought flashed through his mind that her failure to board the return ferry might be connected. There was relief that perhaps she had not deliberately stood him up after all. Maybe she had not even received the message that he had left at the museum? He felt embarrassed that he was even thinking this and then concern for her kicked in. He remembered the museum assistant telling him at the time that Alessandra may have been off sick. What had happened? Where could she be? She had seemed so positive, so full of life, on the ferry.

Nicholas spent a restless night methodically turning things over and over in his mind. He wanted to help and felt he should. The last thing he wanted to do, though, was to inflict more pain on this poor family. The television interview had been difficult to watch.

Next morning he went to Windsor police station to make a statement. He was not sure whether he could add anything to what was already known on Rhodes but felt he had to try. The police were polite and understanding. He told them about his chance meeting with Alessandra on the ferry. He could even tell them the date and time that he had last seen Alessandra that October day. He said she had told him that she was meeting an old friend on the island and that she was booked to return to Rhodes later that day. He was surprised she was not on the ferry. He also said they had agreed to meet the following week for a drink and told them of his fruitless trip to the museum. They took a full statement and his contact details and said they would pass them on to the consulate and the Rhodes police.

Nicholas asked if there was anything else that they could do but was told that the matter would now be dealt with by the Rhodes police. These cases were relatively common and most resolved themselves naturally with the reappearance of the subject, they said.

Nicholas left feeling frustrated and powerless. The Greek police had already closed the case. Was the additional information he had provided sufficient for them to reopen the investigation? Would they consider the Halki connection and interview Alessandra's friend there? There was nothing more he could do.

Driving to work that morning, though, he could not keep Alessandra from his mind. What if something had happened to her and she needed help. He might have been the last person to see her before she disappeared. He had no confidence that the police would pursue it. It was clearly not a priority for them.

For the rest of the morning he kept on turning Alessandra's disappearance over in his mind. He thought back to the museum in Rhodes and his initial feeling that she had let him down. How easy it had been to rationalise her failure to contact him or meet him. If something had happened to her would he now be letting her down by not doing anything more? It had been only one day and one ferry trip, but he had felt a strong connection with her. More importantly it was still possible that their meeting back in October had meant something to her.

Nicholas thought over his own life. He had lived on the periphery, avoiding engagement with everything around him, for too long now. He suddenly felt his choices narrow.

BT Online provided him with the home phone number for a Bianchi in Amersham. He was lucky there was only one listing for that name in the area. He agonised over whether he was doing the right thing, but he dialed the number.

"Hello," said the hesitant voice Nicholas recognised as that of Alessandra's mother from the TV the night before.

"Hello, Mrs Bianchi. My name's Nicholas Adams and I'm phoning because I saw you on television last night and think I may have some information on your daughter for you."

"Oh," Mrs Bianchi's voice was hesitant. She said her husband wouldn't be back from work until that evening.

"I'm really sorry to intrude, but I think I may have some information that will help the search for Alessandra. I met her just before she disappeared." Nicholas wanted to reassure the frightened-sounding woman on the other end of line.

"I can't talk about this. I will need to speak to my husband."

"Perhaps I can meet with both of you and I can tell you what I know. I thought your daughter was a lovely woman. We got along very well."

Mrs Bianchi's tone softened. She said perhaps they could meet the next evening at their local pub, the Plough and Shears, on the outskirts of Amersham at 8.15pm. She took his number and said she would let him know if it was not OK.

Nicholas would not have been surprised if the Bianchis had phoned him the next day to cancel. Hearing nothing, he turned up at the pub, a mock-Tudor building with a car park in need of resurfacing, just after eight o'clock. Outside it was cold and drizzling. Inside, the place, which was festooned haphazardly with tired Christmas decorations, was almost deserted, despite the hour. Alessandra's parents were sitting near the open fire.

"How do you do?" Nicholas extended his hand towards Mr Bianchi. He was thin, even frail-looking, with glasses and thinning grey hair. As he stood, a slight stoop became visible. He was a good two or three inches shorter than Nicholas. Dressed in comfortable brown cords and a baggy fawn-coloured jersey that accentuated his slightness, he looked the part of the college professor. He introduced his wife, speaking with a slight Italian accent.

Both seemed nervous. Looking at Mrs Bianchi, Nicholas could see where Alessandra had got her striking looks. She was slim and elegant, her graying, medium-length auburn hair was tied back revealing a handsome and only slightly lined face. She smoothed the front of her grey shift dress and sat down.

"I'm sorry. This is of course very difficult for us," said Mrs Bianchi, glancing towards her husband, who sat with his arms folded, a guarded expression on his worried face. "We were both," another glance at her husband, "reluctant to meet you." Nicholas noticed Mrs Bianchi's red-rimmed, puffy eyes. "Mr Adams. We are not sure how you can help in any way. Also we do not know you."

"Please call me Nicholas. Yes, it must seem strange, but, as I said, I saw your interview on the local news a couple of days ago. You see, I might have been one of the last people to see your daughter before she went missing."

The news bulletin was the first he knew of Alessandra's disappearance, he told them. He recounted the details of that Friday on board the ferry to Halki.

"We immediately got on and chatted the whole way over. I was on holiday in Rhodes and had decided to visit Halki for the day. Alessandra was going to visit a friend. It was her day-off from work. She told me all about her job at the museum and how important it was for her. Her enthusiasm for what she was working on was so apparent. She told me that she had decided to study further. Clearly, she was very happy living and working on Rhodes. I did get a slight sense, however, that there was something worrying her. I do remember that she kept on glancing towards the stairs whenever someone came up onto our deck. I got the impression she was half-expecting to see someone."

Nicholas recalled the moment when he had last seen her. "She was heading off up into the backstreets of the village to meet up with an old friend who lived on Halki.

"I'm fairly sure it was a woman that your daughter was meeting. I had the impression they had a lot to catch up on. But, the thing is, we agreed to meet up on the return ferry that evening and she didn't turn up. I was sure Alessandra had said she was going back to Rhodes that day, as she had to go to work the next. I was surprised she wasn't on the ferry." He didn't tell them how disappointed he had been. The Bianchis didn't comment. Nicholas noticed that the husband had not made eye contact with him. He had removed his glasses and preferred to examine them throughout the account. He looked uninterested, as if he did not want to be there.

Nicholas continued: "We had made plans to meet up at the museum the following week. Alessandra was going to show me around before we went on for a drink. The woman at the information counter in the museum said that possibly she was sick. They had heard nothing from her. No message had been left for me. I left, thinking it was likely that I would never see Alessandra again."

The Bianchis were silent, so Nicholas said he hoped that, if any of this was new information and provided clues to Alessandra's whereabouts, it might be sufficient to allow the police on Rhodes to continue their investigation.

"As I told you yesterday I immediately went to my local police station to make a statement. They said that they would pass on the information to the police in Rhodes."

Her voice soft, Mrs Bianchi said: "We were taken by surprise by the interest from the press. Mr Adams, please understand we are just normal, quiet people."

"I'd like to be able to help, if there's anything I can do. It must be awful for you. Do you know of anything that may have prompted or be associated with her disappearance?"

The mother looked towards her husband briefly. "We really have no idea why Alessandra might disappear. We do know that she was happy on Rhodes and in her job. There was nothing to indicate that this might happen. As you can imagine, we have thought of little else. Alessandra was so good at staying in touch with us. That's why we first became concerned.

"There was a boyfriend that we did not like the sound of." She again looked to her husband for confirmation. "We had some knowledge of the boyfriend's father from when we lived on Rhodes, but we had never met the son. From what Alessandra told us he had seemed quite domineering. I doubt this is relevant, though, as the relationship finished quite a few months ago. Certainly well before we last heard from Alessandra.

"We also had slight concerns about some of the friends that Alessandra seemed to have made more recently on Rhodes. But it was only a feeling we had. Alessandra has always been such a sensible person. We haven't seen her in more than a year and so any concerns we had were based more on how she sounded over the phone rather than what she was actually saying. Can you understand that?

"I guess it's a mother thing" she continued. "It was more in her tone of voice; her usual sparkle and enthusiasm for things around her seemed to have gone. The last few times we spoke, I remember thinking she was being slightly secretive and distant. As if she was preoccupied by something. It was not like her. She's usually so warm and trusting with us.

"Please excuse me," she said, reaching into her bag for a tissue. Nicholas asked if he could get her a glass of water, which she waved away. Her husband continued to sit quietly, looking into the distance.

Mrs Bianchi eventually recovered enough to continue: "Alessandra had alluded to concerns about her safety. She didn't say much. I remember one phone call quite late at night, some months ago. She said that she might need to come back to the UK. She asked if she could stay with us.

"But the next time we spoke, everything was fine. She told me how much she was enjoying her work as a volunteer at the dog sanctuary at the weekends. She sounded in her element and was back to her old self again. We have told the police all about this. They told us that the Rhodes police hadn't been able to contact the ex-boyfriend. It's believed he left the island some time before she went missing."

Mrs Bianchi said she was upset that the police had asked whether Alessandra was taking or had taken drugs and if any of her friends were involved in drugs. "We are very, very, sure that Alessandra did not take drugs. Nor would she have become involved in anything to do with them. We are very clear on this." She glanced towards her husband for support.

Nicholas intervened: "I completely believe you."

"But we cannot speak for her friends. We had suspicions that the ex-boyfriend may have taken drugs or been involved somehow with them. He did not seem that stable."

Mrs Bianchi turned to her husband: "There was also that call one evening. A man with a foreign accent – I'm not sure what it was – he wanted to speak to you. I gave the phone to you and you spoke to him for a couple of minutes. You said he had got the wrong person. It was another Bianchi that they were looking for." Her husband did not respond.

It felt a bit awkward and Nicholas thought it was time to go. The Bianchis thanked Nicholas. "It was good of you to do this, but there's nothing else you can do," said Mrs Bianchi. "We must be left on our own to deal with this, Mr Adams, so, now, please can I ask that you leave us alone."

They did agree to contact him if there was any positive news. More reluctantly, they also said he could phone them for updates on Alessandra, every so often.

Christmas dragged into the New Year. Nicholas found the holiday period weighed more heavily with the inactivity it invited. He continued to think about Alessandra. He thought over his meeting with the police and the subsequent, rather stilted, meeting with her parents. He felt disquiet. The police did not give him any encouragement that anything would change. Alessandra's parents had come across as passive victims of her disappearance and he had little confidence that they would be able to do anything to help find her. He had heard nothing from them. He wondered whether there had been any ill feeling between Alessandra and her father.

The limbo was punctuated by a visit to his parents, who lived in the village of Chawton, a picturesque village nestling in the folds of the Hampshire fields, near Alton, best known for being the home of Jane Austen. The home is now a museum and it is where she wrote most of her novels, sitting at the small round walnut table in the parlour, looking out on the road and to the world outside.

When they retired, his parents had moved from Southampton and now lived in a low-ceilinged honey-coloured cottage with a long narrow garden that escaped down to a stream at its end.

During the visit, Nicholas enjoyed a rare moment of intimacy with his formal and often distant father. His father had sensed over lunch that something was troubling his son.

"How are things at work?" he asked Nicholas.

Nicholas found himself admitting that his job had lost its allure. "Somehow the challenge has disappeared, along with my enthusiasm. I really feel the time has come for a change. You know, ever since Lynda, I have felt that there is no purpose to my life. It feels as if I am just drifting … as if I were in a river and caught in the current. Sometimes, I feel as though I am hurtling along past everyone and then suddenly I am caught up in an eddy or go off up a side channel." He smiled, feeling slightly embarrassed.

"How can we help?" asked his father.

"Thanks Dad." Nicholas was grateful for this unusually caring response. "This is something that I need to do for myself. I just feel that I have lost control over the direction of my life.

"So, do you know what you are going to do?"

"I think so, but I can't explain it right now. All I can tell you is that I'm going to take a sabbatical from work and I'll be away for a while. I can't even fully explain my motivation, but I hope it will become clearer to myself. When it does, I will let you and Mum know. I will keep in touch, I promise you."

Back home, Nicholas phoned Alessandra's parents. Mrs Bianchi sounded ever more resigned. No, they had not heard from Alessandra, but although the police on Rhodes had drawn a blank, they had agreed to continue with a search on Halki.

Nicholas told her what he meant to do. There was a silence.

"We still hope we'll hear from her soon and we thank you for taking an interest, but we don't think you should get any more involved."

Nicholas was shocked, especially after what she had said about the police and Halki.

"I respect your viewpoint," he said, with more conviction than he felt. "I hope that you're right and do hear from her soon. With or without your blessing, however, one way or another I'm already involved and know what I need to do. I will stay in touch."

Nicholas put down the phone. It was hard to reconcile the strange attitude of her parents with Alessandra's kindness – and vitality. He had to look for her. She had loved life. But was he doing this for Alessandra or for himself? After spending so long with his life being determined by the dead, it was time the living were given their time. Perhaps, he thought, I can make a difference. He felt better able to trust his instincts. It was worth a go.

The next day, he found himself in his marketing director's office, requesting a six-month sabbatical from work. Nicholas wondered whether perhaps they were as indifferent about his absence as he was presently about his job, but it was agreed readily.

So, at the end of the first week in February, Nicholas boarded a flight to Rhodes.

Chapter Five

RHODES TOWN

RAIN SWEPT THROUGH THE DARK STREETS, LEAVING GLISTENING
grey cobbles. The cold northerly wind battered the old buildings,
clawing at shutters and tree branches left exposed. Most of the
restaurants in the Knights' Quarter were closed for the winter,
chairs stacked and secured under awnings. Waiters huddled in the
entrances of the few that were open, smoking, as they scanned
passers-by for trade.

Nicholas turned down Il Forno-Platonos Street towards his
favourite Italian restaurant. He had arrived three days ago and
booked a month's stay in a comfortable white-shuttered hotel on
Oktovriou Street. On his first day he had visited the police station
in Mandraki Harbour, where he had met Captain Petrakis, the
man in charge of the investigation into Alessandra's disappearance.
Nicholas explained his involvement and told Petrakis he had met
Alessandra's parents and told them of his intention to come to
Rhodes to help find her.

Petrakis, short, balding and in his fifties, spoke excellent English. He told Nicholas that he had spent some time in England, studying at Aston University, in Birmingham. He was polite and apologetic, but said there had been no developments. "We went to her apartment, but we didn't find anything there that could help us." Petrakis's manner was brisk and efficient. "We also spoke to her landlord and found she had signed a new one-year lease last July. So, it looks probable that she will return and will be sorry that she hasn't let her friends know she was planning to be away."

"Have you followed up on Halki? In my statement to the UK police I mentioned that she visited a friend on Halki. That was in mid-October and was the last I heard from her."

Petrakis was again apologetic. "I am afraid we don't have a police presence on Halki. I did send one of my men over when we received your report but we found nothing. There were no reports of anyone missing. Unfortunately the island closes down in winter. Not much is open and there are few ferries. Many locals come over to Rhodes during these months." He shrugged. "There was little more that we could do."

Nicholas wondered how seriously the Rhodes police were taking the case. No one seemed to doubt that Alessandra would return, but also no one questioned whether it was in character for her to suddenly take off. Petrakis had said there had been no trace of her mobile phone and, in his view, there was nothing further they could do.

"I expect that Miss Bianchi's case will, unfortunately, be downgraded to a missing person status. I am sorry," he shrugged again.

Nicholas had seen posters of missing people at Rhodes airport. Alessandra was just one more, according to the police. A foreign woman who had decided to take off without telling her family and would no doubt turn up eventually.

Now, crossing the quiet taxi rank, he passed the tourist office, its door locked. His destination was the museum. In the gloom of the narrow cobbled street leading up to the museum, the massive, dark stone entrance was forbidding. Discarded wrappers and cigarette ends eddied in the wind around the large, open wooden door. Nicholas passed the marble statue of Aphrodite Bathing and the wall-mounted mosaics to reach the offices marked "Private Museum Staff". Knocking on one at random, he heard a man's voice ask him to enter in Greek. "Yasas," Nicholas replied "Milate Anglika?" he offered, hopefully, in his guidebook Greek.

"How may I help you," asked the man seated at a large wooden desk, in flawless English. Nicholas explained why he was there. The man seemed surprised, but recovered quickly. "And you are a friend of Alessandra? A very good friend clearly. Well, you better sit. My name is Michael Kamides and I am head of research here at the museum. I was Alessandra's manager." He looked the part: glasses and a jacket with leather patches at the elbows. Nicholas almost expected to see a pipe nestling in an ashtray. He was quite a big man, almost the same height as Nicholas. Kamides said he had recruited her for the research job. She also worked as an archivist across the island.

"Alessandra immediately impressed me with her enthusiasm and passion for our history. We obviously have a rich history here on Rhodes and indeed across the whole of the Dodecanese. She speaks fairly good Greek and was also very thorough in her approach. She had researched the job and came well prepared. She fitted in really well from the start and is … was a popular employee.

"After we received a text from Alessandra saying she was unwell and would be off work, I asked one of her colleagues to go by her apartment to check that she was all right." That was more than three months ago and there had been no further word from Alessandra, he added.

"When the police became involved they obtained a key from the caretaker of the apartments. We believe that they found no sign that she had been there for some time. We thought perhaps she had just decided to go back to the UK. I understand from the police that her passport was missing."

Kamides, on second glance, was younger than he first appeared, but there was something Nicholas was uneasy about.

Alessandra's boss said he believed she had simply returned to England. He was disappointed that she did not tell him that she was leaving or indeed let him know that she might have had any problems that would lead her to do so. As he talked he made sure that the edges of document piles on his desk were all carefully aligned. He then paused, wondering where to move his stapler, eventually settling on placing it on a holiday brochure in his metal out-tray.

"We are a bit like a family here at the museum and we would have done everything we could to help" he resumed.

There was something not right here. Nicholas liked to think that his boss and his colleagues would have done more to check that he was all right if he had not been to work for some time.

Nicholas told Kamides there was no evidence that Alessandra was back in the UK. Even her family had not heard from her since the autumn.

"Can you remember how she seemed or what she was working on in the period before she disappeared?" he asked.

Kamides hesitated. "She seemed her normal self, though a bit distracted. She had been doing work at our Ancient Kamiros site, about 25 kilometres from here, for the early part of the year, documenting some of the recent significant finds. She seemed excited about it."

"What about visits to Halki? Did she go there?"

"Yes, Alessandra did visit most of our surrounding islands over the past few years. I remember that she asked me how to find the old maps of the islands, including Halki, in the library." Nicholas was surprised. He thought that Alessandra had said that the visit was her first to the island. Perhaps he had misheard her?

"When the real summer heat started she returned to her work in the office here. It gets much too hot in July and August for fieldwork."

"Do you know if she had any friends here – or a boyfriend?" Kamides looked away. He picked up his fountain pen, a Mont Blanc, and tapped his teeth in thought. Nicholas wondered if he was nervous.

Turning back to Nicholas, Kamides said: "I feel rather uncomfortable talking about the personal lives of our employees." He paused. "But, yes, there was a guy who came into the museum to meet her a couple of times. I think he was her boyfriend." His voice had become more measured.

"What was he like?" Nicholas asked.

"Well, it is difficult as I was only introduced to him the once by Alessandra. Although he said that he was an academic, with a background in the history of Middle Eastern trade, he came across as one of those rich, arrogant types. I'm afraid I didn't really like him.

"I do remember, on one occasion, there was an argument. I heard shouting. I had to ask the boyfriend to leave. Alessandra was very upset."

Kamides thought the boyfriend had been jealous of her friendship with some of her work colleagues. "He was not Greek – perhaps German, perhaps Eastern European? From what I saw they did not seem well suited." Kamides thought they had split up some time ago. Outside of work colleagues, she had friends she would spend time with at weekends.

"She mentioned a friend she was visiting on Halki. Do you happen to know who that might have been?" Nicholas asked.

"I am sure I do not know. She may have known someone there but I can't recall her mentioning anyone to me."

"Did Alessandra have a car?" Nicholas asked as an afterthought. "When I got back from Halki I did look for a car left behind in the port but did not see one."

"I don't believe that she did.

"When she was working out of the museum at our sites across the island she tended to travel with colleagues who lived in Rhodes town".

Nicholas got up to leave. "Thank you for your time. You have been helpful. Please let me know if anything further comes to mind." Taking his phone number, Kamides said he would. Nicholas paused before he reached the door. "Is there anyone else I should speak to, someone who might know who her friends were or what she did in her spare time?"

"She was very friendly with Eleni Papadakis, another of my researchers. Unfortunately, she is not here today as her daughter is not well. Why don't you try tomorrow, or I could just give her your number."

Nicholas said he might call into the museum tomorrow in case she was back at work. He left wondering about Kamides. He'd had the feeling that there was something he was not being told. Mulling it over, he headed for the fourteenth-century Palace of the Grand Master around the corner. There was nothing more to be done today, so he thought he'd take a look.

The Palace had been originally built by the Knights Hospitaller, but the interior was rebuilt in the eighteenth century, after an explosion caused significant damage. With Alessandra in his thoughts, and reminded of her passion for her work at the museum, he sought out the Ancient Rhodes exhibition. The exhibits celebrated the 2,400 years since the founding of the old city. The exhibition detailed the archaeological research conducted in the city over this period. One exhibit caught his eye. It revealed that Rhodes' strategic geographical position in the sea route between the Levant, Cyprus and the Aegean had led to its development as a naval power and the economy flourished. Evidence had also been gathered from ninth-century BC graves at Kamiros, suggesting a long and significant trade history with Cyprus and Phoenicia.

Stopping for a forgettable moussaka, Nicholas thought over the day and what he had learnt. Buried in the subtext of his meetings, there had been some clues to Alessandra as a person and what might have happened to her. He took out his pocket notebook. He had already scribbled some comments about his visit to the police earlier. Now he wrote:

"Boyfriend???

Public argument in museum

Friends?

Talk to Eleni

Halki?

Work connection to disappearance??

Kamides – Why is he nervous? What is he not saying?"

Nicholas felt Alessandra's disappearance was somehow interwoven with the fabric of this ancient island and its history. He just didn't yet know how.

That night his restless sleep was interrupted by a dream. Alessandra had fallen overboard from the ferry. No one noticed, despite her screams for help. His own shouts also elicited no response. His last sight of her, before she slipped into the deep, was her long dark hair streaming out behind her. He woke with a start, drenched. His disturbed night reminded him of those long months after Lynda's death, when he had been unable to sleep. He had gone to bed exhausted, only to spend each night awake tormented by his thoughts.

The next day he woke to a weak sun filtering through the shutters. After breakfast, he wandered across the drawbridge over the moat and into the old walled town. The artists and fruit sellers who had touted their wares at the entrance during the summer months were long gone. He strolled through the ramparts to the tangle of cobbled roads and alleyways running down towards the harbour. Only a few restaurants and shops were open. Nicholas enjoyed not having to share the streets with tourists. Most of the shops here sold souvenirs, often offering the same wares as their neighbours. He bought a hand-painted salad bowl decorated with green and red peppers for his mother. For himself, he chose a white ceramic candleholder that depicted the Colossus of Rhodes, astride the entrance to the harbour.

He stopped for a coffee in the market, before continuing his walk. As the outline of the Knights' Hospital came into view he turned left into Plateia Mousiou, where the museum stood. He asked for Eleni Papadakis at the desk. After five minutes, a trim, well-dressed woman in black skirt and cream blouse walked across the concourse extending her hand.

"Hello. My name is Eleni Papadakis."

"Nicholas Adams. I assume that Michael Kamides told you about me. It's kind of you to spare me some time." Nicholas followed Eleni to a small staff lounge. "I hope your daughter is better today."

"She is, thank you. I think it was just a winter cold."

She seemed about Alessandra's age, but more reserved. She offered him a coffee and a local pastry. They sat and she took off her black-framed glasses and folded them in her hand. "How can I help you? I understand that you are asking about poor Alessandra. It was a shock to us all here. We all believed that she had returned to England." She was very softly spoken, with a slight accent. Nicholas felt he had to lean closer to hear her.

"I was hoping that you could provide some background to her life here on Rhodes: who she knew, what her interests were outside of work and what you think may have happened to her. The police seemed to have concluded their investigation. They say she is now being treated as a missing person only. I think there may be more to her disappearance."

"Forgive me, Nicholas, but what is your interest in Alessandra? You are not family, clearly, and I assume you are not a current or past boyfriend. I am sure she would have mentioned you."

"It's a fair question. The truth is that I am not sure what my connection really is. I know this may sound strange, but the fact is that I only knew her for a few hours. I met her on the ferry to Halki last year. But, I liked her – she touched something in me. I had a feeling that we shared some past experience, somehow. I think she felt it also."

"I see…" Eleni put her glasses back on to examine Nicholas more closely. They made her look more severe.

"She was going to show me around the Old Town. I was surprised when she wasn't on the return ferry, but we had arranged to meet up a few days later. I couldn't understand why she didn't turn up or why she didn't even leave a message for me."

Nicholas told Eleni how Alessandra had remained in his mind, even after he had returned home. "I could still picture her very clearly. Particularly her smile and her sheer vibrancy. It just seems very wrong that she would just disappear. It's that, more than anything, that has made me want to find her."

He told Eleni how he had seen the news item about Alessandra's disappearance on television and how he had gone to see the police immediately.

"I did not realise that her disappearance had been reported overseas."

"Yes, it was a huge shock seeing it. Knowing that I was possibly one of the last to have seen her. They interviewed her parents, so I contacted them, too, and we met up.

"They were naturally distraught and they seemed confused and powerless to do anything. But, I thought, too, that they were frightened and were holding something back. It was after meeting them that I decided I had to come here. I had to do something. No one else seems to be doing anything – even though the information I gave to the police kept the investigation going for a bit longer, at least.

"It's the strangest thing, but my chance meeting on that ferry has given me a direction and a purpose. I feel, however implausible it might seem to you, I owe it to Alessandra to at least look for her while I can.

"It might be that in the end she will not welcome my efforts and I will of course respect that. I just have this feeling that she needs help. Perhaps not necessarily from me but, as it stands, I'm the only one looking and at the moment I also have the time."

Eleni's glasses were once again clasped in her hands. It felt important to him to convince Alessandra's friend that he was genuine and she seemed to be softening. He told her he had booked into Hotel Anastasia for a month.

"Alessandra's parents mentioned a boyfriend and that the relationship seemed to have ended badly. They said Alessandra had become more guarded and they felt this might have had something to do with the break-up."

Eleni got up, saying she needed another coffee and asked Nicholas if he'd like one. He declined. Eleni seemed to need time to gather her thoughts. When she returned, she looked directly at Nicholas. She seemed to have come to a decision.

"I have known Alessandra since she started here at the museum. We got on from the first moment and she would often spend time with me and also with my family. She was wonderful with children and my daughter loved her. Thea's eyes would light up whenever she knew Alessandra was going to visit. Sometimes Alessandra babysat for us. That was so kind, as my husband and I both work and seem to have so little time together.

"She did have a boyfriend. It was hardly surprising as she was so attractive and open. They started going out over two years ago. I think he was from Russia or the Ukraine. His name was Andriy Solokov, or Sokolov – I was never quite sure which, and I think he was originally an academic back home. Now he is a businessman. He was very wealthy and he liked people to know that. He was staying on an expensive yacht when he was on Rhodes. He was often away on business, though, Alessandra told me."

"Do you know how they met?"

"They met just after he arrived on Rhodes. He was very interested in the history of Rhodes and I have a feeling they first met here at the museum, when he was looking around. Their relationship was quite volatile and Alessandra eventually became a bit withdrawn when she was with him. I didn't like him."

Nicholas sat up. She was the second person to say that. "Why not?"

"I found him quite intense, even a bit menacing. I did not like him visiting us with Alessandra. When I eventually told her I was not happy to have him around Thea, it did have an effect on our relationship. She withdrew from me a bit. I was glad when their relationship ended."

Nicholas was about to ask her whose decision that had been, when Eleni said: "I think it was Alessandra who finished it – because of all their arguments. I think he was jealous of her many friends in the museum. He also didn't like it when she worked away on one of our active archaeological digs out of town. Once he was out of her life she became much happier."

"Do you know what happened to him after they split?"

"No, I don't. Alessandra did not speak about him again. I don't even know whether he stayed here or left the island."

"And her other friends?"

"I don't know much about them. It was only rarely that I could spend time with Alessandra after work. There was something that I do remember, though. Once we went to a restaurant for her birthday. Andriy was there with some of her other friends. A couple of them were from Rhodes and one was from England. But there were one or two also from elsewhere. I think also from Eastern Europe. I really liked Stavros, who was local, and also Caroline, who was the person from England. I think she worked in a travel agency based in Lindos. What she is doing now, out of season, I am not sure." Her voice tailed off.

"Please carry on," Nicholas said. At last some gaps were being filled.

Eleni said the two men from Eastern Europe seemed to be good friends and kept to themselves during the meal. Like Andriy they were quite intense and rude, and she was surprised they were friends of Alessandra. One got drunk and argued with a waiter over his food. She had the feeling Caroline was in a relationship with him because they went off together when he was asked to leave. "I am not sure whether this is relevant."

"It may be," said Nicholas, wondering how the Alessandra that he had met had become mixed up with people like this. "On the ferry, she mentioned to me that she was visiting a friend on Halki. Do you know of anyone who might have known Alessandra and who had moved to Halki?"

"It rings a bell. I remember Alessandra mentioning a friend she had on Halki who she sometimes stayed with. I have a feeling the friend might have worked here some time ago. This would have been before my time. I will get someone in the administration department to check the records and I will let you know." Nicholas gave her his mobile number.

"Away from work, did Alessandra have any particular interests or hobbies?"

"Yes. She did. One thing she loved to talk about was her work with a dog sanctuary – you know there are many stray dogs here on Rhodes. She often gave up a Sunday to help out there. She also read a lot – particularly on the history of ancient Greece and Rhodes – and she loved hiking in the hills around Monolithos and Mount Akramytis, on the west coast.

"Alessandra was very fit. A couple of years ago she also took up diving and was doing a scuba course out of Mandraki harbour. She was passionate about this, particularly after she broke up with Andriy. She told me she was going to dive off some of our surrounding islands."

Nicholas remembered the snorkel and mask Alessandra carried in her green canvas bag.

"Thank you, Eleni. This is so helpful. Do you know what she was working on at the museum before she went missing?"

Eleni told him Alessandra had been researching the old trading routes across the eastern Mediterranean. "Did you know that Rhodes provided a gateway into three continents and had done so over many centuries?" Nicholas remembered his visit to the Palace of the Grand Master and the exhibit that had drawn his attention.

Eleni said Alessandra had started spending time at the Archaeological National Library and the Muslim Library in the town. "She had become very enthusiastic and was spending long hours going through old records and maps. Alessandra had a deep love and interest in the history of Rhodes."

"Did she mention what she was researching?"

"I am not sure what, specifically, she was looking at. Michael might know if there were plans for a future exhibition. Alessandra had become very excited about her research over the last few months. Whenever I tried to get her to talk about it, I got the feeling that she was keeping something to herself."

Eleni rose from her seat. "I'm sorry, but I do need to get back to work." Her face fell as she told Nicholas they were preparing to interview people to fill in for Alessandra and she was due in a meeting with Kamides about it.

"You might want to try the Archaeological Library nearby. They will probably have records of the documents that Alessandra was looking at, as well as the computer search records. It is not open to the public, but if you have permission for research purposes, they will let you use them. They are normally very helpful. Go to the Ministry for Culture, next to the Ministry for Tourism, among all the consular offices on the Knights' Street. Ask for Effie. She knew Alessandra well. I will phone and make an appointment for tomorrow for you."

Putting her glasses on, she said she hoped she had been of some help. She walked with him back to the museum entrance and shook his hand. "I believe your story. Alessandra had that effect on people" she smiled.

Chapter Six

RHODES TOWN

BEFORE MAKING HIS WAY TO THE ARCHAEOLOGICAL LIBRARY, Nicholas walked down to Mandraki Harbour, dominated by its red-topped windmills and the lighthouse of Agios Nikolaos. He looked for diving centres. Aegean Diving Centre's office was shut. On the door was a sign saying they operated only from April to October. He found a contact number in a dusty corner of the window. Frustrated, he carried on along the harbour wall towards the lighthouse. After a few minutes he spotted a boat moored towards the end of the pier advertising Apollon Scuba Diving School. He called out and eventually someone came out on deck.

An unshaven man, dressed in dirty jeans and a thick blue pullover, regarded Nicholas suspiciously. After a pause, he said in halting English that there was no diving. They were closed. Nicholas asked how he could speak to the owner of the diving school, indicating the sign on the side of the boat. The man disappeared below, then emerged with a flyer advertising courses and dive spots. There was a phone number at the bottom. Nicholas thanked him and walked back despondently the way he had come. Although it was a bit of a stretch expecting a dive school to operate off-season, he was disappointed.

Stopping at a café at the entrance to the port, he ordered a pot of Breakfast tea and phoned each of the dive centres. There was no response from Apollon, but a man answered at the Aegean Diving Centre. He said they were closed until April. Nicholas said he understood, but was looking for some help – he was trying to track down a friend who had taken a scuba course over the past year. Her name was Alessandra Bianchi. The man apologized and said he did not recognise the name. There were so many people who enrolled each year to do a course or just to dive for the day. Nicholas said she was not a tourist, but lived on Rhodes and worked at the museum. She was probably about thirty years old, with long dark hair. The man said he was sorry but he had no recollection of anyone like that and rang off.

With an exclamation of frustration, Nicholas slammed his phone onto the table and finished his tea. He set off for the old medieval city and eventually found Platia Agryrokastrou and the building that housed the Ministry for Culture in what was the first hospital of the knights.

At the reception desk he asked to speak to Effie. "She works in the Archaeological library and should be expecting me. My name is Nicholas." Eventually, a tall slim woman, about Nicholas's age, walked briskly down some steps into the reception area. Her long blonde hair was scraped back. "Hi, I am Effie," she said with a confident smile. She extended her hand to greet Nicholas. "Eleni told me to expect you. Come on through to the library and my office."

Her manner was businesslike. She invited Nicholas to sit and closed the door to the small office. Effie said Eleni had told her why he was there. "I feel so upset. We did not know that Alessandra had gone missing. We all thought she had just returned to the UK suddenly. But, I was surprised that she did not say anything to me before she left. Now, I don't know what to think. It is very strange."

Nicholas said that it was only recently that even her family knew that Alessandra was missing. "The police are not completely convinced that she has disappeared. I think they still believe she is elsewhere. That she has her own reasons for not contacting those close to her."

"It is very odd, though," Effie added. "Anyway, let me help you where I can." She told him she had been introduced to Alessandra by Helena Milonas, a former colleague at the library. "Apparently Helena had known Alessandra from her childhood on the island. Rhodes. They had stayed in touch when Alessandra had gone on to boarding school and university in the UK, seeing each other during holidays."

Effie thought Helena had also lived in England for a time and had stayed with Alessandra. "I believe it was Helena who had first contacted Alessandra about the vacant job at the museum." Helena had worked at the archaeological library, which was where she had first met her. "Some time before that, Helena had worked briefly at the museum, which was presumably how she knew of the vacant position. I think she worked for Michael Kamides there, providing him with some administration help. Anyway, she left here suddenly over a year ago and moved away from Rhodes."

Could this be the friend Alessandra had gone to meet, Nicholas wondered?

"As I got to know Alessandra more, we became good friends. Although I am a bit older than her, we have many of the same interests. I love her infectious approach to life – and her sense of humour. I wish I shared some of those qualities ...

"I have always taken things quite seriously and I am often being told to lighten up." She gave Nicholas a rueful smile that made him suddenly warm to her. She was easy to talk to. He suspected that she shared other basic qualities with Alessandra, if not her spontaneity. "We would spend hours just chatting about work and friends. I have really missed that."

"I understand from Eleni that Alessandra had been spending more and more time in libraries here in the town. That she was researching old trade routes around Rhodes for a potential exhibition."

"I don't know anything about an exhibition, but she was certainly spending a lot of time in our reading rooms looking at old documents. She also used the town public library to research old maps. As you probably know, Rhodes and its port were once hugely important commercially across this area of the Mediterranean."

"Yes, I had never realised how strategically important Rhodes had once been."

"Alessandra seemed to have a particular focus on the early trading years – during the first millennium. Sometimes I helped her to find documents. She used the computer system in the main Greek archaeological library in Athens."

Nicholas asked if there might be a search record of documents Alessandra had accessed. Effie said she would check all the records as soon as she could. "It is so kind of you to give up some of your time searching for Alessandra. I would really like to help you in any way I can," she said.

"Your help is invaluable. You knew Alessandra. My only knowledge of her was from the time spent with her on the ferry. It's not much to go on, and her parents were not particularly forthcoming – for whatever reason."

Nicholas asked Effie about Alessandra's friends. He said he was aware that she had had a wealthy boyfriend called Andriy and that the relationship was quite volatile. Effie said she had met him a few times, usually after work with Alessandra.

"I expect he found me a bit boring compared with Alessandra," she said. Her mobile phone rang. She looked at it, hesitated, then turned it off. "It can wait. I will get back to them. Anyway, he said he was an academic studying early trade in the eastern Mediterranean. I think he said he was from Minsk. He had a large boat moored in the port, which I think Alessandra had been on several times.

"He was certainly knowledgeable about ancient commercial routes through the Holy Land and across the Middle East. We had some interesting discussions."

Effie said Alessandra had brought him to the library a couple of times and they had spent quite a lot of time studying some of the documents in the reading room. She thought this shared interest explained how they had first met and started going out. "He was quite difficult and demanding and I was never sure what Alessandra really saw in him. However, knowing her, she always saw the positive in people. I was not surprised when it ended, though, although Alessandra had a hard time. Even though she ended the relationship, Andriy would not leave her alone. She told me at one stage that she was becoming a bit afraid of him."

"So he stayed here … in Rhodes?"

"I think his business interests took him away quite often." Effie said she had seen Andriy only once after he and Alessandra had split up. "I bumped into him in a street in Lindos one weekend, but he barely acknowledged me. I think his boat disappeared from its usual berth in the harbour here soon afterwards."

"And her other friends?"

"Alessandra was also very friendly with Eleni, who you have already met. Alessandra often spent weekends with her and her family. Her daughter worshipped Alessandra.

"There were also a couple of men that Alessandra occasionally socialised with when she was with Andriy. I never felt comfortable around them. They were not particularly friendly. I tried to make sure I was never alone with them. There seemed to be a contained aggression about them, although they never did anything to me. It was just an odd feeling I had. I am not sure how Alessandra felt around them. They talked very little about themselves. The rest of her friends were mainly from work. I know that, after she broke up with her boyfriend, Michael Kamides kept on asking her out for a drink, which she found a bit awkward."

Effie walked with him to the entrance and shook his hand, saying, "I wish you well Nicholas". They agreed to meet at the end of the week.

Nicholas's mood had lifted. Perhaps it was just the sharing of the search effort or because he felt he could really talk to Effie. He could see how she and Alessandra had become such good friends. They complemented each other. There was an unexpected vulnerability about Effie that he found attractive. He hoped they could work together to find some concrete clue to reveal Alessandra's whereabouts.

He took out his phone and dialed Apollon Scuba Diving. He was surprised when the call was answered and he was greeted in English. "Hello, this is Demetrius, OK. How can I help you?

"Hello, Demetrius. I am hoping you can help me. I am looking for a friend who has gone missing. I know she did a scuba-diving course in Mandraki harbour over the last couple of years, so I am speaking to all the scuba schools on Rhodes, hoping to trace her."

"OK, I will help you, if I can. What is her name?"

"Alessandra Bianchi, she is about thirty, slim with dark hair."

"Yes, I remember her. She was always friendly. She took her PADI course with us more than a year ago and then did some dives at sites around the island. I took her for her first dive in St Paul's Bay at Lindos. It was where she wanted to go.

"She told me she would like to dive off some of the other islands, OK. She wanted to know whether these islands had their own dive centres. She was a very confident diver, yes." He told Nicholas that she had also said she would like to learn cave diving, but it's not something they offered. "The last time I saw her was August, maybe September, last year. I hope you find her, OK."

Nicholas returned to his hotel. He phoned Alessandra's parents and explained that he had made contact with their daughter's friends on Rhodes. They reluctantly agreed to let him visit her apartment in the New Town. They would contact the caretaker and ask him to open the apartment for Nicholas. He wrote down the address and the caretaker's name.

"We were very surprised that you went back to Rhodes," Mrs Bianchi said. She sounded weary. "Captain Petrakis phoned us to let us know that you had come in to see him about Alessandra, but they had no new information. Surely there is nothing you can do that the police can't. You should come home and get on with the rest of your life."

"I'm sorry, but I don't feel that I can do that, now."

"So, how much longer will you go on looking?"

"I don't know. I haven't found anything yet that I didn't already know. I'll keep searching for a while."

As he was ringing off, her voice softened. "Please be careful then." Nicholas put his phone down, thinking that this was an odd thing for her to say. Why would he need to take care?

Chapter Seven

RHODES TOWN

ALESSANDRA'S APARTMENT WAS IN A TRANQUIL, TREE-LINED street, away from the busy main roads that circle the Old Town and the business district. The rain had returned and people were hurrying along the uneven pavements, sheltering beneath umbrellas. Nicholas crossed the road, avoiding an overflowing drainage ditch, and looked up at Alessandra's building. It was a square, white, three-storey block, surrounded by a small garden of orange and lemon trees. He found the path to the entrance and sheltered in a small covered porch while he rang the caretaker's bell. A voice answered in Greek. Nicholas asked if he spoke English. "Small, a little," came the gruff reply. Nicholas explained that he wished to see Alessandra Bianchi's apartment.

"Wait, I come now," came the response. Eventually, an elderly man with disheveled grey hair, and wearing an old white shirt and black trousers, opened the door. He indicated with a nod that Nicholas should follow him. They climbed slowly – one of the old man's hips seemed to trouble him – to the top floor. He searched ponderously through a large bunch of keys. "Oopa!" he grunted, as he finally selected the correct one and opened the door to a large, light-filled apartment. Nicholas entered and looked around. He hadn't been sure what to expect. On first glance the apartment seemed more functional than bohemian. The furnishings were sparse. The walls were painted a standard off-white, with light-grey tiling on the floors. It did not feel lived in and his initial feeling was that Alessandra did not spend much time there. He recognised flashes of her personality in the bright yellow curtains in the main room and a patterned silk scarf draped from a mirror by the front door. The caretaker indicated that he would remain in the doorway. Nicholas wondered if this was on the instruction of her parents.

He didn't know what he expected to find out from her apartment. It felt invasive going through her things and he felt uneasy. He had to admit, however, that he was interested in how she lived and what it might tell him about her. He was not sure how to start or what he was looking for. He decided to search the least likely areas for clues first and give himself more time where it might matter. Off the living room were a bedroom and a kitchen. There was also a small bathroom. Nicholas's eyes were drawn to a diagonal crack in one of the tiles in the hallway.

The bathroom and kitchen suggested that Alessandra did not intend to stay away. The bathroom was cluttered but tidy. Her toiletries and two bottles of perfume were still there – as was a toothbrush. Nicholas spotted a bottle of blue nail polish on the shelf. He moved on to the kitchen. The fridge yielded the same conclusion. It was fairly bare: there was an opened bottle of white wine, a full bottle of Perrier, a jar of olives and a mouldy plastic-wrapped loaf of wholgrain bread at the back of the shelf. Nicholas also found a small portion of dried-up cheese and a paper packet containing rotted tomatoes. He removed them and put them in a paper bag that he found.

Otherwise, there were no dirty cups or plates lying around. He was pleasantly surprised to find that Alessandra was neat and orderly. Beside the fridge were four sealed packets of dog food. She must have been planning to take these to the sanctuary.

The bedroom was just as tidy. The bed was carefully made, and covered with a blue and mauve patchwork duvet. There were no clothes strewn around. A watercolour of a colourful market scene hung over the bed. Nicholas could not identify the location – possibly it was French. A gaily coloured throw covered the chair in the corner. There was an old suitcase under her bed. It was empty. He looked in her chest of drawers and could see nothing out of place. It felt strange to be looking at intimate items. Unsettled, he hurriedly searched through each drawer and then closed them. He opened a wardrobe that contained an array of dresses and print skirts, but few trousers he noted. A selection of turquoise and emerald green bead necklaces, that looked as though they might have come from India, hung from a hook in the door. To one side of the cupboard were a couple of winter coats. Would Alessandra have left without a coat? He would not know whether any of her clothes was missing, but it did not look as though she had packed hurriedly. At the bottom of the cupboard her shoes and boots were neatly stacked. He also found a bag containing scuba and snorkeling equipment.

On a cabinet next to the bed stood an alarm clock, phone charger and a small brown photo album. He flicked through the album, peering closely at each picture. Did they contain any clues? He wondered if the police had removed any of the photos to assist them in their initial search. Some photographs were obviously taken around the island or in Rhodes Town. In one he recognised Alessandra with her parents in the Old Town. Others were more difficult to identify, but were taken somewhere around the Greek islands. Some were underwater shots of various fish and the murky outlines of coral and rocky structures.

He removed a photo of Alessandra smiling, dressed in a bright, patterned red skirt. Judging from the cobbled lanes and the pale brown stone of the surrounding buildings, it was taken somewhere within the Old Town. He took another, a group shot, showing Alessandra with her friends in the apartment. Everyone was sitting around the table in the living room, smiling or laughing. The table was covered with wine bottles, glasses and a typical local meze of cheese, bread, olives, tomatoes, tarama and tzatziki. A man with dark hair sat next to Alessandra – it must have been Andriy – his arm draped around her shoulders. He recognised Eleni. One of the last photographs in the album was a selfie of Alessandra and another woman, who looked Greek. She was slightly bigger than Alessandra, with shorter dark hair. Both were standing at the edge of a small harbour. Behind them was the sea with a small rocky island in the background. Nicholas could just see the tip of a Greek flag flying from a mast. He wondered whether the picture was taken on Halki and also whether the woman was Alessandra's friend Helena. As an afterthought he took it as well.

Tucking the photographs in his pocket, Nicholas moved on to the lounge. To one side was the table in the photo. On it were orderly piles of papers and another of Alessandra's brightly coloured scarves. There was a large green couch and a comfortable armchair. None of the furniture looked new or to what he imagined would be Alessandra's taste. She must have rented the apartment furnished. In the corner was a small television. No phone was evident.

Nicholas started his search with the metal bookcase near the entrance. Along with modern fiction, he found books by Lawrence Durrell and Graham Greene, as well as travel guides to Rhodes, the Dodecanese and Greece. There were manuals on scuba diving, as well as illustrated guides to dive locations around the world. Alessandra's collection included books on Greek and Rhodian archaeology and history, as well as a volume on Ancient Greek mythology. All looked well used. A section of the bookcase was devoted to maps, including detailed maps of Rhodes and the wider Dodecanese. On the top were maps of Symi and Livadia.

The caretaker interrupted Nicholas's search, signalling that he had to go downstairs. "Soon, yes," he said, indicating that he would be back shortly. Nicholas concentrated on the piles of papers on the table. One contained bills. Alessandra had marked not only whether they had been paid but also when. There was also a receipt for the payment of the lease on the apartment – for a year. He searched the bills for signs of unusual purchases, such as airline tickets. There was nothing. There was also a large pile of unopened mail. Nicholas assumed that it had been put there by the police or the caretaker. He left it unopened.

To one side was flyer advertising the dog sanctuary. He wrote down the phone number. He would contact them to find out whether they had heard from Alessandra.

He turned to the third pile of papers, which seemed to be a collection of notes and articles on areas that Alessandra was researching. There was a writing pad with notes on the old trade routes around Rhodes. He flipped through and found details on early trade with Syria and Turkey. Further down the pile of papers he came across notes on dive sites around the coast. Included was a brochure of sites in Lindos. At the bottom was a clear plastic folder containing photocopies of maps of old trading routes around the Dodecanese, as well as old documents written in Greek that he could not understand. Another folder contained copies of academic and archaeological articles.

Nicholas could hear the halting tread of the caretaker making his slow way up the stairs. He had just unearthed a folder with articles on the archaeology of the old harbour area, the Acropolis of Rhodes and the great earthquake. He had no time to read it, so he put all the folders in a large envelope he found on the table. He sealed it and tucked it inside his jacket. Turning, he made a final search for a laptop, diary and any other notebooks. He found nothing.

Nicholas asked the caretaker whether anyone else had visited the apartment. Only one person – a Greek woman – had asked if she could enter the apartment. She said she was a friend of Alessandra. He had not let her in and could not describe her to Nicholas, other than that she sounded local.

By the time Nicholas left the rain had softened to a drizzle. He zipped up his jacket to protect the envelope. It was early evening, so he stopped in a bar for a beer and a snack on his way back to the hotel. An English Premiership football match from the previous evening was showing. He was not a football fan, but it provided a diversion. Two hours later, having watched a tepid nil-nil draw, he emerged into the gloom feeling dispirited and left.

—

The barman asked Nicholas if he would like another drink. The question jolted him back to the present. He shook his head and looked around the room. Everyone had left and the music had finished some time ago. He was still shaken by the chill of the woman's calm threat.

Back in his room, it felt as though the air had been disturbed. Immediately he saw things were not right. The room was as meticulously tidy as he had left it, but everything seemed to have shifted – very slightly. The book he had been reading was in a different position on the bedside table. Opening it he found the envelope he had used as a bookmark was not where he had left it. He looked in his bedside drawer and found his sunglasses, car keys and headache tablets had been pushed into one corner. The maps of Rhodes town and the island, his guidebook, his notebook containing the notes he had made on Alessandra's friends and their phone numbers, the paper with the contact name and phone number for the Rhodes police were jumbled, as though someone had been hurriedly searching through them.

He went to the cupboard. The shirts, which he had folded neatly into a pile when he had unpacked, had been moved and were now all slightly askew. He checked the safe in the cupboard.

It was still locked. He entered the combination and looked inside. His passport, airline ticket and money were still there. Nothing obvious had been stolen. He put the envelope containing the documents and notes taken from Alessandra's apartment into the safe, reset the combination and locked it again.

He went into the bathroom. When he left the hotel earlier his room had already been cleaned. He opened the mirrored cabinet above the basin. His toiletries had been moved. He looked into his wash bag and saw someone had been through it.

Nicholas returned to the bedroom and sat on the bed. He felt invaded. His hands were shaking. He wished he had brought a second brandy up to his room. When he had finally recovered his composure he started to feel a sense of outrage. He caught the lift down to the lobby, where he asked the night manager whether anyone had asked for him or for his room number.

"A woman did come in some hours ago and asked for you by name," the manager replied. "I told her you were out, sir, so she said she would wait. I think she went and sat in the lounge." He described the woman who had met Nicholas at the bar. "Of course, the hotel has a policy of not giving out the room number of guests," he said.

Nicholas told him that someone had been in his room and gone through all of his things. The manager said he would need to report this. He had come on duty at 6pm and it might have happened before that. He continued to assure Nicholas that no one was allowed access to guest rooms without their permission. He looked a little less self-important now.

"How would someone have obtained access without a key?" Nicholas persisted.

The manager shrugged. "Has anything been stolen?"

"Not that I could see. But that is not the point." Nicholas said he assumed the police would be informed.

"Certainly," the manager replied. "But, if nothing is missing, they will not come immediately. I am sorry. I will make a report now and when you come down tomorrow you can speak to the hotel manager. He will also inform the police. This is very unfortunate."

Nicholas returned to his room. It was now half past midnight. He went to bed and lay there, thinking. To dispel the feeling of invasion he had opened his window wide. The sound of late-night traffic outside drifted into the room. There must be a connection between the searching of his room and the threat from the woman, he thought. What had they been looking for? He turned over the possibilities in his mind.

His search for Alessandra had taken a serious turn and there were more questions than ever to be answered. How had anyone learned that he was looking for her? He had been in Rhodes for less than a week. Since arriving he had spoken only to the police and those who knew her. He had presumed they all had her interests at heart.

More important, why would anyone be concerned about someone searching for a person who was merely listed as missing? It did not add up. The one thing he couldn't ignore was the menace behind the earlier warning. The obvious course of action would be to heed the advice and leave things well alone. After all, finding Alessandra was not really his responsibility. Many people, including the police, had already told him as much.

An owl called in the trees outside. Nicholas continued to turn over all the options. He eventually fell into a troubled sleep at about three in the morning.

Chapter Eight

RHODES TOWN

NICHOLAS SAT IN THE POLICE WAITING AREA. CAPTAIN Petrakis was taking his time. The Rhodes police did not seem to be overburdened with cases that morning. Nicholas was alone in the drab room lined with plastic chairs, with only the peeling green paint to contemplate. His habitual politeness deserted him, as he became increasingly irritated by the wait. Eventually, a door opened and he was taken along a similarly depressing corridor, painted in the same shade of green, and shown back into Petrakis' office where the Captain was waiting behind a battered-looking table. Declining a coffee, Nicholas pulled up the grey plastic chair and told the policeman why he had come back. Petrakis listened politely, but no hint of emotion crossed his world-weary features. He acknowledged that a report of the incident had been made earlier by the hotel, and asked whether anything had been stolen. He seemed sympathetic about Nicholas's concerns regarding the threat from the woman in the bar and agreed there could well be a link with the break-in to his room, but said there was no evidence that the events were connected to Alessandra's disappearance.

"Mr Adams, as you say nothing was stolen from your room, I am afraid that all I can do is make a note of the incident," he said, in a manner that suggested he had more serious issues requiring his attention.

"We will of course question the barman at your hotel, as well as the person who cleaned your room yesterday. Perhaps they have seen someone suspicious on your floor."

He did at least ask for a description of the woman from Nicholas and said his officers would talk to the hotel staff.

"Thank you for coming in and I'm sorry I kept you waiting," he said, as he shepherded Nicholas towards the exit. "We will contact you if we obtain any further information from our enquiries." Nicholas was not going to hold his breath.

He walked out of the soulless police headquarters into a weak sun that echoed his mood. The rain of the day before ran in the gutters at the side of the street. As he walked past the graffiti-covered concrete walls of a school sports ground, the shrieks of children and the thud of a football being kicked behind it, sounded more sinister than cheering. He found a sidewalk café where Saturday morning traffic buzzed past and phoned Effie. They agreed to meet later at a bar in Orfeos Street, in the Old Town.

"I should be able to get away. I will come straight from work and will meet you there," she said.

It was good to hear her voice. Nicholas realised how much he was in need of a sympathetic ear. He felt deflated. Back in his hotel room, he could see that nothing else had been disturbed. He removed the envelope containing Alessandra's documents and notes from the safe and sat down to read.

He began with the articles and the copies of documents. One offered a brief history of Rhodes town. It said that, since ancient times, the island had been a main intersection between the Mediterranean and Aegean seas and was an important economic hub. Towards the end of the Peloponnesian War, in 408BC, three of the island's ancient towns – Kamiros, Ialysos and Lindos – were merged to take advantage of the island's best natural harbour and became Rhodes town. The resulting increase in trade meant the city flourished for the next fifty years until the island was conquered by Mausolus of Halicarnassus. Shortly afterwards, it fell into Persian hands for a brief time before it was captured by Alexander the Great.

Ancient history had always intrigued Nicholas – like Alessandra, he rather wished he had taken a course in it rather than the chemistry major at Southampton. He read on. Rhodes then decided to enter into an agreement with Egypt to cooperate against a common enemy, Antigonus Monophthalmus of Macedonia. In 305BC, Antigonus sent his son, Demetrius, to capture and punish the city of Rhodes for this alliance. Demetrius attacked with a huge army of forty thousand men and a year-long siege began.

Nicholas leant back on the bed and stretched. It had been a hell of a hundred years for the poor inhabitants of the city. He read on. Ptolemy of Egypt then sent a relief force of ships to help defend Rhodes and Demetrius finally abandoned the siege, leaving behind most of his equipment. To celebrate the victory, the city sold the siege equipment and used the money to build a massive statue to their sun god, Helios. This was the Colossus of Rhodes, which was to become one of the Seven Wonders of the Ancient World. Not long afterwards, in 227BC, an earthquake devastated the city and toppled the huge statue.

Nicholas was surprised that the great Colossus had stood for such a short time. He turned back to the article, which eventually took the reader all the way through to the 20th century, when, in 1912, the Italians occupied Rhodes until their surrender in 1943. Four years later, it became part of modern-day Greece, along with the other Dodecanese islands.

Nicholas got up and looked out of the window. What an amazing and chaotic history Rhodes had endured. He began to feel some of Alessandra's passion for its ancient past and a developing curiosity about the history of the Colossus.

He needed exercise and fresh air, but he had plenty of time before he was due to meet Effie and, taking an orange juice from his mini-bar, he sat down again and turned to the article on the earthquake of 226BC. It told him that Rhodes lay on the boundary of the Aegean Sea, known as the Aegean Arc, and the continental African tectonic plates. The earthquake of 226BC was known to be associated with a catastrophic uplift of the fault-line of more than three metres.

Alessandra had made notes in the margin. He wondered what her interest was. They indicated that the epicentre of the earthquake was estimated to be in the sea just south of Symi. Nicholas knew Symi lay just off mainland Turkey. Some accounts suggested that the earthquake also caused a tsunami, although there was no concrete evidence. Significant damage was done to large portions of Rhodes town. The harbour area, including its commercial buildings, was destroyed and the Colossus was toppled. It lay in pieces near the port for centuries.

The ancient writer Strabo's account was among Alessandra's documents. It said that the citizens of Rhodes consulted the oracle of Delphi because they feared the huge statue had in some way offended Helios, who had used the earthquake to destroy it. According to Strabo, the oracle instructed the citizens of Rhodes not to rebuild it.

Finally, Nicholas turned to a paper on the history and archaeology of the Acropolis of Rhodes. He had visited the site, a couple of kilometres from the city centre, the last time he had visited the island. It was set in a park on a hill behind the city. He had walked around the remnants of a temple and a stadium. Excavation work was being carried out in the Acropolis archaeological park. Alessandra must have spent some of her time there.

He got up and stretched again. It was now early evening and he was due to meet Effie soon. He gathered up all of Alessandra's papers and notes and put them back in the safe.

It was dark and there was a slight chill in the air when he emerged from the hotel and walked towards the Old Town. Turning down Orfeus Street, Nicholas found the bar Effie had recommended. In its dimly lit interior he saw her waiting at a table to the side. She was wearing her work clothes, a neat white top and black skirt, but her long, blonde hair was loose and she looked less formal. He kissed her on both cheeks. "You look lovely," he said.

Effie smiled and touched his arm. "Thank you. You, I'm afraid, look a bit tired".

"Yes, I probably do. I have been studying."

They ordered a bottle of local red wine that Effie chose. A fire in the grate warmed the room. Nicholas began to relax and said it was really good to see her. Explaining all that had happened, he told her of his visit to Alessandra's apartment and how it had appeared that she had intended to return from her trip to Halki. He told her he had taken documents and notes he had found, looking for clues about her disappearance. "There is a lot of reading and information to go through. It's going to take me some time. That's probably why I look tired, although I didn't have the best night's sleep last night."

Nicholas showed Effie the group photo he had found in Alessandra's flat and asked her if the man with his arm around Alessandra was Andriy. Effie held the photo to the candle and said it was and that the man at the end of the table was one of Andriy's friends. He also showed her the harbourside photograph of Alessandra with another woman and asked if that was Helena. She took her time. "She looks a bit older in this than I remember her. Her hair is also different, but, yes, it's her."

Nicholas told her what had happened to him after he had left Alessandra's apartment. "I was really shocked. It took me by surprise, being threatened like that. It must have been connected with Alessandra's disappearance. Why else would anyone want to warn me off, though they never said what it was about. Then, when I went to my room and found someone had been through my things ..."

Effie looked horrified. "Oh Nicholas, I am so sorry. How terrible for you." She squeezed his hand in concern. "How are you feeling?"

Nicholas said he was fine now and had reported it to the police.

"Who did you speak to?"

"Captain Petrakis."

"Ah yes, I know the good Captain. So what are you going to do now?"

"I am booked into the hotel for another week, so for the moment I will continue my search. I'll decide at the end of the week whether there's anything more I can do."

"And what about the threat? Are you not a bit nervous?"

"In truth, yes I am. I've never experienced anything like that – at work I might have the odd difficult customer – but to be threatened is a first for me. It did shake me. I'll be more careful now. For the next week I'll do my best to look like any other tourist – just enjoying the sights." Nicholas tried to make light of it, snatching up his mobile phone and taking a photograph of her with glass in hand, but Effie wasn't to be diverted.

"I feel nervous for you. Please take care. If it is your decision to stay I'll do my best to help you."

Finishing their wine they decided to go on to a restaurant where Effie knew the owner. Nicholas welcomed the company. The owner of the restaurant was delighted to see Effie and Nicholas was charmed by the warmth and ease that only comes between old friends. The owner beamed as he showed them to their table. After they ordered their food, Nicholas summarised what he had found among Alessandra's documents.

"I am sure you know most of this history. I found it fascinating, though I'm not sure what it is telling me. It feels like looking for a needle in a haystack at the moment."

Effie surprised Nicholas by admitting that she had never heard that phrase before and was intrigued with its explanation. Swapping English and Greek idioms in the warm, friendly atmosphere of the restaurant where Effie was so much at ease made a pleasant diversion. While they were chatting, Nicholas appraised her. He liked this woman, although she could be quite serious and direct. He felt he was party to a rare moment when she allowed herself to fully relax.

The mood switched again and she became businesslike once more. She said she had had some news for him. She had got hold of information on the computer searches Alessandra had made at the institute. "I was a bit surprised. They seemed to concentrate on the time of the building of the Colossus. She had also done a search on the recovery and sale of the remnants of the statue, hundreds of years later. Rhodes was captured by a Muslim caliph in the middle of the seventh century," she said. The remains of the Colossus were sold to a Jewish merchant from Syria who had realised how valuable they were because of their metal content. When the merchant removed all the pieces, it was alleged that he had to use almost a thousand camels for the transportation. "What finally happened to all those remnants after their removal no one really knows."

"I was rather thinking of all those camels," laughed Nicholas.

"Who knows what happened to them," said Effie, more seriously. "Apart from the camels, it has always amazed me that not one authenticated relic has ever been found of what was once considered a wonder of the world. It seems there is very little recorded, but Alessandra did manage to find a story dating from the 13th century, in Edessa, about the Arab pillage in Rhodes. Effie took a folded paper from her handbag. She said, with a smile, that though she knew a lot of the story she had had to make some notes herself.

"Apparently, the sole source of all the accounts of the sale and removal of the statue is someone called Theophanes the Confessor. All that is really known is that camels were used to carry the fragments to merchant ships and it is thought they were transported back to Syria. I guess that might explain some of Alessandra's interest in Syria."

The food arrived and Effie folded her notes on the table. "This looks delicious," Nicholas said. They chatted about Rhodes and Effie's day at work. Nicholas asked whether she had any brothers or sisters.

"One sister," Effie replied. "She is younger, married and lives in Prasonisi which is right at the bottom of the island, past Lindos. She and her husband run a windsurfing business there. They always seem blissfully happy," she said, without a hint of wistfulness. "See. It can happen. And they are doing exactly what they always wanted to do."

Nicholas felt he should return the gesture and tell Effie a bit more about himself, something that did not come naturally to him. "I still find it quite difficult to talk about, but I was married for quite a few years. Lynda was wonderful and I still miss her. She died almost two years ago ... of cancer. It was very hard, particularly the last few months."

"I am so sorry," Effie said, leaning towards him.

"I still struggle with it. I think it has had some effect on my relationships, particularly with women."

Effie reached out and touched his arm. Her concern was genuine and the physical gesture reassuring. They ate in silence for a while.

When they had finished their meal, Effie unfolded her notes. "Are you OK with me going on, or should we do this another time?"

"Yes, please do. I am fine."

Effie tried a lighter tone. "The Statue of Liberty guarding the entrance to New York and the New World was based on the dimensions of the Colossus. Did you also know that your William Shakespeare was fascinated by the story of the Colossus? He used it as a metaphor – is that how you say it? – to describe Caesar in "Julius Caesar". He also alluded to the statue in other plays. The huge statue that was meant to have straddled the entrance to Rhodes harbour has fascinated the outside world for many hundreds of years. Of course, we now know that it is unlikely to have spanned the port entrance. That idea was a product of the rich medieval imagination.

"I didn't know that Alessandra was researching the Colossus," Effie continued. "She certainly never spoke to me about it. I assumed that all the time she was spending in the library was related to what she had been working on at the museum – the excavation going on at Ancient Kamiros."

"Let's assume there's a link between all this and Alessandra's disappearance. What's the best way to find out more about the Colossus?" Nicholas asked. "Perhaps it would provide some further clues."

Effie thought for a moment, then frowned. "I just don't see it."

Eventually she offered, "If you want to look into it my suggestion would be to start at the public library. It is in Aristotelous Street. There is an English historical section. You will also find old maps that go back to ancient times.

"If you have the time you might also visit the Muslim Library on Platia Arionis. It is right at the top of the Old Town, near the Suleiman Mosque. Some of its important manuscripts describe the siege and conquest of Rhodes by the Arabs and then the Turks. You might have to ask for some help."

Nicholas thanked Effie, saying he was sure this would all be useful somehow. He then said: "Effie, has anyone asked about me by any chance?"

She seemed taken aback. "No, why do you ask?"

"I just want to know how the woman who threatened me knew how to find me and what I was doing."

"No one has spoken to me." She seemed thrown by the question and looked uncomfortable. Nicholas, worried that he might have offended her with his clumsy questioning, sought to change the subject. After asking whether she would like some coffee, he returned to safer ground. "You speak very good English, but can I hear the faintest hint of an American accent?"

Effie said her father had worked for an international company and she had learnt English at international schools in Athens and briefly in the US.

"I wanted to be a doctor, once, and also to live in America."

"What stopped you?"

"I got married and it was disastrous. I wasn't able to study. The marriage didn't last long. He was an idiot. It just took me a bit of time to see it. Luckily, I got over it and just got on with my life."

Nicholas found her straightforward manner refreshing. He was interested to know more, but there was something closed about Effie and she obviously had nothing more to say about her marriage. She began searching her handbag for her keys.

As they left the restaurant, she said that she would be happy to help Nicholas look for her friend. Nearing her street she said, cautiously "I had a good time tonight. I am so sorry about your wife, but I do find you attractive. I also enjoy your company. What I am saying is that I would like to continue to see you if you are alright with that."

Nicholas hesitated, confused by her. He enjoyed her company. He had thought, though, that she was just being helpful in trying to find her friend. She was an intelligent woman, so she must realise that a large part of the reason for him returning to Rhodes to search for Alessandra was that he had feelings for her that he could only hope were reciprocated. He eventually said: "I would like that. I enjoyed this evening. It is good having a friend here."

They parted at the entrance to her apartment building, promising to meet again soon. Nicholas said he would follow up on Alessandra's research and would phone Effie in the next day or so. As he walked back to his hotel, warmed by the ouzo and wine, he wondered whether he had misunderstood Effie's intentions. Perhaps she had read something into what he had said? He was reluctant to trust his instincts these days. His confidence had taken a blow when Alessandra hadn't turned up for their meeting and, even if he now knew the reason, he had been left feeling uncertain.

He knew women found him attractive. Since Lynda's death, a few had given him hints, but, in his grief, he had no interest in any emotional attachments. He had always erected barriers with women, anyway, even before Lynda.

At the moment he felt that whatever charm he might have had once had long deserted him. Lynda said she had married him for his charm rather than his boyish good looks. Alessandra had been the first to awaken feelings that had been well hidden since Lynda had died. Perhaps the fact that he had been so attracted to her meant the barriers were starting to come down. It was a new and not entirely unwelcome feeling.

He had to admit that he did find Effie attractive, too, as any man would. He felt something, but what it was he was not sure. He shook his head. He could well imagine what his grief counsellor would have made of this, but he knew he needed an ally and someone to confide in.

Chapter Nine

RHODES TOWN

THERE WAS A BUSTLE TO THE STREET MARKETS OF THE OLD Town. One or two more shops were opening and Nicholas noticed the odd tourist on the streets. The public library was housed on the ground floor of the "Kastellania" – a medieval building that had been the meeting point for the merchants of Rhodes.

Nicholas was guided to the English language section and given the access code for the online records. Selecting some books, he settled down at one of the long wooden desks and began reading one. Early medieval engravings showed the naked Colossus as a huge man, torch in one hand, flame billowing, and holding a spear in the other. The statue wore a spiked crown. The straddled legs, each foot resting on a giant pillar, allowed masted ships under full sail to pass beneath. These were the images that Nicholas was most familiar with. The record explained that the reality was more prosaic. Had the statue straddled the harbour entrance, the port would have had to be closed to trade for the twelve years it took to build. A cross-reference to another study also noted that the ancient Rhodians did not possess the means to dredge and reopen the harbour after construction. Recent archaeological evidence suggested that the Colossus might have stood on the hill overlooking the harbour. An article by an archaeologist proposed that the Colossus might even have been part of the Acropolis overlooking the port. An alternative theory that had also gained some credibility was that the sandstone floor of the harbourside Fortress of St Nicholas, with its lighthouse, was originally the foundation for the marble base of the Colossus.

Nicholas found a translation of a text by Pliny the Elder, who described the statue's construction. The architect was Charos of Lindos. His ambitious brief was to build a statue twice as tall as any that had ever been built. Sadly the unfortunate Charos became so ashamed when someone noticed a slight design fault in the construction that he committed suicide shortly before the statue was finally completed.

The base of the statue had supposedly been built of white marble. The structure was made around an iron and stone framework. Much of the iron and bronze used in the construction came from the weapons of the defeated Macedonian invaders. A captured giant enemy siege tower, nine storeys high, provided the scaffolding for the project. It was claimed that silver was used to make the spikes surrounding the crown. When completed, the Colossus was more than thirty metres high, each thigh three metres in width. After it was destroyed in the earthquake the statue remained on the ground until its sale in AD653. As Effie had described, the remnants were transported by boat to Syria, where it appears they disappeared for good.

Nicholas felt he had learnt all he needed to about the Colossus. It must have been a magnificent sight to both friend and invader. It amazed him that it had stood for only about fifty years. He imagined what a draw it might have been to this incredible city had it remained. Alessandra's notes had revealed her interest in the statue, and she had been researching it, rather than her work project. He was beginning to feel that her disappearance was somehow interwoven with the history of the Colossus, but how was not at all clear. He needed to read up on the period 800 years later when the statue was taken to Syria.

First he needed some fresh air. He gathered up his reading matter and asked the library assistant whether he could leave them somewhere and return to them later. Nicholas walked out of the library into the bright sunshine of the square outside. While he was thinking about what he had read, his phone rang. It was Eleni from the museum. "Hello Nicholas. I promised to get back to you if we turned up any old employees with connections to Halki," she said.

"Yes?" Nicholas was suddenly focused.

"Well, I spoke to our administration department and they found that someone who worked for us briefly, about three years ago, went to live on Halki. Her name was Helena Milonas and I believe she also knew Alessandra. Alessandra had certainly mentioned her name to me. They had a phone number for her. I did try it earlier, but there was no reply."

Nicholas remembered the selfie taken with Alessandra. Eleni gave Nicholas the phone number and Helena's address on Halki, cautioning him that these details were three years old. Nicholas tried the number but got no response. He looked around him. He was still worried that someone might be following him. He saw no one acting suspiciously.

A tour company was offering trips around the harbour, so he walked to the port, enjoying the chance for some exercise. At Mandraki, a glass-bottomed boat tour was leaving soon, so he paid and went aboard. There was only a handful of customers and he settled down at the rear of the boat. He hoped the tour might add perspective to the dry descriptions of the old port in the reference books.

He was glad of his jacket as the wind increased. From the water, the coastline of mainland Turkey emerged on the horizon, reminding him how close the two countries were. The tour guide provided a commentary in English as they moved slowly through the harbour. Little evidence remained of what was once a rich and successful commercial port. Superyachts now mingled with traditional fishing boats in the marina. Larger tour boats offering trips to Symi and Nisyros lay idle, waiting for the summer season to start.

The boat headed along the quay towards the harbour entrance. Late-night bars and cafes lined the quays. A Spanish couple sitting in front of Nicholas asked the guide about the buildings on the right of the boat. Nicholas saw the three windmills, standing like pepper pots along the breakwater where merchant ships had once offloaded their cargoes of grain. The guide explained that the windmills were one of the few reminders of the port's commercial past. At the head of the harbour the boat came alongside St Nicholas Fort, with its lighthouse, Greek flag fluttering in the wind. Looking back Nicholas saw the minarets and castle turrets pierce the skyline over the medieval walled city, evidence of the rich tapestry of the city's past.

His thoughts drifted back to the phone call from Eleni. It now seemed likely that the friend Alessandra had gone to meet on Halki was Helena. It was also likely that she had disappeared soon after this visit. What could have happened? Coupled with his belief that his research was leading somewhere, the call made him feel he was a step closer.

The tour boat continued slowly through the grey-green water towards the harbour mouth. The guide announced that this had once been dominated by the Colossus. Nicholas felt the weight of ancient history enveloping him, drawing him in. Today the guardians of the port and town beyond were the twin bronze statues of Elafos and Elafina, the male and female deer that symbolised the island, sitting atop slender stone columns.

Back on dry land, Nicholas returned to the library via one of the quayside cafes. As he passed through the old stone arch leading to the old town, someone bumped him from behind. He jumped and, despite the apology offered by the American tourist, his heart raced. Only when he was seated at the desk he had occupied earlier, did he feel his heart rate slow. He settled down to read about the history of early trade and the trade routes between Rhodes and Syria. In the first two centuries, Rhodes had thrived as the leading trading centre of the eastern Mediterranean. When it was occupied by the Islamic Umayyad forces of Caliph Muawiyah I in 654, it was claimed that the remains of the Colossus were sold to a salesman from Syria for an amount, in today's currency, equivalent to the current cost of a mid-range family car. The remains were transported to a town now known as Homs and were melted down on arrival in Syria to make bronze coins. Other accounts suggested that the pieces were transported across Asia Minor. Some accounts also claimed that fragments turned up for sale years later, after being found the length of the old caravan route. None of these theories could be corroborated.

Nicholas remembered that Effie had suggested he visit the Muslim Library and he resolved to do so. Turning to the last document, he read that there were ports, including Lindos, trading between Rhodes and the eastern Mediterranean. However, most commercial transport came from Rhodes Town. At this time Syria and Turkey were key trading partners. The principal routes tended to be north from Rhodes to Turkey, sailing past Symi, or east to Cyprus and the Syrian ports.

Nicholas returned the books and documents and emerged into dusk. Lights were starting to come on in the shops, bars and restaurants. He strolled up Sokratous Street looking into shop windows as he passed. The eerie feeling that he was being followed returned. Perhaps he was just being paranoid. He went into a shop selling ceramics and looked out.

There were passers-by but no one stopped. He came out of the shop, but could not identify anyone that he might have seen earlier. He was cross at being so jumpy. He needed a beer and went into a bar. Choosing a seat near the front so that he could keep watch, he sat down and ordered. Thinking that Effie should have finished work he gave her a call. She picked up straight away, sounding delighted to hear from Nicholas. It was reassuring. Nicholas told her what he had found at the library. Effie said she had phoned Eleni to discuss what Alessandra was working on just before she went missing.

"I thought she was meant to be working on the excavations at Ancient Kamiros and cataloguing the artifacts at the museum. Eleni seemed to think Alessandra was working on something else. Something she was very enthusiastic about, but kept to herself." Eleni thought Alessandra had started looking at some of the trade routes around Rhodes. "She said Alessandra's interest was focused more on the islands around Rhodes, rather than Rhodes itself."

Nicholas recounted the phone call earlier from Eleni. "You mentioned the old friend of Alessandra called Helena Milonas," he said. "Well, it transpires that she is living on Halki." He told Effie what Eleni had uncovered at the museum. "It would seem likely that the friend Alessandra was visiting when she disappeared was Helena. You also said that she had worked there for Michael Kamides."

Effie was silent, then said: "It is interesting." Nicholas wondered at her tone, there was something enigmatic about it and it was not the encouraging response he expected. He said he had tried to phone Helena, without success. Eleni had also tried. "However, we do have an address."

"Leave that with me," Effie said. "I will see what I can find out."

The next day was a Saturday and he asked whether she would like to go to Lindos for the day. "I want to follow up on a couple of things that Alessandra mentioned to me on the ferry." He also wanted to try to speak to a friend of hers who lived in Lindos. He looked at his notebook. "I think you said her name was Caroline and she was in the tourist industry there. Could you see whether you can find her work or even a home address. Also a phone number, if you can. I have a feeling that she is a part of this puzzle."

Effie said she would love to go with him and would see what she could find out. She would look through her phone and address book. She had a car and would pick him up from his hotel at 9am. He finished his second beer and got up to leave. He had not mentioned the feeling of being followed. He did not want to worry her. When he emerged from the bar, he looked both ways.

Chapter Ten

RHODES TOWN AND LINDOS

EFFIE'S DRIVING WAS CAUTIOUS. "I AM NOT THE GREATEST driver," she confessed with a quick sideways glance. "I really don't drive that often." Nicholas was surprised at this admission. She seemed so confident in so many ways, but the vulnerability he had detected was showing itself.

"Honestly, don't worry on my part. You are doing fine."

"I am also nervous of some of the driving here. I think you could best characterise it as aggressive – or perhaps interesting – if you are feeling charitable."

The traffic was heavy on the narrow roads leading out of the town. Eventually, they emerged onto the two-lane section of motorway leading south from Rhodes town. They drove past the tacky neon-lit bars and restaurants serving "traditional Greek food", signifying the outskirts of Faliraki. It looked forlorn out of season. When Effie felt she could relax she said she had forgotten to tell Nicholas the other evening of another search Alessandra had made.

"She researched a report in 1987 that the remains of part of the statue had been found in Rhodes harbour. Apparently, a Dutch clairvoyant had visited Rhodes and predicted that the remains would be found lying on the seabed, six hundred metres off St Nicholas Fort. This led to an intensive underwater search of the area. The divers found a giant fist on the seabed. It weighed over a ton and was six feet long. When archaeologists examined it, though, they cast doubt on the idea that it was part of the Colossus, as it was found to be made of limestone."

"Ah. Rather an anticlimax," Nicholas interjected.

Effie smiled and continued. "Yes, somewhat. Later on it was determined that the hand was really just a huge lump of rock. Apparently, the knuckle shape had actually been gouged out by a mechanical digger and the rock had been dumped in the sea. So the mystery continues." They laughed at the thought that a stone, probably discarded by one of the many property developers, could have excited such international interest.

After a while, the road turned up into the hills and soon the sea appeared to the left. They passed the turn-off to Pylona where Nicholas felt everything had all started.

The first sight of Lindos is always spectacular. They came round the corner from Vlicha Bay and there was the Acropolis cresting the cypress-covered hill and dominating the whitewashed town below. Effie pointed to a round structure on the hilltop, to the left, on the opposite side of Lindos Bay. It reminded Nicholas of his time at the villa he had rented and the long hot walk out to visit the tomb of Cleobulus.

They turned off into the steep, narrow road that led to the town. Effie said she had managed to find a phone number for Caroline and had given her a ring the previous evening. She was aware Alessandra had left Rhodes, but did not know she had been classified as missing. "She was very upset when she heard," Effie said.

Caroline had suggested that they meet at an address in the town. "She is taking over a small tour company operating out of Lindos and said she would be in the town this morning. They are renovating the office, ready for the start of the new season."

Turning down the road to the beach on Lindos Bay they parked and walked the short way up the hill. Nicholas noticed that Effie was wearing a blue floral dress this morning – a change from her usual, formal black and white work clothes. She looked good. Nicholas was disconcerted when he found himself admiring her long legs. Goats grazed on leaves from the lower branches of scrubby olive trees lining the road, as they walked past the closed tavernas and bars. A few visitors mingled with the donkeys taking tourists up the steep steps of the approach to the Acropolis. Their musky smell pervaded the warren of narrow streets, lined with whitewashed buildings.

At the address Effie had been given by Caroline, there was no sign over the entrance. Inside, it was evident a renovation was taking place. Knocking, they opened the front door and found a woman in jeans and a T-shirt, on her knees, putting brochures into a bookcase. She seemed pleased to see Effie. Effie introduced Nicholas and they all sat around a desk in the office. Caroline apologised for the state of the place. "I am afraid we still don't have electricity, so I can't even offer you coffee," she said in a soft Welsh accent.

Effie explained why they wanted to speak to her, filling her in on what they knew so far about Alessandra's disappearance.

"I've spoken to her parents a couple of times," said Nicholas, wanting to let Caroline know that he was bona fide. "I've also spoken to the police here and I think it's now clear that she has not returned to the UK. I've spent the past few weeks trying to understand what Alessandra had been researching – all of which might provide some clue as to where she might be."

Caroline said she had not heard from Alessandra since last September. "We would often go months before seeing each other, though, so I wasn't surprised at first when I didn't hear from her, but it's been a while now and I was starting to get worried. I tried to phone her a few times. The last time I rang it sounded like the number was no longer in use, so I phoned her friend Eleni. She told me that they thought at the museum that Alessandra had gone home to England.

"To tell the truth, I was a bit distracted at the time. My boyfriend had just left me. We were meant to be going into this business together and he just disappeared one day. I have not heard from him since. He was a friend of Andriy, Alessandra's boyfriend. He and Alessandra broke up some months before. I haven't heard from him, either."

"Nicholas and I would like to know anything Alessandra might have said – whether there was anything unusual – before she disappeared," Effie said. "Was there anything odd or out of the ordinary that you noticed?"

Caroline thought for a moment. "Well, as you know, she had become very interested in scuba diving. She and Andriy were both keen. They came to stay with me one weekend and spent most of the time diving in and around St Paul's Bay, on the other side of the town. Do you know it?" she asked Nicholas.

"I do. It's the small bay with the pretty white church that everyone seems to photograph."

"That's the one. Anyway, from what they said, they seemed to be looking for old artifacts in the bay. They seemed convinced they would find something."

"Vitaly, my boyfriend at that time, was sure that they were looking for the Colossus of Rhodes, or at least parts of it. Andriy was obsessed with finding it and believed it had been hidden away. Vitaly was sceptical. He believed it had all been removed and sold."

Nicholas leant forward, suddenly alert. Perhaps there was some basis for his theory that Alessandra's disappearance was linked to the Colossus. "Please tell us more. Is there anything else that you can recount about Alessandra, or indeed Andriy? Was there anything that stood out?"

Caroline thought about this for a moment. She remembered that either Alessandra or Andriy had tracked down a stone used in the original construction of a wall in a bar in Lindos. "They got very excited because they found the name of an ancient architect who came from Lindos inscribed on the stone."

"Perhaps that was the reason why they thought they might find part of the statue in St Paul's Bay, as it is just behind the Acropolis," added Effie.

Nicholas suddenly remembered Alessandra mentioning a bar here that she had often visited.

"It's called the Captain's Bar and is one of the original buildings in Lindos," said Caroline.

Nicholas asked whether the bar might be open. It was approaching midday, perhaps they could get a coffee there? Would Caroline be able to leave the shop and join them?

"Actually, without electricity and a phone line, there's little more I can do here. So I'd love to, thank you. It will also be good to catch up with Effie," she said, turning to her.

Caroline locked the shop and they continued up the labyrinth of passageways, following the directions to the Acropolis. The Captain's Bar was open. The interior was cool and shaded. Taking a table in the pebble and mosaic courtyard, under the dark vines draping the trellis, they ordered coffees and a beer for Nicholas. On the table stood an ancient-looking ashtray in the shape of a turtle. Nicholas remembered Alessandra saying this was one of her favourite places and he imagined her sitting across the table from him chatting, in the animated way she had, about her work.

Shaking off the thought, he began asking Caroline about the history of the building. The bar was not busy and, when the owner overheard, he came over. He said the building had been in his family for more than two hundred years. It was believed to be the oldest surviving building in Lindos, dating back to the sixteenth century. There was a small museum to the rear, where he took Effie and Nicholas.

"It is believed to be the first of the old sea captains' houses built in the town," he said. Proud of his heritage, he showed them early photographs and a collection of maritime artifacts. Parts of the building were much older he told them and pointed to the ornate courtyard pillars, which were said to date back to the time of the great earthquake. He said that a piece of stone near the entrance was found recently to have the name of Charos inscribed on it. They bent down to examine the white stone with its faint inscription in one corner. "Charos was a famous sculptor from Lindos and was responsible for the great Colossus in Rhodes town," the owner said.

They thanked him and finished their drinks. Nicholas suggested he buy them all lunch. They walked back down the winding streets and found one of the few tavernas that were open, with views across the bay. Caroline said if they had time afterwards she would show them the area of the bay where Alessandra and Andriy had dived. "Both times they asked me to drop them off with their scuba equipment at the same spot."

Caroline and Effie spent much of the lunch discussing old friends and what had happened to them since they last met. Nicholas was happy to let them get on with it, until the discussion turned to Andriy. Caroline said she did not like him. Her boyfriend, Vitaly, had seemed scared of him. "Andriy could often appear distant and arrogant … I never got used to him." She paused for a moment, brow furrowed. "He didn't seem to be Alessandra's type at all. She was always so warm and open. I always wondered why she was with him. I can only think that it must have been their mutual interest in Greek history and archaeology.

"I think that is how they first met. However when they came to stay with me they were already arguing a lot. They broke up soon after. I got the impression from Alessandra that she had already determined to leave him by this stage."

"Perhaps she had found out that he was not quite as he seemed…" Effie responded enigmatically.

After lunch they walked the steep footpath to the Acropolis. Reaching the battlements built by the Knights of St John, they were rewarded by the far-reaching view along the east coast of Rhodes. Despite the much-improved weather, few tourists had made the arduous climb. Effie explained the history of the Acropolis to Nicholas. She said that major restoration work was carried out on the site during the time of the Italian occupation. Unfortunately it had been poorly done and caused more harm than good.

"Large areas were just covered in concrete and inscribed blocks were moved from their original locations and used to restore the walls." She was proud to say that archaeologists from her department had been working with the Greek Ministry of Culture to restore and protect the site.

They walked on down to the cliffs behind the Acropolis, where there was a view across the heart-shaped St Paul's Bay. From behind the fortress, they could see where the turquoise of the sea shelf disappeared into the deeper blue of the waters beyond.

"This area is a popular spot for diving and snorkeling. There are many underwater caves and the sea floor has dramatic rock formations. St Paul's Bay is considered one of the most beautiful on Rhodes. In summer the beaches at either end are covered by sun loungers and parasols," Caroline told Nicholas. "I'm sorry, I can't help sounding like a tour guide," she laughed. "I love living here."

Across St Paul's Bay lay the picturesque whitewashed St Paul's Chapel. Caroline said the saint landed there in about AD50, after a storm. He preached Christianity to the inhabitants of Rhodes. Andriy had believed this landing to be linked to the removal of important historical artifacts from Rhodes town. "The church was a once a wedding venue for overseas tourists, but, after some unfortunate incidents, foreign weddings are banned there," Caroline told them.

They walked the perimeter of the Bay. Caroline pointed towards a huge cavern at the massive granite base on which the

Acropolis was perched. It was used to shoot some of the scenes from *The Guns of Navarone*, the 1960s film starring Gregory Peck and Anthony Quinn. This was where Alessandra and Andriy had dived, she said. "It is quite deep there." The cavern plunged dramatically into the bay. Nicholas wondered what they had been looking for and whether they had found it.

Back in Lindos they said their goodbyes. On the journey home Nicholas and Effie were quiet. As they neared Rhodes town the streetlights were coming on. Making her careful way through the busy evening traffic Effie broke the silence.

"Would you like to come back to my place – I think I have enough in my fridge to make us a meal, and I have some cold wine." Nicholas agreed, though after their contemplative silence, her offer came as a surprise.

Effie's apartment was modern, decorated in sleek Scandinavian furniture and there was little clutter. It fitted his impression of her as someone who was both efficient and organised. She also turned out to be an able cook and Nicholas complimented her on the salmon and broccoli pasta. They drank wine and chatted over the meal, before moving to the sofa. Effie seemed relaxed. She put on some music and sat down next to him. Kicking off her shoes she turned to Nicholas.

"I really enjoyed today. It's a shame for it to end. I was wondering whether you might like to stay and help me finish this wine," she asked, leaning towards him. "I will understand if you are tired or you have an early start tomorrow" she added quietly.

Nicholas waited before replying. He wasn't sure how to respond to the invitation. He felt a range of conflicting emotions. He was meant to be looking for Alessandra. He felt a disloyalty. It had been Alessandra that had first awakened in him the need again for physical closeness. Along with the confusion there was also a nervousness: this would be the first time he had slept with anyone after Lynda. He found Effie attractive, and he also enjoyed being with her. And here he was, sitting close to her. "Yes, I would like to," he said. "Thank you." Embarrassed about his hesitation, he turned towards her. Effie looked into his eyes, searching. Nicholas cupped her face and kissed her lightly, hesitantly at first. She responded tenderly. He felt the longing for a connection with a woman after so long, and she responded with equal ardour. The kiss went on for a long time.

They said little as they moved to her bedroom and undressed each other slowly. Their lovemaking was slow and silent. Finally, there was no need for words. They held each other protectively. Suddenly, Nicholas did not feel so alone.

Sunlight filtering through the curtains woke Nicholas the next morning. He felt good. Stretching, he felt Effie beside him, fast asleep. He lay quietly enjoying the scent and feel of a woman next to him. It had been a long time. After a while he got up carefully so as not to disturb her. Collecting up the wine bottle and two half-empty wine glasses he went through to the kitchen. Returning with a cup of tea, he gently kissed Effie on the forehead. He smiled as she slowly opened her eyes and he offered her the drink. "Good morning. I wasn't sure whether to wake you or just let you sleep."

"Good morning Nicholas" she murmured, still only half-awake. He sat next to her on the bed as she slowly sipped her tea.

"Don't get up. I need to be on my way shortly but I really enjoyed last night."

Needing some fresh air to clear his mind, he walked back towards his hotel. Church bells were sounding around the town. He thought about what had happened. How did he really feel? Should he have accepted her invitation? Had he taken advantage of her vulnerability? Making love with Effie had felt good and natural. She was a considerate lover. He was glad that it had happened. It felt like a turning point, but he was somehow uncomfortable that it was with Effie. He could not stop himself from feeling that it should have been with Alessandra.

Stopping for a coffee he bought an English newspaper. The news from back home wasn't cheering. He found it hard to dispel a lingering feeling of guilt from the night before. He decided to give his parents a ring. They were home and not enjoying the heavy snow that had just arrived. It made him feel privileged to be sitting outside a pavement café enjoying the early spring sun.

"When the snow has cleared, would you mind going to the cemetery and leaving some flowers for me on the graves. I feel far away." They said they would leave Lynda's favourite flowers with her. Nicholas said he would see them soon.

The sun and the vibrancy of the street sounds made him feel more positive. The scent of fresh baking from the kitchen buoyed his mood. He thought about Effie. She was beautiful and caring. Had he been fair with her? She seemed to know what she wanted – and she wanted to help him. Perhaps she would be good for him.

Later, Nicholas took the brown envelope containing the papers from Alessandra's apartment and sat at the desk in his hotel room to read. He concentrated on Alessandra's notes. The first set covered the old trade routes around Rhodes. They focused on routes between Rhodes and Turkey, Syria and Egypt. Notes in the margin referenced the grain-trading monopoly Rhodes had built up between the Black Sea and Egypt. Later on, this trade was supplemented by the export of wine, well into the second century. Nicholas could picture the cargo vessels plying their trade across this busy corner of the eastern Mediterranean. There were also copies of old maritime charts around Symi and Halki, showing currents and sea depths. The charts detailed surrounding islands and even small rocky outcrops.

In a red notebook she had listed the dives she had made around the coast, noting the location, depth and water visibility. There was also a description of the sea life found and interesting topography. He looked at the dives completed around St Paul's Bay. Two had taken place around the cavern under the Lindos Acropolis. The notes on the first described a rock formation at a depth of seventeen metres that had required her further investigation. The outcome of the second was a disappointment – the dimensions were recorded as incorrect. The following entry was for a dive planned for the island of Symi. There was a contact number for a dive centre on the island, together with details of boats for hire. Bays that Alessandra intended to investigate were also included. One containing an ancient shipwreck had been highlighted. The last entry was for a series of dives completed off Halki in early August. One had been at a small island just outside the harbour entrance; the other was a dive at a cave called Charidimos. There were descriptions of the marine life, but it was obvious she was looking for something else.

Nicholas realised Alessandra had not been entirely truthful with him. She had said she had not visited Halki before, when her notes showed she clearly had. What had she been hiding? The entries detailed currents around the island, as well as the location of caves. Alessandra had highlighted some with a star. Nicholas wondered what that meant. Were they places where something had already been found? Or were they places of particular promise? And where was Andriy? Had they split up by this stage? Surely Alessandra was not diving by herself. Nicholas knew little about scuba diving, but enough to know that was regarded as irresponsible and dangerous. He turned the page and saw that the next few pages had been torn out of the notebook. He wondered whether he had left some key papers back at her apartment. He would need to go back at some stage.

He knew, however, what his next step should be. He also needed to be far more careful than he had been so far.

Chapter Eleven

HALKI

NICHOLAS HAD TO GO BACK FIVE MONTHS TO HIS LAST sighting of Alessandra, to perhaps retrace her steps. He needed to establish what happened after she waved to him and disappeared around the corner. He found himself back on Halki. He was pleased: he had enjoyed his day trip that October. The port of Emborio was slumbering. A single yacht was moored in the bay alongside the fishing vessels. The expensive-looking motor cruisers had gone. Only one or two tavernas and cafes were open. The gelateria was firmly shut.

He had checked out of his hotel in Rhodes, hoping that whoever was following him would assume he had gone back to the UK. Before he left, he had telephoned Captain Petrakis, who told him they had no leads on his hotel break-in. "We interviewed the barman, as well as the cleaning staff. Unfortunately, we have been unable to gather any information that might aid an identification," Petrakis had said. It seemed to be the end of the investigation. He apologised that there had also been no progress on Alessandra's case and no sightings had been reported since her disappearance. He wished Nicholas a safe flight home.

Over dinner the previous evening, he had told Effie what he planned to do. She said she would not be able to get away from work at short notice. Something had come up that required her urgent attention. She would try to make it over for a couple of days. "I am going to miss you," she said. "Please take care. I am just getting to know you." They promised to talk on the phone. She stressed that he should update her if he found out anything.

His choice of hotels on Halki was limited. Most were closed for the winter. He found one with a view of the harbour, where he was given a room with a sea view. He said he was staying for a week. It was starting to get dark, so he unpacked and left the hotel. Armed with the address for Helena that Eleni had obtained for him, his Halki guide, and a street map the hotel had provided, he headed off into the town. The wind was picking up and the flickering street lighting was starting to come on in the tangled thoroughfares behind the houses and restaurants lining the port. The narrower alleyways remained unlit. Picking his way carefully in the rapidly disappearing natural light he made his way towards Helena's narrow street. Her house was a two-storey cottage, midway along. A smell of cooking emanated from the open kitchen window of a nearby house. The yellow shutters of Helena's cottage were closed. He rang the bell. There was no answer, so he knocked loudly on the white door. There was still no reply. He had tried to phone earlier without success. He would come back tomorrow.

Near the port, Nicholas found a welcoming bar, protected from the sea breeze, where he could enjoy a drink. He sipped his beer while looking out to sea as the last rays of the winter sun disappeared. Finishing his beer he strolled along the windswept quayside, where he found a bench facing away from the sea and sat down, pulling up the collar of his coat. Perhaps it was because it was early in the year and most things were closed, or maybe it was the poor lighting that left most of the passageways in shadow, but just as the island appeared hulking from out at sea, it now seemed to be as forbidding onshore. Nicholas shivered. He got up and continued his slow walk back to his hotel.

The next morning the wind had died. Retracing his walk to Helena's house, he rang the bell, then knocked. There was again no response. Many of the other houses in the street also had closed shutters. There was a small supermarket around the corner, someone there might be able to help. "Yasas," he said. "Milate Anglika?" he asked hesitantly, still not sure of the correct pronunciation.

The unshaven shopkeeper replied: "No, only little, yes," with an apologetic shrug.

"I am looking for Helena Milonas," Nicholas said. He repeated her name again, slowly. He pointed to where he had come from and showed the shopkeeper her name and the address on a piece of paper. "I am a friend. Do you know if she is living here now?"

The shopkeeper said she came to the shop regularly, but had left some time ago. He did not know where she had gone. Perhaps she had returned to Rhodes, perhaps she would return in the summer. He eventually shrugged in apology. Nicholas took out Alessandra's photo and asked if he recognised her. The shopkeeper said he did not think he had seen her before. He shrugged again, "Many pretty women come to Halki." As an afterthought, Nicholas showed him the group photograph he had taken from Alessandra's apartment. The shopkeeper peered at it and shook his head in apology. "Efharisto," said Nicholas and left.

That evening Nicholas walked into the village centre and found a bar that was open. It was early and it was almost empty. Ordering a beer he asked the barman if he spoke English.

"Of course," was the response, "I worked in Leeds in my brother's restaurant for two years." Nicholas asked if anyone had heard of a woman going missing on the island last year. The barman said it had been in the newspapers and on television. It had caused some excitement on the island. The police had even come over from Rhodes. "She was English, but working on Rhodes. She was meant to have been visiting someone on Halki when she disappeared," he said.

"That's correct. She is a friend of mine. I am here trying to find her. What did people say here about her disappearance – were there any rumours?"

The barman considered that for a moment as he removed glasses from the dishwasher under the bar. "At the time, people thought that it was probably to do with a man. Isn't that usually why women disappear?" He stopped and looked up at Nicholas. "It was also suggested that it might have been connected to a drugs ring operating across the islands. Some thought that she was part of that. There was some talk that Russians were involved. Certainly Russians spent some time here last year. They were probably only innocent tourists, though," he laughed.

Nicholas ordered another drink and bought one for the barman. He showed his photograph of Alessandra and Andriy together. The barman shook his head and said that he did not recognise either of them. "The woman in the photo is Alessandra Bianchi, the woman who disappeared."

Nicholas also asked about Helena. "Yes," the barman said, "she came in once or twice. but I did not know her well. Try Taverna Milos around the corner. She used to go there sometimes."

"Thanks, you have been very helpful," Nicholas said. "Could I ask you a couple more questions?"

"No problem. I am not busy," he gestured to the now empty bar. "I am not sure that I know much more."

Nicholas told him Alessandra was a scuba-diving enthusiast. "Who would she have used on Halki to go diving with? I did not notice any signs advertising dive trips when I walked along the harbour yesterday."

"Well, of course it is still the low season for tourists. We only have one dive operator normally here in Halki. I think he does scuba and snorkeling trips around the island, but he closes in October and goes back to Rhodes for the winter."

Nicholas asked if the barman had an address or phone number for him on Rhodes. "I think I might have a business card for Spiros at home. Last year he rented a room from my sister. I cannot leave the bar now, but will look for it when I get home. Are you here tomorrow?" Nicholas said he would come by the following evening.

"Is there anyone else here on Halki I should speak to who might have any further information?"

The barman took Nicholas's money to the till. Returning, he said: "Speak to Yannis at the taverna I suggested earlier. Also, there is an English lady who lives here even during the winter. She is an artist and has her own gallery. She knows everything that is going on." He wrote down her name and explained how to find the gallery. "It is often open, even in winter, because she paints there."

The gallery was down a side street, not far from his hotel. It was open. Paintings, mostly views of the town and port, filled the walls in the small space, interspersed with a few portraits of characterful locals. A woman in a long, flowing, Indian-print dress, her unruly grey hair secured by a scarf, sat behind a small desk. She greeted him. "Hello, my name is Nicholas. I assume you are Catherine? I hope you don't mind, but I obtained your name from the barman at a bar on the harbour."

He told her why he was there. "I am really looking for any clues that might help in my search for Alessandra."

"I would of course prefer that you were a customer," she said, with a disarming smile. "Things have been very quiet over the winter, but I will help you any way I can. Your barman probably said that nothing passes my notice on the island." She looked amused. I have been living on Halki for 27 years and I know everyone who has lived on the island. Come and sit down. I could do with some company, anyway."

Nicholas took out his photo of Alessandra and Andriy. "Yes, I have met both of them. The woman here is the one that you are looking for?" Nicholas said, yes, the picture was of Alessandra.

"However, the other one – the man next to her – I met later and he was with a different woman. Her name is Helena," she said, handing the photograph back to Nicholas.

"Can you tell me what you know about all three of them?"

"Well, I only met Alessandra on a few occasions. She was absolutely charming, a lovely young woman. I can well understand your interest in her." There was a twinkle in her eyes. "I was first introduced to her here by Helena. Alessandra was staying at her house. I believe she was into scuba diving and was diving around Halki. I only saw her on the two or three times when she popped into my gallery. I probably first met her 18 months ago. She was very polite. She showed real interest in my art, which was kind of her. It is hard to believe that she has gone missing. I have heard all the talk about drugs and drug smuggling, but I don't believe that she would have been involved. She was just not that type."

"I don't believe those rumours, either," Nicholas said.

"Her friend Helena was different," said Caroline, frowning. "She often comes across as quite a difficult woman; someone who has a chip on her shoulder. I think she originally came from quite a wealthy family on Rhodes, but had fallen out with them over something or another. She never seemed able to hold a job down for too long, hence the reason I think she moved to Halki. She has been here on the island for a couple of years now. When she first arrived she tried to open a café, but it didn't take off. She was not close to many people and chose to keep to herself."

Catherine offered Nicholas some tea. "Some British habits never die. Let me guess – milk, no sugar for you?" She disappeared into a studio to the rear of the gallery and Nicholas heard a clattering of crockery. When she returned with the tea, she sat down and tapped the photograph in Nicholas's hand, "This one, I really did not like," pointing to Andriy. "When I met him in a taverna with Helena he was rude and dismissive towards me. He had come across on one of those expensive boats that you see showing off and clogging up all the island ports in the summer. This must have been early to mid October last year. Most of the tourists had gone by that stage. One day he actually came into the gallery with Helena and said that my work was 'colourful'. Colourful," she snorted. "I was glad when he left a few days later. Luckily, I have not seen him since".

"Did you know that Alessandra worked in the museum in Rhodes?"

"Yes, I think I did."

"Did she ever ask you about the archaeology on the island? Whether there had ever been any interesting finds?"

"Yes, she did. She said she knew Halki had a long and interesting past. She asked if I knew anything about the early shipwrecks that are supposed to have occurred around these islands many centuries ago and if anything had ever been recorded here. I remember telling her that there were various stories of shipwrecks off the coast in storms in ancient times. This area of the Aegean is notorious for the Meltemi – the violent storms that can come almost from nowhere.

"The only museum we really have here is called the Traditional House, on the outskirts of the town. However, you could also look in some of our old churches. In all likelihood, though, any artifacts of historical interest have probably found their way back to Rhodes."

Catherine asked Nicholas if he would like some more tea. He thanked her, but said he had taken up too much of her time. She said it had been a real pleasure. "What I could do – if you feel it may help – is to look through all my old documents and diaries at home. I absolutely love this island and have noted down all manner of things over the years. Anything of interest that has happened over the last 27 years will be recorded there somewhere."

Nicholas thanked Catherine and said he would take up her offer to go through her records. She gave him her address and directions to her house. He said he would see her in a couple of days.

Walking back to the hotel there was much he needed to figure out. Alessandra had visited Halki several times. She had split from Andriy, but here he was on Halki with one of Alessandra's friends who, coincidentally, also seemed to have disappeared.

—

Looking out of his hotel window towards the small, uninhabited island to the right, Nicholas thought of the millennia of history surrounding these barren and mysterious islands. He was even more convinced that Halki held the clues to Alessandra's disappearance. Later, lying in bed, he thought of Lynda. They had been so happy when they learned she was pregnant with their first child. Then, cruelly, just weeks later, she was diagnosed with breast cancer. Lynda was still in the first trimester of her pregnancy. At first they were told that the treatment was not likely to affect the health of their unborn child. That was until they discovered, with further tests, that Lynda's cancer was more advanced than first thought; it had already metastasised through her lymph nodes. She was advised to terminate the pregnancy but refused.

Eventually, they understood that the baby was unlikely to survive if the same treatment continued. The cancer was aggressive and the specialists could not guarantee that a change to a less invasive form of treatment would be effective. Lynda could not be persuaded not to have the baby and decided to discontinue the treatment. Nicholas knew in his heart that she was also thinking of him; that, in the awful event she did not survive, he would still be left with the child they had both longed for. There would be a legacy of their time together.

Over time, doctors advised them of the possibility that the early treatment that Lynda had received had increased the likelihood of some abnormalities in the foetus. As it turned out the baby's lungs were found to be underdeveloped. At the end of the pregnancy, with Lynda rapidly weakening, the baby had developed acute respiratory difficulties. An emergency Caesarean was required in a last-ditch attempt to save the child.

Nicholas would always remember those first moments when he was told by the doctors, who had fought so hard to keep Lynda alive, that neither mother nor child had survived the birth. He had felt that he was in a dream, watching this happen to someone else. He did not recognize the woman lying quiet and peaceful, her baby beside her on the bed.

He sat with them for hours, hopeless, tears cascading down his cheeks, holding Lynda's cold hand. He remembered a kindly nurse hugging him and helping him from the hospital room for the last time. He had always excelled academically as well as at sports. He had become accustomed to feeling in control. Suddenly, it was taken away from him and the first months after their deaths were the most difficult of his life. In the midst of his grief, he felt directionless. His once purposeful life seemed empty and meaningless. Not for the first time he wondered why he had not been able to give his dead daughter a name.

As always, he woke with a heavy feeling, as if pinned to the bed. To shrug it off he went for a run along the harbour. The sun was just starting to rise and, in the dawn light, he passed boats that had just returned from a night's fishing. Nicholas sat and watched the early morning activity in the port. Exhausted fishermen were slowly unloading their catch. As the sun began to rise above the horizon, the catches were being dumped on the dock in crates. It was not yet seven, but already there were customers arriving, haggling over the prices. What remained in their crates was taken away to be delivered to the restaurants and hotels later. Fishermen and locals departed, some for a coffee and a stronger drink, others to their beds.

He continued to sit, thinking about the everyday scene he had just witnessed, his eyes focused on the horizon. As the sun began to climb, he pondered over the comforting, often mundane, rituals of ordinary life that are repeated daily everywhere across the world.

Chapter Twelve

HALKI

A PHONE MESSAGE WAITED FOR HIM BACK IN HIS HOTEL ROOM.
It was from Catherine. She had just recollected a particular visit
from Alessandra to her studio. "If you are free, why don't you
come around this afternoon," she said.

After breakfast Nicholas set off to explore the little town. He
had time to kill. He passed the impressive white town hall with
its large, blue-painted windows. A winding staircase led up to the
entrance. He walked on through circuitous alleyways, past red
and mauve bougainvillea cascading from balconies and arches. All
around were the sounds of the morning: the excited chatter of
children and dogs barking, making their own contributions to the
daily ritual. Now and then he came across elderly women, dressed
in black, and he greeted them with a friendly "Kalimera". He
received wide, gap-toothed smiles in reply. Passing large waterfront
villas for rental, their shutters closed, he reflected that there was an
air of decayed grandeur about the town, reflecting its past glory

and prosperity. Eventually, he found himself down by the water's edge and selected a shady taverna where he could sit and watch people wander by for a while.

Catherine's house was one of the grander Venetian-style mansions on the island. It was painted a pale yellow and blue shutters framed enormous windows overlooking the bay.

"Please come in." She looked pleased to see Nicholas. "It is so very nice to have a good-looking man coming to visit me. That hasn't happened for a few years."

Nicholas smiled. "It's my pleasure. Thank you for inviting me." He accepted a glass of wine and admired the view over the bay. He asked about the paintings. "A few are mine," Catherine said, "but the majority I brought over from England many years ago when my parents died. There is the one that I wanted to show you. I only remembered this after you left."

She took Nicholas through to a more formal dining room. "This is one of mine," she said, standing in front of a watercolour landscape of ruined stone buildings set against a steep hillside. Behind the buildings, in contrast to the grey of the hillside, was an elegant, vaulted white church. It had a tall cypress tree guarding the entrance to the walled surrounds.

"I remembered that Alessandra came into my studio one morning, about a year ago. It had been a miserable rainy day and there were no tourists around. It was only the second time I had met her. She was admiring this painting of the abandoned village of Horio, which is up on the hills behind us. You could tell by her eyes that she was excited. Alessandra pointed to one of these old houses in the painting and told me she had been doing research on the village. She had just spent the day there among the ruins taking photographs. Set into a wall, inside one of the ruined buildings, she had come across a stone with a particular marking."

"I think I may have an idea what the marking might be of," Nicholas said.

"Apparently it had confirmed a theory she was working on. It was exactly what she had been looking for in the old village. She was reluctant to say more. Hopefully, you can make some sense of it."

"I don't know the site, but if it was the original town of the island I imagine it covers quite an area. Did Alessandra say exactly where the ruined house was, I'd like to try to find it?"

"All I remember is her pointing at the church in the picture – the Church of the Holy Virgin Mary. She said the building was below and to the right of the church." Catherine pointed to a collection of houses in the painting. "About here."

"If you are going to go up there, the church is below the castle. It's about a third of the way up. I think she mentioned that it was near a stone with a blue cross as a marker. It should be close to the pathway going up to the castle. I also think it was one of the few houses that still has part of its own roof."

Nicholas said it was certainly worth a visit.

"In the summer months there is a small bus that takes tourists up to Horio and the castle. I suspect, however, that you are going to have to walk up there. You should take some cold water with you and you'll need a flashlight. I can lend you one."

They returned to the living room and sat down. "Can I top up your wine glass," Catherine asked. Nicholas said he was fine.

"Did you know that the island, which is also spelled Chalki, by the way, originally got its name from a copper workshop that used to be on the island."

Nicholas could see that Catherine loved nothing more than sharing her knowledge of the island. He was happy to listen to her stories.

"I don't know if you know any ancient Greek mythology. If you do, you will probably remember that, before the Olympian gods, the Titans were meant to have ruled the world. The king of the Titans was called Cronus. When Cronus was dethroned by his son, Zeus, the Titans were then banished to Halki. So, according to ancient mythology, this tiny island assumed a huge importance in the world." She smiled. "Don't forget that while you are here.

"Staying with mythology, I did go through some of my old papers. There have been significant wrecks in these waters, but one story has been passed down repeatedly through the centuries. It dates from the time of the Arab conquest of the eastern Mediterranean, when there was significant trade between Rhodes and Syria. The story goes that one vessel was transporting a valuable cargo of looted treasure from ancient Rhodes. It got into trouble during a violent storm.

"At that time the island of Alimia was used as a haven from bad storms during a Meltemi. The boat carrying this treasure was making for the island, when it sank. The claim, as far as I can see, has never had any physical or documented proof. But, it was also rumoured by locals that, over the years, artifacts from the wreck have turned up every so often, particularly after a severe Meltemi storm. Mostly it has been pottery, normally fragments of vessels, but, occasionally, there have also been bronze figures and coins. Sometimes even human bones. Have you heard of the Meltemi?" she asked Nicholas.

"Yes I have," replied Nicholas. "Is it similar to the Mistral you get across the south of France?"

"It's far more violent. Meltemi is the Greek name for the strong, dry winds that blow in from the Balkans. In Greek mythology the wind is said to be under the control of Boreos, who is the God of the north winds. It's a natural phenomenon of the Aegean, and in particular around these islands. Sailors fear it, as it seems to come almost from nowhere. You can have clear skies and then suddenly violent winds whip up and churn the water."

"I have heard that the ferries around Rhodes will not sail when the Meltemi is blowing," said Nicholas.

"Absolutely. Sometimes we can be cut off for days without fresh food and water on Halki during a Meltemi. Tourists are not able to come to or leave the island. The winds can whip up the sea to the extent that the waves cascade over the quayside and have, on occasion, flooded some of the bars and restaurants."

Nicholas looked at his watch. It was late. He got to his feet, thanking Catherine for sharing her knowledge. "Telling tales of the past is part of our tradition here on Halki," she chuckled. "I guess that I am part of that tradition now. We have very little written or recorded history. So what there is largely folklore, passed down through the generations by word of mouth. Occasionally, some history is included in old folk songs and that is how most of these tales of shipwrecks and treasure have survived." Catherine rummaged through a cupboard in the hall and found a small flashlight.

"Can I ask you one further thing?" he said. "On a very different subject."

"Of course. Ask away."

"You know this island intimately. Is it possible that anyone could be held captive here without anyone getting to know?"

"It would be impossible. There's only one small village on the island. Everyone knows each other and someone would notice something unusual, even if it were just a change in shopping habits. It is a very tight-knit community – and, of course there are only 400-odd of us, outside of the summer months."

Nicholas took his leave, kissing her on both cheeks. He promised to call into the gallery and return the light before he left the island. On his walk back down the hill towards the port he wondered about the myths. Of course, they often took on a life of their own, with the story subtly changing with each generation, but was there something important in them that could help his search? He passed Helena's house. The shutters remained closed and again there was no response to his knocking. She was obviously not on the island. He remembered that he had said that he would stop off at the bar and made his way towards it down the cobbled lanes.

The barman of the previous night was there. This evening the place was busier and he had to wait to be served. Fleetwood Mac's "Don't Stop" was playing in the background. Rumours seemed to be following him around the islands. Eventually, the barman came over and recognised Nicholas.

"Yasas," Nicholas said. The barman gave him a beer and said "I did not forget. I phoned Spiros this morning. He remembered the woman you are looking for well. She hired him for the whole day a few times. She was diving at Charidimos Cave, in Trachia. You can only reach there by boat. He also said that he took her to Alimia a couple of times. He told me he is happy to speak to you. How long will you be on Halki? Spiros said he would be back in mid April."

Nicholas said he would be leaving in the next few days.

"No problem," the barman said. "I have written down his address when he is in Rhodes. Do you know Faliraki? He works in a hotel there during the winter. Let me get it for you."

When the barman returned, Nicholas had another beer. Some things were finally starting to make sense on this mysterious island. He needed to meet Spiros. Later, sitting at a nearby taverna, over a meal of fried local fish, he phoned Effie. "Hello," she said, sounding cautious and on edge: "Oh, Nicholas. I am so pleased to hear from you."

"What has happened? You sound upset."

"While I was walking home, I swear I was being followed. There was a man walking on the other side of the road. I couldn't see his face, but I was sure that he was keeping pace with me. He followed me all the way back to the apartment. I didn't know what to do. I have just looked out of the window, but I can't see anyone there now."

"Is your door secure?"

"Yes, I have also put the chain on, but then, just five minutes ago, my phone rang. I could tell there was someone there, but they didn't say anything. After a while, they rang off."

"I think you should phone the police."

"I would, but I know they will tell me there is nothing they can do."

"If you have a caretaker for your apartment you could ask

them to look around outside for you. Tell them you thought you were followed from work."

Effie agreed to do so.

"Phone me the moment they get back to you," Nicholas said.

Twenty minutes later his phone went. "Hi, it's me," said Effie. "The caretaker did take a look around. He walked all the way around the garden and then down the street. He saw no one, so I feel better now."

"Good. You will be safe inside," Nicholas said. "Don't open your door to anyone tonight. You're not working the day after tomorrow, so why don't you come over to Halki and stay the night? I think there is a ferry on Saturday morning. I could come back to Rhodes with you on Sunday."

Effie seemed happy to be invited. She said she was going out to dinner with friends the next evening. "I will ask one of them to see me back to the apartment when I leave. I am really looking forward to seeing you."

They chatted some more. Effie sounded more settled. Nicholas told her what he had found out since coming back to Halki, including that Helena seemed to be missing. "You haven't heard from her recently have you?" Effie hadn't.

"Also, did you know that Helena was a friend of Alessandra's boyfriend, Andriy?"

Effie was surprised. "It's likely that she met him through Alessandra, but it sounds like she was with him on Halki, well after he and Alessandra had split up. It's crazy. It makes no sense."

Effie thanked Nicholas for taking her fears of being followed seriously. "It may be I just imagined it. The poor man was probably just walking home, minding his own business. Anyway, see you on Saturday morning."

They rang off and Nicholas finished his meal. Was Effie being followed? Were they both under threat? He didn't want to expose her to any danger, but it seemed more and more likely that all of this was connected to Alessandra's disappearance?

Chapter Thirteen

HALKI

PASSING THE SMALL, WHITEWASHED CHURCH OF AGIOS Nikolaos on his right, with the shimmering blue of Pondamus Bay on his left, Nicholas began the long walk up the steep road towards the abandoned village of Horio. The morning heat elicited the insistent humming of the cicadas, bringing the promise of spring to Halki. After a half-hour climb he stopped to catch his breath and to admire the view below. Beyond the horseshoe bay of Emborio were the scattered islands of the Aegean, fanning out from Halki. To the left was the coast of Turkey. He looked at the map in his guidebook. The old village seemed to be about three or four kilometres from the port. He continued upwards along the winding, stone-paved road, passing crumbling stone goat pens, abandoned huts and a scattering of rusting vehicle parts and machinery. Olive trees, interspersed with prickly pear and fig, flourished in the barren, rocky soil of the fields to either side of the road. The scent of herbs pervaded the air, punctuated by the occasional cry of goats.

Rounding a bend, he saw the ruins of the village rise up around and above him. He stopped to catch his breath and have a drink of water. He was glad he had taken Catherine's advice. It had taken over an hour to make the relentless climb and it was starting to get hot. He walked past an old cemetery with its ancient graves. Beyond it was what looked like an old school and a couple of dilapidated churches. The road came to an end at the lower perimeter of the old settlement. In front was a Ministry of Culture sign detailing Horio's history, together with a map of the area. Many of the buildings dated back to the fourth century BC. Above him, he saw the old village tumbling down the rocky hillside. At the top, the ruins seemed to stop immediately below the imposing Castle of the Knights of St John.

In medieval times the threat of sea piracy had forced the inhabitants of Halki to move away from the coast to the hills. When Horio was the island's capital, it was once home to three thousand inhabitants – eight times that of modern-day Halki. Horio had reached its peak in the eighteenth century, but the site was abandoned a century later. By that time the threat of piracy had largely receded. Emboldened, most inhabitants moved down the slopes to the natural amphitheatre that was Emborio, leaving their former homes to decay.

Entering the ruins, Nicholas looked across the crumbling houses. There was an air of desolation. The atmospheric ruins were scattered over the precipitous rock-strewn slope. In between, tall cypress trees pointed to the sky. Nicholas remembered that they were classical symbols of mourning and long associated with death and the underworld. A feeling of morbidity pervaded the hillside. Nicholas could almost sense the ghosts of its ancient inhabitants moving silently through the ruins. He thought he could identify a rocky path winding up through the settlement to the castle. It looked like an arduous climb.

The houses were simple small square structures. Goats, bells tinkling, grazed on the brush and bushes growing around and out of the abandoned structures providing a stark, almost biblical, vision.

He began the sheer climb up the path towards the brooding ruined castle, where, after a while, he came upon the Church of Panagia Horiani, also known as the Church of the Holy Virgin Mary. Dating from around 1400 it was noted for its magnificent frescoes. On the metal gate at the entrance was the outline of a cross. Entering between the stone pillars, he tried the door, but it was locked. He sat for a while on a bench in the shade of a cypress tree looking down the hillside. The cool breeze from the mountain above was welcome in the midday heat. He sat, soaking up the views below. To the left of the church, beside the path below, was the faint outline of a blue cross, etched on a stone. Rousing himself he headed towards the marking.

Nicholas looked across the hillside. To the left were three small houses, their pale red roofs partially intact. Leaving the path, he edged towards them through the jumble of boulders strewn between the ruins. The breeze was starting to strengthen as he picked his way across the exposed hillside. He entered the first house, using Catherine's flashlight to orientate himself. There were three small rooms. Despite small windows in two of them, the interior was almost pitch dark. He felt his way past ancient rubble and vegetation and played the light on the walls of the room at the rear. They were a rough mixture of stone. Stumbling over a rock, he grazed his arm on the wall and cursed loudly. He examined each wall meticulously without success. Weeds and creepers obscured parts, but he was satisfied there was no inscription.

Nicholas studied each room in the same manner. It was painstaking. He realised his careful examination of the first house had taken almost half an hour. He could imagine Alessandra doing the same thing, perhaps in this very ruin. On his own, among these old stones on a desolate mountainside he felt close to her.

Inside the house the flashlight cast shadows across the walls. Occasionally, he had to scrape lichen from the surfaces or move stones leaning against walls, to ensure he did not miss anything. He repeated the process for the second dwelling. Entering the third, he saw that part of the roof had caved in. Following his earlier method, he worked carefully, clockwise from the entrance, to the small back room. He had an idea he knew what he was looking for.

Suddenly, out of the darkness, a black figure hurled itself at him. He fell backwards, dropping the flashlight as he hit the floor hard and lay there, winded, waiting for the blows he knew would come. He held his arms over his face for protection and lay there for a while. It took time for his breathing to return to normal. He tried to stand and stumbled towards the opening, arms raised to fend off another attack.

Nicholas emerged into the glare of the sun, bruised and disoriented. There, some metres in front of him, stood a glowering goat. His assailant was black, with a white blaze on its chest and its amber eyes, with their unnerving slitted pupils, were fixed on him. He felt both stupid and relieved, then was embarrassed to find that he was shaking from the encounter. He felt his head – he had hit a stone on falling – and encountered something sticky. He was bleeding. He held his handkerchief to the wound. Grazed, and with blood pouring from his head, he sat down unsteadily on a rock and stared back at the goat. "Fuck you," he said. The goat maintained its impenetrable gaze.

When he felt he could actually smile at the incident, he dusted down his clothes, then, steeling himself, he went back into the building, feeling around for his flashlight. The light was still on. Recovering it he continued his exploration, still holding the bloodied handkerchief to his head. He examined the other small room and turned back towards the entrance to check out the last one. On the second wall he found it.

There, chiseled in the corner of an oblong stone was a faded, man-made mark. He became excited as he made out the inscription for Charos. In the beam of the flashlight it was clearer than the one he had been shown in the bar in Lindos. He took a photo as best he could with the flashlight on his phone and walked out, thankfully, into the sun.

Nicholas still felt bruised from his encounter with the goat. His bleeding scalp had eased off, and, after resting in the shade of a crumbling wall, he decided to look around the imposing castle far above him. He climbed through ruins up the narrow, winding stone pathway. Again, he thanked Catherine inwardly for insisting he take water, as he sipped from his bottle.

The regular castle ramparts contrasted starkly with the ragged grey of the mountains behind. The breeze had become a buffeting wind. Approaching the entrance, he walked up the worn marble paving. There was an air of foreboding about the place. Above the gate were various coats-of–arms. The castle's history stretched back over two thousand years. It had been built on the site of an ancient acropolis. He walked past the foundations of ancient temples and the remains of walls dating back to Hellenistic times. Inside the walls the ruins had remained untouched for centuries. Nicholas wondered how much of the tumbled stone was used to build the dwellings of the town below. Could there be stone fragments from the Colossus contained within the medieval buildings?

The view from the ramparts was breathtaking. From this height the coast of Rhodes looked within touching distance. To the left he could see the whaleback island of Alimia. All around were barren cliffs and the shimmering sea, hundreds of metres below. He walked along the battlements. Far below was the peninsular of Trachia, where Alessandra had dived with Spiros. From this height it was impossible to see the cave the barman had referred to.

In the centre of the castle stood the remains of the medieval church of St Nicholas. It was built in the familiar vaulted Halkian style, with whitewashed walls and a terracotta roof. The impressive wall paintings had been dated back to the fifteenth century. Climbing the stairs, he was greeted by a musty scent as he opened the door. Lizards scurried up the walls, retreating from the light.

There was little to see of the interior, apart from the murals on the ceiling. He shone his torch upwards and noticed that one, missing some plaster at one corner, depicted a single-masted boat foundering in a turbulent sea. The faded mural showed the battered ship stranded on rocks, the pounding sea washing over it. And there, on the roof of the ancient world, Nicholas comprehended the violence portrayed in this single image. He walked out. There was an air of desolation about the grey mountain that he wanted to be rid of. He emerged from the gloom of the castle and followed the path around to the other side. There, facing towards the west, he found the Throne of Zeus and Hecate. The stone structure was carved out of the rock to resemble two benches with armrests side by side. Nicholas remembered the myth Catherine had recounted about Zeus toppling his father, resulting in the Titans being banished to Halki.

A young Australian couple were enjoying the view. They explained to him that, according to legend, the throne was positioned so that Zeus and Hecate could both enjoy the magnificent sunsets. Nicholas smiled and said: "I really don't blame them. If I ruled the place I would choose the same spot. It is an impressive view."

Buzzards were soaring above the serrated crags, behind which dark clouds were starting to form. There was a growing chill in the air as the northerly wind tugged at his clothing. He turned and began the sharp descent to the port, glad to leave the sinister mood of the castle behind.

Chapter Fourteen

HALKI

NICHOLAS SIPPED A COFFEE AS HE WATCHED THE MORNING ferry from Rhodes approach. He was looking forward to seeing Effie, but wondered whether he had done the right thing in inviting her to Halki.

The sudden storm of the night before had passed, the strong winds now a gentle zephyr. The ferry sidled up to the dock and the gangway was lowered, Effie was one of the last off. They embraced. "I have missed you," she said, continuing to hug Nicholas. She stepped back to look at him, removing her sunglasses. "My God, what has happened to your head – and your arm?"

"It's all very embarrassing. I was viciously attacked by a goat yesterday, when I was exploring the old abandoned capital. In my defence, it was a large goat in a very bad mood – and it was dark."

Effie laughed. "I can see who came off worse."

"Let's drop your case off at the hotel and you can tend to my wounds – and my self-esteem. Later we can wander around the island if you like." Nicholas took her case and they walked the short distance to the hotel.

Inside the room they kissed again. As with the first time, there was an urgency to their lovemaking. Later, they took their time to explore and enjoy each other. Finally exhausted, the windows open to the sea, they lay naked on the bed.

Some time later, while Effie slept, Nicholas gently disentangled himself and turned to lie on his back. Gazing at the ceiling, he once again experienced conflicting emotions. Was he starting to fall for Effie? Or was there a message among those desolate ruins the day before? As vulnerable as he was after Lynda's death, he still felt as though he was taking advantage of Effie. His brief time with Alessandra on board the ferry was the only occasion when he had felt close to anyone since Lynda. This unexpected intimacy with Effie felt like a release, but, as wonderful as it was, it somehow seemed wrong. She was fun and caring, she was attractive and she was helping him. It felt almost dishonest. The day before, in that ruin of a house, he had experienced an intense closeness to Alessandra that went beyond mere physicality. It felt almost as if her very being was being carried on the Meltemi wind that blew in. He drifted back into a fitful sleep.

The cooling breeze woke them both. Sitting up, Effie examined Nicholas's wounds. "Our first stop when we leave the hotel will be the pharmacy. You need something on these scrapes. Don't worry, I will look after you," she said, looking amused.

They emerged from the hotel feeling hungry. "I know where there is a small pharmacy," Effie said. They bought supplies to treat Nicholas's wounds then headed to the beach at Ftenagia. It was approaching midday and the temperature had climbed into the mid-twenties. Navigating the alleyways behind the harbour-front houses, they passed a tiny white church, then followed the narrow coastal path, skirting the rocks. Here they came across a quaint seaside taverna. It had just opened for the season. Three men sat chatting, smoking and drinking coffee at a table in the corner. One of the older men, dressed in black T-shirt and trousers, rose. "Come in my friends," he said.

Only two other tables were occupied. Nicholas and Effie chose one facing the tranquil turquoise waters and the tiny unnamed island, just offshore. There was a light warm sea breeze. They ordered a bottle of chilled, local white wine and relaxed.

"You know, there is something I have always wondered about," said Nicholas, adopting a mock-serious expression. "These chairs," he pointed to the slatted wooden chairs with their rush seats. "They are the same wherever you go in Greece. Is there some factory that manufactures identical chairs just for taverna use – and are they specially designed to be equally uncomfortable wherever you go?"

Effie laughed. "You could well be right."

"Being serious, though. How are you feeling after the other night? Did you notice anything else yesterday?"

"No, everything seemed normal. A friend dropped me off in his car last night. He waited until I got to my entrance. You know, I probably just imagined being followed. After what happened to you I have felt a bit on edge. It all probably just got to me."

Nicholas did not feel so sure but said nothing.

They ordered and, shortly afterwards, a wonderful vegetarian meze arrived. They took their time, enjoying the food and the views across the bay.

"Let me tell you what I have been doing since I arrived here," Nicholas said, eventually.

"Please do, but why not start with the goat and work backwards from there."

Nicholas smiled. "Of course. I wouldn't dream of spoiling your fun." He described his encounter with his hairy foe, embellishing a little and pausing for dramatic effect. Then he told Effie about Catherine and what she had told him. "I promised to visit her before I leave to say goodbye. Perhaps we can pop into her gallery later on." He told Effie about his find in one of the ruined houses at Horio. "Here, I took a photo of the inscription. It looks very similar to the one we saw in Lindos."

He described his visit to the castle.

"I know it," said Effie "but I have not been up there. It is a pretty steep climb. That must have been quite a walk from the town."

"It was. I discovered I was not as fit as I thought I was. It was worth it, though. But the whole place was somehow ... eerie, mysterious – rather creepy. I was quite glad to leave." Nicholas told Effie of the myths and folklore surrounding the island that Catherine had recounted. She said she was aware of some of the stories.

"When I visited Halki last year I popped in to the Traditional House very briefly. It was on the way to the beach," he said. "However, then I was more interested in the every day life of the locals and did not pay much attention to these old folk tales. I wouldn't mind visiting again. With your background and, of course, your Greek, we can probably get a better insight into these traditional stories."

"I would love to," said Effie. "I last went many years ago, so I am sure that they have added to it. In any event, I love learning about our islands. Each has its own culture and mythology."

The grey-haired owner came over to ask how the lunch was. They said it had been really good. "Can I bring you some baklava, or I have some special orange pie for you?" They both thanked him saying they could not manage another thing. Effie asked how long he had been running the taverna.

He smiled. "Over twenty years. My father built it after moving across from Alimia." They both sat up. Nicholas said he understood that Alimia was uninhabited. "It is now," the restaurant owner replied. "My father was one of the last to leave. That was the end of the 1960s. Since then we all live here."

"What did your father do on Alimia?" asked Effie.

"He was a fisherman. Before that he was diving for sponges."

"Do you know all the stories of ships sinking in these waters in ancient times?" asked Nicholas.

"For sure. Sometimes they were carrying treasure from Rhodes to the Middle East."

"Did your father ever find anything in his time as a fisherman? Or possibly when he was diving for sponges?" Effie asked.

"Many things. A lot were of course modern, probably lost from the ferries or the boats going between the islands. But he did find old coins, also some pottery and amphora. Once he also found a small marble figure, which he sold to a collector."

"Do you still have any of his finds?" Effie asked. "I am involved in historical research at the library on Rhodes and my friend here is very interested in our archaeology."

"Wait here a moment," was the response. "Let me see."

He disappeared for a few minutes and then came back with a pottery urn and what seemed to be a corroded lump of metal. The urn was decorated with a vine pattern and Ellie said that it was likely to be Roman. They studied the pitted, corroded piece of metal. It was five or six inches long and a couple of inches thick. It had a green patina, but there were no inscriptions or markings. It looked old.

"You know, this looks like bronze," Effie said. "Do you know where it was found?"

The restaurant owner knew only that it was found off the coast of Alimia. "My father found it a long time ago. We first thought it might be gold, but we know now it is not."

They thanked him for showing them the finds and asked for the bill. While they were waiting, Nicholas said: "You know, it is entirely possible that we have just held in our hands a fragment of the great Colossus of Rhodes." They became silent.

Walking back to town they discussed what the find might mean. Did it have any significance in Alessandra's disappearance? The Traditional House was on the other side of the town, just off the road to Pondamus Bay and beyond. The white-fronted, double-storey house had brown shutters. Through the iron gates and up some steps, they entered the cool of the museum and paid. Inside was a collection of antique furniture. Another room had a display of costumes and handmade dolls. They smiled at the pairs of old lace drawers lovingly enclosed in a glass case. Nicholas remembered most of the exhibits, though his previous visit had been cursory. This time he paid more attention. In the third room was a display cabinet with small pottery bowls and painted pottery fragments, together with spindle bottles and alabaster vessels. Another showed a collection of amphorae, recovered from shipwrecks off the Halki coast, some dating back more than two thousand years. There was no sign of any metallic objects.

"I think any finds of significance would have been sent to the museum on Rhodes or even the national museum in Athens," said Effie as they wandered back into the street outside.

They found Catherine in her gallery. She was talking to a customer so, while they waited, they studied the paintings on display. Effie admired a panorama of the harbour-front with its elegant sailing boats anchored in the bay. To one side the graceful, pastel-coloured villas cascaded down the hill towards the seafront. "Halki is just made for artists," she said. The customer left and Catherine greeted them both warmly. "So you are the Effie that Nicholas has told me about," she said. "It is lovely to meet you. Do I gather, Nicholas, that you are both about to depart our island?"

"We will be leaving in the morning. I am returning your flashlight, but we actually came to invite you for dinner this evening, if you are free."

"That would be lovely. Can you give me half an hour to close up and I will meet you."

Nicholas remembered the barman from the other night recommending Taverna Milos as a place where he might find out more about Helena. They arranged to meet there at seven.

Nicholas and Effie watched the sunset with a drink while they waited for Catherine. Effie said, when they got back to

Rhodes, she would try to find out whether Alessandra had come across any ancient artifacts in the museum, particularly any bronze pieces from these waters. She could ask Eleni, but she would probably ask Michael, as he had a greater knowledge of this period of antiquity.

Nicholas said he planned to visit the Muslim Library to see if there was any more documentation on the removal of the ruin of the Colossus. There must be some records of how they were transported, the intended destination and whether any of the ships had gone down in a storm. "I'll probably need your help. You'll know where to look. You might also be able to translate some of the records. I also need to go back to Alessandra's apartment to check through the remaining papers. It's possible there is something that confirms what we have learnt here."

"Oh, and I almost forgot, I have the phone number and address of the dive operator on Halki whose boat Alessandra chartered to dive around here. His name is Spiros. Out of season he works in Faliraki. I might ask for a lift there if that is OK?"

Effie said of course she would give him a lift. They finished their drinks and walked to the taverna. Catherine was not yet there, but they were shown to a table near the entrance. Nicholas asked the waiter if he was Yannis and was shown a thick-set, middle-aged man sitting by himself reading a magazine near the kitchen entrance. Catherine arrived moments later.

They looked at their menus. Catherine said: "Halki is famous for its handmade pasta. Here they have koulia. If you prefer seafood, I can recommend the fish soup, if they have it." They ordered and Nicholas asked if he could speak to Yannis. The waiter whispered to the man sitting by the kitchen and nodded towards their table. Yannis came over. "Catherine. Lovely to see you here," he said, then turned to Nicholas and Effie. "Welcome," he said.

Nicholas asked if he knew Helena Milonas.

"Of course. I know her quite well. But she has not been here for a long time. I think she went with her boyfriend back to Rhodes."

Nicholas took out the photograph of Alessandra and Andriy. "Is this the boyfriend?" he asked, indicating Andriy.

"Yes, that is the one. They left with two of his friends on his boat. This was last year. In October, I think, after all the tourists have left. I have not seen any of them since. He was a Russian. I think his friends were also Russian. They were not here for long, but no one really liked them," he explained, adding "the boyfriend was obviously very rich."

"Do you, by any chance, remember the boat at all?" asked Effie.

"Ah, it was of course big, expensive." He used his large hands to emphasise its size. "I remember that it was registered in Italy. I think it said it came from Genoa, or one of those Italian ports, but I cannot remember the boat's name.

"I remember one night when he came in with some of his friends. They got very drunk on ouzo and vodka and were very loud, shouting at each other and offering everyone drinks. Someone sitting nearby asked him what he did for a living. He said he bought and sold old things, but he did not look like an antiques dealer. I think people on the island thought he was another type of dealer. He had that look about him."

Nicholas asked if Yannis remembered ever seeing the woman in the photograph. He pointed at Alessandra. "This lady here. I have seen her before. A few times, I think. She was a friend of Helena." He looked more closely at the photograph. "Was she the woman who disappeared here last year?"

"Yes, this is the woman. Her name is Alessandra Bianchi. We are trying to find her, or at least to trace her movements on Halki."

"I am sorry I cannot help you with that." Yannis shrugged. "Perhaps they all left on the boat together."

They finished their meal with ouzo. Outside the restaurant they said goodbye to Catherine and thanked her for her help.

"No doubt I'll visit Halki again and you'll be the first person I come to see," Nicholas said, hugging her.

Chapter Fifteen

Halki

"WHAT ARE YOU GOING TO DO?" ALESSANDRA ASKED. "KEEP me a prisoner here?"

"I am going to do whatever it takes," he said softly. "You are not going to go anywhere until you have told me everything. I know you have found it."

"That is just an assumption. You have no way of knowing what I may or may not have found. And I have no intention of telling you – ever" Alessandra stated.

"Believe me you are going to tell me exactly what you have found," the man said menacingly.

"And what if I refuse?"

"Then you will never get away from me."

"That is rubbish," she snapped. "People will know that I have gone missing. I have got a job for heaven's sake. The museum will know immediately. My parents will also know. They will inform the police and they will come looking for me. You will not be able to get away with this."

He said: "You know what resources I have. All these things will be taken care of. Helena will also help me in this. Please believe me that no one – not your parents or your colleagues – will come looking for you. I can make you disappear – for ever if needs be."

"I don't believe that you would do this to me. I know you are capable of certain things, but not this."

"Alessandra, listen to me carefully. This is my business and it is too important to let anything get in its way. In a way, I have been looking for this my whole life. Nothing, not you, not anything, will now stop me."

Helena interjected more softly, pleading with Alessandra. "We know that you have found the site. Please make things easier for yourself and just tell us."

"I cannot do that," she repeated. "I have investigated a number of sites and have found nothing."

"I do not believe you," the man said, striding restlessly around the room. "I believe you know exactly where it is and you will show us."

"Even if I did know, I would not do that. It doesn't belong to you. It belongs to the world. You will only steal it and sell it. It would then probably disappear into some wealthy person's collection, never to be seen again. I would never let that happen."

"I am very sorry then," he said. "I feel I am going to have to convince you."

As frightened as she was Alessandra also felt herself getting ever more angry. She pushed past him and said: "We are getting nowhere. I am going to go. I am not going to be threatened by either of you." She started to open the door.

As she did he stepped back across her and hit her with a closed fist, hard, across her face. She spun away to the side with the force of the blow and crashed over the chair beside her. Lying on her back she felt herself be dragged roughly across the room to the stairs. Before she lost consciousness she heard Helena scream.

Some time later, Alessandra remembered coming round. She was in one of Helena's bedrooms. Her nose was still bleeding and she was handcuffed by one wrist to the bedstead. She wiped her face with her free arm and saw fresh blood. Her nose hurt and the side of her face was numb. The room was dark. The window and heavy shutter were closed and she knew that there was no point in calling out. She looked for her bag and realised it was probably downstairs. She remembered the room well. It was the bedroom she used when she stayed with Helena. Her arm was at a strange angle and she tried to get more comfortable on the bed.

Alessandra heard the door being unlocked and Helena entered. Wordlessly, she set a glass of water and packet of painkillers beside her friend. Alessandra said nothing. She didn't bother to look up. There was no point. She waited until Helena had left and then took a couple of the tablets with a large gulp of water. Her jaw hurt and she felt sick. She imagined she looked a sight. It must be evening. She could no longer see any light filtering through the cracks of the shutters. She heard some sound from downstairs and then the heavy tread on the stairs. The door was unlocked and he came in, turning on the light. He brought a chair over to the bed. "I am hoping that you have had time to reconsider your position," he said. "As you can see you have no bargaining power. I know you have principles. Just show me the site on the map that was in your bag. We will then let you go."

She remained quiet.

This seemed to infuriate him. "Look, I know you can be stubborn. And I understand that you believe that what I do is wrong. But I really did care about you."

"You are joking," retorted Alessandra finally. "When I first met you I thought we were similar in many ways; that we shared the same interests, the same passion. I thought you were so knowledgeable about archaeology. I really thought that you understood that archeology is integral to its own country, that it is part of the fabric of its heritage. How wrong I was."

It was the man's turn to remain quiet. "I realised that you are none of these things," she continued. "You had the huge advantage in studying in these places, for heaven's sake. You, above anyone, should have understood this. The past does not belong to one person or a group of people – it belongs to all the people. But, underneath everything, you are just a crook, a common criminal. At heart you are immoral. I came to realise that you are capable of many cruel things. I find you utterly repugnant," Alessandra's eyes flashed with anger. "I am not frightened of you."

"I am really sorry that you feel that way," he finally responded. There was still an air of suppressed violence about his words. "You are nothing to me now. I would suggest that you do have good reason to fear me. One way or another, you are going to help me. You can make this difficult for yourself, or you can put your own morals to one side and cooperate with me. I am a patient man and I will wait to see what you choose."

"Can I have my bag back?" asked Alessandra.

"You can. I will ask Helena to bring it up for you. We have of course removed certain items. You will not get your mobile phone back. Helena is going to contact your work, saying that you are unwell and will not be back for some while." He smiled. "We will also send a text message to your parents letting them know that you have met someone and that you intend to take some time off to go travelling. I rather think they will be relieved that you have finally got over me," he said laughing.

"We will send a couple more texts in a week's time or so and then will deposit it in the Aegean, together with your laptop, which we have also removed. So, no one will be looking for you Alessandra."

Alessandra felt a chill. She suddenly realised how much danger she was in. This man would be ruthless with her. "Helena will take you to the bathroom if you need to go. You don't look too good," he observed. "Don't worry, she will be handcuffed to you the whole time. We don't want you to try to escape, do we? I have to go back to the boat. I will come up and see if you have changed your mind a bit later." He went downstairs.

Some time later, Helena came up the stairs, bringing Alessandra's green canvas bag with her. She gave it to her and indicated she would accompany Alessandra to the bathroom. She unlocked the handcuffs and attached one to her own wrist.

Reaching the bathroom Alessandra immediately threw up into the toilet. When she had finished retching she stood up shakily and went to the sink. Running the water over her face, she managed to clean some of the drying blood from her nose. Helena passed her some tissues. Alessandra noticed that the blow had split her lip. There was also a swelling on the side of her face. The painkillers had helped, however. Helena took her back to the bedroom and reattached her to the heavy bed. She left, saying that she would bring up some tea and a sandwich.

Alessandra looked through her bag. Along with her phone, her computer and passport, the maps and documents were also missing. She was glad that she had sent the important documents to her parents, where she hoped they would be safe.

Sometime later Helena came upstairs with the tea and something for her to eat. Helena had given up trying to engage her in any conversation. For that Alessandra was grateful. She still felt nauseous and was not hungry. She had a couple more painkillers. Alessandra could hear sound downstairs and movement on the stairs. Her assailant came back in and looked at her. He examined her face. "I am very sorry that I had to do that," he said. "However, I am prepared to do it again and again until you understand."

Alessandra believed him. She tried once again. "Why don't you just let me go? You know you will never get away with this."

"You know I cannot. This is too valuable to leave alone. My partners, in any event, will not allow it. We already have a number of buyers lined up. The only way that you will be allowed to leave will be when I find what we have been looking for. When you go free, I give you my word that I will leave you alone, as long as you give me your word that you will not go to the police or the authorities. That you leave me and my business alone."

She did not believe that for one moment. She knew she already knew too much. "I cannot do that for you. You are going to have to find it for yourself."

"Believe me, this approach of yours will help no one. You can save us a lot of time and trouble by cooperating with us. If you don't, we will eventually get the information from you." He clenched his fists. Eventually, he turned away and left the room.

It was quite late. Alessandra drifted off, despite the raised voices from below. She woke with a start when the door opened and the light was turned on.

"Unfortunately, you have left me no choice," said the man, his voice cold. "I had hoped it would not come to this." Helena held her arm, while Alessandra tried to fight them off. Between them they subdued her and the man produced a syringe. Alessandra felt the sharp prick of the needle as he injected her, then a fizzing in her head and then nothing.

Chapter Sixteen

RHODES TOWN

BACK ON RHODES, NICHOLAS PHONED SPIROS. "ANDRES, from the bar on Halki, told me that an Englishman might phone," Spiros said. "OK, how can I help you?"

Nicholas explained.

"I remember Alessandra well. She hired me several times for the whole day to take her diving around Halki."

"Was it just Alessandra – on her own?"

"Mostly, yes it was. The first time she had her boyfriend with her. He was quite difficult. He was not as good a diver as she was. I took them diving around Trachia and also to Charidimos cave. The boyfriend was very nervous about entering the cave. He was not so brave."

"Did Alessandra give you the impression she was looking for something?" Nicholas asked.

"Yes, she did. Not the first time we went out. But the last few times she asked me to take her to Alimia. These times she was without the boyfriend. We went twice one weekend, and then once more in September, last year. It was just before the end of the season. I always go back to Rhodes at the beginning of October.

"She seemed to know exactly where she wanted to go on Alimia. The first time she had charts and maps. She also took a lot of photographs with her underwater camera. She dived on her own and I waited on the boat. That is what she wanted.

"The last time we went out she wanted to go back to where she had dived before. That time she only needed a snorkel. After that I have not heard from her again."

"Is it possible for us to meet up in the next few days?" Nicholas asked. "I would be very grateful if you could indicate on the charts where Alessandra was diving – on Halki and Alimia."

"That is possible, yes," Spiros said. "I work in the evenings in a hotel in Faliraki, but I could meet you on Wednesday at the hotel before I start work." They agreed a time. Nicholas gave Spiros his number in case something came up.

Nicholas had made a week's booking in a different hotel in the town. He hoped no one would realise he was back. Effie had offered to let him stay at her apartment, but he felt uncomfortable with that arrangement. Besides, he didn't want to expose her to any unnecessary danger. When they parted she said she would phone Kamides. They agreed to meet for drinks on the Thursday evening.

The next day he walked to Alessandra's apartment. It was late morning and warmer than a week ago. He pressed the bell for the caretaker and the familiar, gruff voice answered. The caretaker remembered him and pressed the door release. He met Nicholas at the entrance and they began the slow walk up to Alessandra's apartment. The caretaker gave Nicholas some new mail for Alessandra, then left him, this time saying he should just shut the door when he was finished.

It did not feel as though anyone else had been there since his last visit. He put the new mail on the table and looked around the other rooms to make sure he had not missed anything from his previous visit. The kitchen and fridge were as he had left them. Nothing had been moved in the bathroom. He took more care in the bedroom and went through the photograph album again. As far as he could see there were no other photographs from Halki or Alimia. He also checked for any sign of a camera but there was none.

He moved through into the living room and looked through her mail. Apart from a couple of bills, the rest was junk mail. He opened the mobile phone bill and saw that it was a final reminder to pay. The bill showed that no calls had been made for a number of months. Some calls, including overseas ones, dating from before Alessandra's disappearance, were itemized. He recognised two of these calls made to her parents back in September. The last two entries recorded were for text messages sent in late October and then early November. After these there was no indication of any further phone usage. He put the bill to one side to take with him and went through the rest of the mail. In the middle of the pile, Nicholas noticed a receipt for a registered package sent from the Rhodes Town Central Post Office. The recipients were her parents in the UK and the receipt indicated that the contents were documents and photographs, with a value not exceeding a hundred euros.

The receipt showed that the package was sent on the 20th September last year, a few weeks before he had met Alessandra. Nicholas put the receipt with the phone bill. The final pile of documents contained papers and notebooks related to her work. In one notebook were details of her recent work at Ancient Kamiros. He left that, but took one filled with notes on the destruction of ancient sites in Syria after the war. As an afterthought, he added an article outlining Russian involvement in the country.

Nicholas left and went down the stairs and knocked on the caretaker's door to let him know that he was leaving. He thanked the old man. On the walk back to his new hotel in the early afternoon sun, he wondered about the package Alessandra had sent to her parents. What could have been in it and why had they not mentioned it to him?

Later Nicholas walked into the Old Town to meet Effie. Evening was approaching and the lights in the shops were starting to come on. Nicholas walked up Sokratous Street, lined with tourist shops, towards the bar Effie had suggested. More shops had opened since the last time he was in the Old Town. The bar opened into a shaded garden providing a tranquil haven from the bustle of the street outside. It was less than half-empty, but he still could not see Effie. He ordered a beer and took it across the courtyard to a table next to a fountain, giving himself an unobstructed view of the entrance. Gradually the garden started to fill with office workers, celebrating their release from a day spent sitting in front of a computer. The noise level began to rise. He checked his phone. There were no missed calls. Nicholas supposed Effie was held up at work. He ordered another beer and watched the crowd. Half-an-hour later, he started to worry. Effie had always been punctual. It was strange she had not phoned. He went outside into the street to call her. The phone rang for a time and switched to her voice mail. He left a message and went inside to finish his beer.

An hour later there was still no sign of Effie. He had tried her phone again, with the same result. He decided to get something to eat. When she phoned he could redirect her to the restaurant nearby.

While he waited to be served by the busy waiter he called his parents. His mother sounded relieved to hear his voice. He realised he had not spoken to them for a few weeks and apologised.

His mother said they were both fine. It was so like her to minimise their troubles, because then she told him she had found a lump in her breast and had been for a mammogram. She was waiting for the results, but she assured Nicholas there was nothing to worry about. Despite the reassurance, Nicholas felt a familiar dread. "How are you feeling?" he asked. "How has Dad taken this? I am sorry that I am not there for you at the moment."

His mother said that all was fine and changed the subject. They were relieved that spring was on its way; they increasingly found the winters harder as they got older. She brought him up to date with life in the village and Nicholas felt calmed by her account of the mundane activities that determined his parents' lives. It sounded so solid and English. Any nagging anxieties he had were soothed by her positivity.

His father came on the phone and Nicholas explained briefly where he had been and what progress he had made. He did not mention the threat or his feelings of unease. He rang off, promising to phone them the following week.

It was after ten when he had finished his meal. He had tried Effie's phone once more. He could only assume she had forgotten their arrangement and had switched her phone off.

Nicholas was undressing for bed when the phone finally rang. It was Effie. "Hello," she said. "Can you hear me?" Her voice was faint and she spoke with difficulty. The reception was poor and he moved closer to the window. He could just make her out.

"I am at the hospital. I have had an accident."

"Are you all right?"

"I'm at the general hospital. I was hit by a car this evening and my ankle is badly broken. The doctors say I will be going in for surgery in the morning. I just wanted to let you know where I was. I will be OK." Nicholas was not reassured. He said he would be there as soon as possible. "That's very sweet, but it's late. They are putting the lights out in the ward. I am fine, really. I am quite comfortable." She continued in a businesslike manner. "In truth I would just prefer to go to sleep, if I can. I have been given painkillers to get me through the night. Come in the morning when I have had the surgery. I will then explain what happened."

Nicholas relented, saying: "OK, I do understand. Try and sleep and I will see you tomorrow."

He called a taxi at nine the next morning and was at the large, modern hospital in fifteen minutes, where he was directed to the waiting area on the first floor. Effie had had her surgery and was in the recovery area. The nursing staff said they would call him when she was back on the ward. He waited for an hour, staring at an old copy of Reader's Digest that he had found, without really reading it. Eventually, a nurse came over and told him that Effie would be fine. The surgery had gone well.

She took Nicholas to a small ward with two other beds. A sleeping elderly lady lay in the bed near the entrance. The bed opposite was empty. At the third, nearest the window, Effie was sitting up, looking pale and groggy. Nicholas gave her a careful kiss, squeezed her hand and sat down next to her. He gave her some water and she smiled. "Hello," she said, weakly, trying to smile.

Nicholas sat with her while the last of the anaesthetic wore off. Eventually, he was able to ask her how she was feeling.

"A bit bruised and a bit tired. My ankle feels all right at the moment. I guess the pain will come later."

"Can you remember anything about the accident?"

Effie took time replying. "I was cycling home. I had left work early to go and change, before coming back into town to meet you. I was close to home and a car came from behind me." She closed her eyes for a moment, trying to remember. "It seemed to suddenly veer towards me. I saw it at the last moment out of the corner of my eye. The next thing I knew I was flying through the air. I was just lucky I was wearing my helmet, but I came down badly on my ankle. I was told last night that it was fractured in two places. The doctors said it was lucky that they did not need to put a pin in it." She looked down. "As you can see I now have a sexy cast. They said it should heal fine, though."

"Did the car stop to help you?"

Effie shook her head. "I didn't really get a good look at it, either. It all happened so fast."

"Did anyone else see what happened?"

"I really don't know. I think my bike was lying in the road. It was quite mangled. Someone came along in their car a bit later and saw the bike and then saw me."

She stopped and Nicholas poured her some water. He helped her to sit up. "Relax," he said. "We can talk later. I can just sit here beside you."

"No, I am fine, really," Effie smiled at him. "I was lying on the side of the road. It was just starting to get dark. A nice young man with his girlfriend helped me off the road and called an ambulance. They waited with me and I think they also called the police."

"God, it sounds awful. Were you conscious all the time?"

"I think so, although I can't be sure. It could have been worse I guess."

"Is there anything I can bring for you from home?"

Effie thanked him, saying: "My mother is coming in with a change of clothes. I am hoping that when the doctor sees me I should be able to go home later. My mother will help me with that."

Nicholas sat with Effie for the next hour. They were chatting when a nurse came to say that the police were outside. Did Effie feel up to answering a few of their questions? Nicholas said he would go, but would phone Effie later. As he was leaving two policemen came into the ward. They seemed to know Effie.

That afternoon Nicholas phoned Spiros and they agreed to meet at a hotel on the beach side of the main road in Faliraki later. He took a taxi to the resort, twenty minutes away. When he walked into the hotel, he saw a wiry, grey-haired man in his sixties drinking coffee in the lounge. They shook hands. Spiros offered Nicholas a coffee and explained that in the off-season he worked on the night shift in the hotel. In passable English he said: "I have just under an hour before I am back on duty."

Nicholas told Spiros of his search for Alessandra. "I am really interested in her diving. I think it will provide some clues as to why she has disappeared."

Spiros looked at Nicholas, questioningly, then took out a couple of crumpled, folded sheets from his pocket. They were charts of the waters around both Halki and Alimia, showing sea depths, offshore rocks, currents and points of interest for divers. In places there were hand-written notations in Greek.

Spiros asked Nicholas if he had tried diving.

"I actually did a PADI course some time ago in the Caribbean," Nicholas said. "But, I haven't been diving for the last few years."

Flattening the first page on the coffee table, Spiros explained that this was a chart for Halki. "There are some popular diving sites that I usually take my customers to. Alessandra and her boyfriend were really only interested in one – this one here at Trachia, below the castle." He pointed.

"It is called the Charidimas Cave and they spent a lot of time diving around the cave entrance, as well as inside the cave. If they were looking for something, I don't think they found it. The water is also quite deep around that part of the island.

"The next time I heard from Alessandra, she asked me if I knew Alimia well. I told her I did and had done a few dives there. Most of my work is around Halki, however. Most people don't know about Alimia. It is a protected island about forty-five minutes from Halki. Anyway, she booked me for the day and was only interested in diving around there. This time she was by herself.

"She had a map of the island with her and she pointed to where I had to take her. I was a bit surprised because most people who go diving around Alimia just want to explore the wrecks of sunken ships. She knew precisely where she wanted me to take her and that is what I did."

Nicholas said he only knew Alimia from having passed it on the ferry to Halki.

"Ah, yes," replied Spiros. "Well, this is the route the ferry normally takes." He traced a route to the east of the island.

"The first dive was to a site here on this east coast," he indicated a position on the chart with a nicotine-stained finger. "There was a small bay there. The second time I took her here to this spot." He pointed to a larger bay to the south-west. "I know the bay. It used to have an old settlement on it. During the war the Italians used it as a port and built barracks for their troops." He pointed to an area on the opposite side of the bay. "This side, I do not know well and I have never dived there. Alessandra said there were underwater caves she was keen to explore. Boats are warned to keep away from that area of the bay. The water is shallower on this side and it is dangerous to shipping because there are strong currents and sharp rocks there. See, I have marked this particular area on the map for you. This part of the bay is honeycombed with caves and underwater cavities. It is a bit like a … a Swiss cheese. Is that how you say it?"

Nicholas nodded in agreement. "Did she dive by herself or did you accompany her?"

"No, on each occasion she insisted on diving by herself. It was fairly safe, as the boat was quite close and she was not diving to any great depth. In fact, at the second location, she only needed a snorkel."

"Would you be able to find all these dive sites again?"

"The first site on Halki is no problem. The second is a big problem as there are hundreds of caves. It will be impossible to say which of the caves she explored. I am back on Halki in a few weeks and I would be happy to take you close to all these spots."

"Thanks Spiros. That would be good," said Nicholas. "I will phone you.

"Can you remember whether Alessandra ever found anything at these sites?" Nicholas asked. "Perhaps some pieces of pottery?"

Spiros thought about this. "It is hard to say. She did not say anything to me and did not bring up anything on board unless she had put it in her dive bag. If it was something small, like a coin, I would not have known. She did not say anything to me."

It was time for Spiros to start his shift, so Nicholas took the folded charts and thanked him warmly. He said he would be in touch and would see him on Halki.

Back at his hotel, Nicholas phoned Effie. She was home. The hospital had released her earlier and her mother had taken her back to the apartment. She was resting on her couch and her mother was cooking her something to eat. "She is being very sweet. I have crutches to get around and at some point I will need to go back to the hospital for physiotherapy."

"Is the ankle painful?" asked Nicholas.

"I have been given some quite strong painkillers, so I feel quite laid back. Which is not me, normally – as you well know. Seriously though, it is manageable. I am meant to take it easy for the next week."

"How were the police? Did they have any news for you?"

"No. So far they have no witnesses. All they wanted from me was a statement of what happened. I couldn't really provide much detail. It all happened so quickly. At least they have my bike for me," she said, ruefully. "I think it is a write-off, though."

Effie said her meal was ready. "I feel quite tired, though. I am just going to eat and then go to bed. Can you come round tomorrow morning? I would love to see you and you can help me practice with these crutches."

"Of course. Just take it easy and I will see you then."

Chapter Seventeen

RHODES TOWN

Effie answered the door on crutches. The bruise on the side of her forehead was darkening. "I am slowly getting used to these things," she said. "I have stopped knocking things over. I must really look a sight."

"You look fine." Nicholas kissed her gently. "Can I get you anything? I brought you a couple of magazines and a newspaper. I'll go down to the supermarket in a moment to get you a few things for the apartment. First let me make you some tea and you can then tell me what you need."

She made her way slowly to the couch. "That's so kind of you. I don't think I am quite up to stairs at the moment."

While Nicholas was making the tea, Effie said that, as a result of the accident, she had forgotten to tell him that she had phoned Michael Kamides. "He wasn't particularly helpful. I asked him whether the museum had a collection of ancient artifacts recovered from sunken ships around Rhodes. He said they did. It was largely pottery, but they did have a collection of old coins and amphorae. I asked whether Alessandra had shown an interest in them. Also whether she had brought any finds from around Halki into the museum."

"What did he say?"

"He could not recall her showing any particular interest. It was certainly not what she was meant to be working on. He was adamant about this. However, he knew diving was an interest of hers. She told him that she occasionally came across artifacts while diving."

Effie stopped to adjust the position of her leg. Nicholas placed another cushion gently under it. "He said that finding old relics was not really surprising. The coast in this area is littered with shipwrecks. With the amount of artifacts to be found around here, there is seldom any value in them or any interest by the museums. Michael thought that whatever she might have recovered would have come from her wreck diving off Symi, rather than Halki. I questioned him on that and he said he was sure that Alessandra had told him that it was around Symi. As far as he was aware, she did not bring anything to the museum for verification."

"That is odd," said Nicholas. "Did Kamides say when she had retrieved these artifacts?"

"No he didn't, but I got the impression it was sometime last year."

"I guess we now need to figure out how, or where, Symi fits into the equation then," said Nicholas.

"There is one other thing ..." said Effie. "After I spoke to Michael, I thought I would walk up to the Muslim Library, I told you about. I think I had more success there."

"Yes, I remember you suggesting it would be worth a visit. It's one place that I haven't been to yet."

"No problem, but I think I found something that might be of interest." She seemed excited by her discovery. "I made copies of a couple of old parchment documents. One will need translating from Arabic, but I think it provides an original account of the sale of the pieces of the remains of the Colossus to a Jewish trader from Edessa. I believe it contains details of the loading and transportation from Rhodes. It also records the types of ships used and the planned routes back to Syria. It amounts to quite a few pages and I was only able to partially translate it.

"The second document details a bad storm that interrupted the transportation. I have translated it for you as best I can. It tells of a number of ships having to flee the storm and seeking safe harbour in Alimia."

"One of the last dives that Alessandra made before she disappeared was on Alimia." Nicholas's interest was piqued.

"At the time of the Arab conquest of Rhodes, Alimia had been used for years as a deep-water harbour for the Rhodian fleet. The document records that boats were wrecked off the coast, with significant loss of life. It's very interesting, don't you think? It also fits with what we learnt on Halki."

Nicholas agreed. "It really does. It links in beautifully. Let me go through these documents in detail. Perhaps I can find someone around who can complete the translation for us."

He finished his tea and made sure that Effie was comfortable on the couch. She was tiring again, so he brought a pillow from the bedroom for her head. Taking a list that he had compiled with her help, he left to go to the nearby shops.

On his way back with the groceries, he wondered about Effie's accident. Was it an accident? Hopefully, the police would establish a lead on the car involved. While packing away the shopping in her kitchen, he asked: "Can I make you something for lunch?"

"I am not feeling hungry right now. I will probably have a salad a bit later," Effie said, pulling herself up on the couch.

"Fine," said Nicholas. "Salads are my speciality. I'll make one and leave it in the fridge for you." They chatted for a while, but Effie's eyes were starting to close. Nicholas said he would leave her to rest. "Thank you. I still feel quite bruised from the fall, so I'll just lie here on the sofa for a bit."

Nicholas said he would phone her later to find out how she was feeling. "Try and stay off your feet for as long as possible," he said, as he let himself out.

Back in his hotel room, he put the documents from Effie in the safe and was thinking of phoning the Bianchis, when there was an insistent knocking at his door. He opened the door to find two men outside. One he recognised immediately as Andriy. "May we come in?" he said, in his accented English. Nicholas let them in. Andriy was bigger than he looked in the photographs. He had a broad chest and powerful build. His confident posture signaled that he was used to being in control.

"How can I help you?" asked Nicholas.

"I think you know," said Andriy. "We have already warned you to stop interfering. You did not take our warning seriously. We know that you have carried on with your stupid investigation. We even know that you have just got back from Halki looking for heaven knows what. You are getting in the way."

"Why don't we go downstairs, sit down and talk about this," Nicholas's room had taken on an air of menace. "I am sure this is all a misunderstanding."

"I don't think so, but why don't you sit down on the bed." Andriy sat in the chair nearby. He reached past Nicholas and picked up some of the papers on the table and glanced through them, "You are stumbling into something that you do not understand." He deliberately let the papers cascade onto the floor.

Nicholas's mouth felt dry. "I don't know what you are talking about?"

Andriy sighed. "We know that you are looking for Alessandra. I don't know why. She certainly never mentioned you to me. You don't look her type." Nicholas noticed that Andriy wore a thick gold bracelet on his left wrist.

"I met her briefly last October on the ferry going over to Halki. I subsequently heard that she had gone missing when I was back in the UK and thought that I would contact her parents. I spoke to them just before the end of last year. Her parents believe that she has disappeared. I am just trying to help them."

"I don't think so," said Andriy. "I know her parents wish to stay out of this. They will not get involved."

"How on earth can you say that? She is their daughter."

Andriy laughed. "She might be, but her father knows what is best for him. We own Mr Bianchi, you see. He knows that Alessandra is safe for the moment, but I cannot guarantee that will continue. He will not do anything and he certainly would not encourage any investigation."

Nicholas replied quietly: "I am not frightened by a thug like you. You cannot dictate what I can or cannot do. I want you both to leave now."

He made to stand up, but was pushed back onto the bed by the other man. "I think you need to stay seated," said Andriy. "And don't think of calling out, either."

Nicholas looked up. A large black gun was being pointed at his head by Andriy's accomplice. He had never seen a handgun in real life. It was large and evil looking. He nodded his assent and tried not to let it show that his hands were shaking.

Andriy turned on the television and raised the volume. "Let me explain the situation very plainly – and for one last time. We will not hurt you now unless we need to. If we do need to hurt you, you will be hurt very badly – very badly indeed," he said softly. "Please do not underestimate us. We know most things about you. We are not fools and we have resources. You cannot escape us. Neither can your girlfriend. Please consider what happened to her two nights ago as a final warning. I have met Effie. I suspect that there are a few things that you do not know about her."

"What do you mean by that?" Nicholas asked.

"She is also a threat to our business," Andriy replied, ignoring his question. "The point is that, if you don't do exactly what we tell you to, a lot worse will happen to her, I promise you."

"Why are you doing this?"

"For me, this is just business. Believe me you don't need to know any more. Somehow you have managed to get involved in something you do not fully understand."

"And what is Alessandra's involvement in all of this?"

"Unfortunately, she became caught up in something – unknowingly. We were working on a project together, but after a while we did not see eye to eye on it. She did not understand my position and she became a threat to us. Like you, she also did not understand what she was getting involved in. Then she made the mistake of threatening to go to the authorities."

"What was she getting involved in?" asked Nicholas.

Andriy ignored the question again. "It is very unfortunate, but we could not let her go free. She knows exactly what we are looking for and I also believe she knows where it is and how to get it. We are still hoping to persuade her to show us. We hope she will be sensible. We are holding her and cannot let her go until we find what we are looking for."

"So, you have kidnapped her."

"Please trust me in this. For sure, she will get hurt if you continue to look for her. I guarantee also that you will not find her – even if we do have to hurt her."

Nicholas felt chilled. The gun had not wavered from his face, but it was the cold malice conveyed by the calm words that frightened him the most. "Can you at least tell me where Alessandra is and whether she is all right?"

Andriy ignored Nicholas. "You need to listen very carefully. Please believe me that we have no problem with hurting people. It is what we do, and we do it well. This is also part of our business. If you continue your search with Effie, the next time, I promise you, your girlfriend will not see the accident coming. The question is only how bad will it be for her." He smiled. "We can make it very bad, but still it will look accidental.

"Your search for Alessandra is over. You will now need to find some way to convince Effie that you wish to end the relationship. Perhaps tell her that it has run its course. You can find the right words, I am sure. You are not to see her again and you need to leave Rhodes as soon as possible. In any event, we know that she will be out of action for some time. She was lucky. But, we know all her movements and she will remain very vulnerable.

"We expect you to leave Rhodes tomorrow. You will not come back. This shall be the last time we will ever speak to you."

"I need to see Effie, before I go" Nicholas said. "I can't just disappear without saying goodbye. It will look very suspicious and will cause more questions to be asked."

"You may phone her and give some plausible excuse for why you are leaving tomorrow. I am sure you can think of something. Perhaps you have a girlfriend back home who is getting suspicious?" He laughed. "It will be up to you to make it sound convincing. Her continuing safety will depend on it.

"One last thing before we go. There is no point in going back to the police. They are unlikely to believe you and I would suggest that you really don't know who to trust here on Rhodes. Go back home and forget you ever came to this island. It will be much safer in England. Have a good life, Mr Adams," he smiled. "This will be the last time you hear from us. If you return, we will do what we have promised. Don't even consider not catching the flight tomorrow. We will be watching at the airport."

Both men left. Nicholas sat for a while. He was shaken but he could still think clearly. In a way, he was not surprised by what had just happened. He had felt a heavy air of disquiet around him since he had arrived on Rhodes. He had not been able to shake off the feeling that he was being watched and it seems he was right. Now he knew who it was who had been following him. The enemy had a face. If Andriy and his men saw Nicholas as a threat to their business operations, it meant he was getting closer. He also now knew that Alessandra was alive and unharmed, at least for the moment. He was surprised by just how important this knowledge was to him. It would determine what he did next.

He needed to prioritise. First he had to minimise the risk to Effie. It seemed possible there was an organised Russian criminal connection to Alessandra's disappearance. He had read about the growth of the Russian mafia influence across the Mediterranean. He did not know whether Andriy had such connections, but it seemed likely and, if so, that would double the risk to Effie. She was an innocent party and deserved whatever protection he could provide.

Nicholas puzzled over Andriy's enigmatic comments about her being a threat to their business, then put them to one side. They were not relevant to what he now needed to do. He opened his laptop and booked a flight to Gatwick for the next day. Next he had to work out what he was to say to Effie. Nicholas waited a while before phoning her. He was going to have to put some distance into their relationship and there would be no advantage to disclosing what had happened. It would not help her to know of the threat against her. It was better that she believed her injuries were caused by an accident.

When he did phone she sounded happy to hear from him. She said she had slept and was feeling much better. Did he want to come round? Nicholas told her in as neutral a voice as he could summon that something urgent and unexpected had come up at work. He must cancel what he was doing on Rhodes and hurry back to England. The lie made him feel uncomfortable and he tried to keep the content vague. He endeavoured to convey that the seriousness of the issue back home would, unfortunately, require his full and immediate attention. He said he was truly sorry he would not be able to see her before he left. He had a lot to arrange in a short time. He was careful to keep emotion out of his voice. It all sounded a bit trite, even to his ears. Effie sounded shocked. Too shocked to ask him more searching questions, for which he was grateful.

She asked when he was to go and he told her he had booked a flight for the next day. "Could I at least see you before you go? Perhaps you could stop briefly on your way to the airport?"

Nicholas could not take the risk. He would probably be watched. He told Effie it would not be possible. He was going to be preoccupied with work and was booked on conference calls until the last minute. He said it would be better this way. In any event, it would be too hard to say goodbye. They would stay in touch though he promised.

Effie went quiet. "I think I understand. Whatever is going on and whatever your real reasons, you still mean a lot to me. I have enjoyed our time together, Nicholas, and I have no regrets."

"Please just trust me in this," said Nicholas. "Give me a week or so to deal with what is going on at work and I give you my word that I will phone you." He did not know what more to say. "Take good care and look after your ankle," he said and rang off.

Chapter Eighteen

ENGLAND

Back home Nicholas felt lost. The purpose that had dominated his life over the past few months had been abruptly wrenched from him. It was true that now he did not need to look over his shoulder all the time but, with a few months left of his sabbatical, he felt directionless. He still had time to decide on what he was going to do. The company had been fair with him and they deserved to know when he might be back. He resolved to go and see them the following week. He felt ambivalent about leaving Effie in the manner he had. He worried about her and felt that he should have been there in Rhodes to look after her. However brutal his departure had seemed, the outcome regarding their relationship was the right one.

He had tried to begin tidying up the house. He had even thought of visiting those friends that still remained but Alessandra, Effie and the events on Rhodes and Halki dominated his thoughts. Today, he planned to go down to visit his parents.

Now, sitting with his mother, he asked: "Have you had your test results back yet? She replied that the tests had been inconclusive and she had to go back into the hospital for further examination.

"But I am not worrying and you shouldn't either." Nicholas felt that she did not wish to discuss it further. His father smiled in support of his wife.

"Are you returning to work?" his mother asked.

"I am not sure at this stage. I still have some time left of my sabbatical. I need to do a couple of things before I make a final decision." He was careful to exclude all mention of the threats he had received. He showed them the photos he had taken of the islands, starting with his time on Rhodes. When he came to a picture of Effie in the taverna in Lindos, smiling at him with her dark eyes and looking pretty in a simple dress, it gave him a jolt. Could she forgive him for leaving so suddenly. He fought an urge to call her to find out how she was. What had they done to each other? He moved on, swiping past more scenic shots, until he came to photographs taken on Halki. He showed his parents images of the picturesque harbour, almost deserted, save for a few small fishing boats moored at the quayside. He remembered how different the harbour had looked last year and then thought back to the photos he had taken at that time. Swiping hurriedly back, he came to what he was looking for, stopping at a couple of photographs of the harbour taken on his first visit. In them were two expensive-looking motor cruisers, moored by the stern, displaying their names and registration. He looked for the names of the boats but the images on the phone were small and indistinct.

It was an exciting discovery. Nicholas thought he might know what to do. Later, in his study at his home, he enlarged the images on his phone and the names became slightly clearer, but were still indistinguishable. He plugged the phone into his laptop and uploaded the pictures. Zooming in on the stern of the boat nearest the camera he could read clearly the name "Esperanza". Underneath it was written "Fort Lauderdale" and he assumed this was the port of registration. The second boat's name was slightly obscured by the gangway. The next picture was clearer and showed the name "Lady Gabrielle" and "Genoa". Above it he could see an Italian flag. He tried googling the name and port of registration but found no matching entry.

This must be Andriy's boat. It was silver grey with tinted windows. The rear deck was covered and he could make out a large table with seating surrounding it. The top of the boat sprouted all manner of telecommunications and radar equipment. It looked very expensive; Andriy's business was obviously profitable. He trawled the internet until he found a site offering a guide to yacht registries in Italy, where he found the Lady Gabrielle registered to the port of Genoa. The registration details revealed that the owner was Boris Solokov. Hadn't someone said Andriy's surname was Solokov? Was this his father? Was he using daddy's yacht for business as well as pleasure?

Nicholas googled Boris Solokov. He was listed as CEO and majority owner of a Russian minerals company, part-owner of an Italian football team, married with two sons and resident of Minsk, capital of Belarus. He also owned property in Cannes and Sardinia. Perhaps he wasn't using his boat at the moment. Or perhaps he had another registered elsewhere in the Mediterranean?

—

At the imposing stone entrance to the cemetery in Windsor, Nicholas bought two bouquets of spring flowers. He passed the old cemetery chapel, with its tall spire and high stained-glass windows and turned right down a sloping path, and there they were, shaded from the rain under a tree. His parents' flowers lay on the smooth stone of the graves. He removed the faded blooms and replaced them with his flowers, placing them on the two graves, side by side, within touching distance, as if they could hold hands. Baby Adams's grave was tiny beside Lynda's. Nicholas stood for a long time in the rain looking down at his family. He remembered the laughter, the hope and all the plans. He smiled. He would always hold those memories.

Walking back, he disposed of the dying flowers. On a whim, he entered the old chapel. It was cold and empty. Despite the temperature, he sat for a long time, alone with his thoughts.

Nicholas phoned the Bianchis on his return. Mrs Bianchi answered and he asked if he could meet them. "I have spoken to someone who has told me Alessandra is fine. I also believe that she is still somewhere on or nearby Rhodes," he said. "I'd like to speak to your husband, if that would be all right."

Mrs Bianchi seemed hesitant, but eventually a time was agreed for the following evening. Nicholas could come to their house in Amersham. She provided him with directions from the pub where they had met in December.

Later, as he pulled into the car park at work, Nicholas knew he was making the right decision. He had phoned his manager to say he would like to come to see him. Nicholas smiled at the receptionist, as he waited for the lift to come back down to the ground floor. He did not recognise her and assumed she was new. The lift stopped at the fourth floor and the doors opened. He walked down the familiar corridor to his manager's office. Richard seemed delighted to see him. "In truth, Nicholas, when you phoned, I hoped you were going to tell me that you were coming back to work early. We have missed you."

Nicholas smiled and said: "Richard, I appreciate that. I have actually missed it – as well as working as part of the team. I wanted to confirm that I will be returning, but I'll need to take the full period of time off you kindly agreed. I feel more clear-headed now than I have felt for a long time. Certainly since Lynda died. So the break so far has done me good. I think I just needed some time out."

"I can see a difference in you. There seems to be a new positivity," Richard said. "We'll all be delighted to have you back in the next few months. We have some new clients and your return will coincide well with the launch of our new anticoagulant. You remember? You did some initial work on the therapeutic usage with NICE. You'll take the lead on this and I'll look to find you a substantial new challenge in due course. Perhaps a secondment to one of our European operations might suit you?"

Nicholas promised to stay in touch. They shook hands. "Thank you. I have appreciated your support, Richard," Nicholas said.

Before he left the office, he walked around the floor greeting his old colleagues. He caught up on who was doing what, who had left and anything else that had happened in his absence. It all felt refreshingly familiar. He drove the route home that he knew so well. It had stopped raining and the sun had emerged. He loved the seasons, but particularly the onset of spring in England. It was full of promise, of the summer days ahead, and he welcomed the sense of renewal. Trees were starting to come to life, daffodils and crocuses sprouted on verges and in gardens. Everywhere seemed brighter, more optimistic. He smiled.

That evening he did something he had not done in a while. He had never been good at staying in touch with friends, particularly since Lynda had died. He very much regretted his lack of contact with the friends who had provided so much care and support while she was ill. It was time to repair those relationships, to show that they meant something to him. Going through his phone contacts, he called the friends that remained important to him. Those he managed to speak to sounded pleased, even relieved, to hear from him. He promised he would be better at staying in touch in future and told them that he would value their continued friendship and support.

The following evening, he knocked on the Bianchis' front door. The house was fairly modern and set at the end of a cul-de-sac, not far from the town centre. Mrs Bianchi invited Nicholas in and showed him into the living room, where her husband was sitting. Nicholas shook his hand and they all sat. If anything, the

Bianchis looked even more dejected and defeated than they had before Christmas. Nicholas noticed a framed picture of Alessandra on the mantelpiece. He looked at Mr Bianchi: "As I explained to Mrs Bianchi on the phone, I have heard that Alessandra is fine and is still in Greece. But I think you know that."

The Bianchis looked at each other.

"Mrs Bianchi, would it be possible to have a few words alone with your husband?"

She looked at her husband and he nodded. She left, saying she would be in the kitchen if he needed her.

"Don't worry. I will be fine," he said.

"I met Andriy Solokov. Or, rather, he came to my hotel room in Rhodes, just over a week ago. He threatened me. I believe you know our Mr Solokov. His accomplice pointed a gun at my head. Do you know what that feels like, Mr Bianchi?"

Mr Bianchi shook his head slowly.

"Andriy told me that Alessandra was safe, but was being held somewhere. He, and whoever he is working with, were waiting for her to cooperate to help them locate something. I believe it to be an ancient Greek relic of immeasurable value and importance. I think Alessandra had been close to discovering its whereabouts. That is why the stakes are so high. He told me that unless I stop my search for her and leave Rhodes immediately, both she and a friend of hers would be harmed. I know that this is not an empty threat. That is why I am back here. And that is also why I am here talking to you."

Mr Bianchi looked ashen. He started to say something, but Nicholas had to finish saying what needed to be said. "Andriy said something very interesting. He said that you would not intervene in the search for Alessandra. That you owed him something."

Mr Bianchi's eyes moistened. He nodded and said, quietly: "I don't feel proud about this. I have never been sure that I made the right decision." He stopped.

"I'm sure you had your reasons for what you did," Nicholas said, more gently. "I am also absolutely sure that you have had

Alessandra's safety as your priority. However, it might help if you explain everything that happened, from the beginning. You would be getting it off your chest."

Mr Bianchi slumped in his chair. "Some years ago, I had my own architectural consultancy on Rhodes. For years it was very successful and I employed three other architects. We did design work over the whole island. As we expanded, we entered a partnership with a firm of estate agents, who also commissioned housing developments across the island. Then came the banking crisis, back in 2007. It hit Greece very hard. All building work came to a sudden stop. The estate agency had overextended itself and went into administration, leaving a significant debt. At the same time, the demand for architects started to dry up. The only way the business could survive was to obtain a loan."

He looked to Nicholas for understanding. "I had been introduced to a wealthy Russian, a Boris Solokov, who was looking to invest on Rhodes. He lent me an amount to repay the debt and to keep the business afloat for a period. By that stage, I was the remaining architect in the business. I had to let the others go. We only managed to last for another year until we had to close. I had to sell our house on Rhodes to pay back part of the loan."

"I am sorry," Nicholas said.

"That was when we left Rhodes and came back to England. I still owed Boris some of the original loan. He told me not to worry. I could repay the balance when I was able to. Of course, I now know that there were strings attached."

"And, of course, Boris Solokov is Andriy's father," Nicholas finished.

"Yes. I do not know if Alessandra meeting Andriy was pure coincidence or whether it was planned. I had never met him and I am fairly sure that Alessandra did not meet Boris. Our relationship was purely business and he never came to the house."

"Have you tried to contact Boris?" asked Nicholas.

"Yes I did. Andriy phoned me soon after we realised that Alessandra had gone missing. From memory, it was about a week after we first notified the Rhodes police that she had disappeared. He explained that he was Boris's son and had been Alessandra's boyfriend for a period. We did know that. Andriy said Alessandra was well, but that I should not try to find her. I immediately contacted Boris. He was abrupt, almost dismissive. He said I should do exactly as his son asked. He reminded me that I was still in his debt. Boris added that if I looked for Alessandra, he could not guarantee her safety with Andriy. I finally appealed to him as a father and he just laughed. He said, 'You do not understand the Russian way of business. Do not contact me again'. And he hung up."

"Did your wife know about this?" Nicholas asked, quietly.

"Not at first. I tried to keep her out of it, as much as possible. All I said at the time was that a friend had phoned me to say that Alessandra was all right. I did not tell her about the threat until some time later. I felt embarrassed. You can imagine how worried we both were when Alessandra's disappearance was reported on the local news in December. We could not say anything. We were frightened that Boris or his son would hear about the interview and that Alessandra might be harmed. When you contacted us, we tried to discourage you from getting involved. We did not know what else to do."

When he finished talking, he looked up, exhausted. He got to his feet to get a drink and asked Nicholas if he would like something. He poured himself a large glass of red wine.

"Just water will be fine," replied Nicholas.

Sitting back down, Mr Bianchi took a large sip of his wine and continued. "Please believe me, it is not the money that is important. I have to believe Boris and his son that they will not harm Alessandra. She is all we have."

From his own experience and from all that he had heard, Nicholas did not share the belief. His encounter with the cold brutality of Andriy did not give him confidence. Alessandra was likely to be expendable, if Andriy felt she had no further purpose. He said nothing; he did not wish to add to her parents' anxiety.

At that moment, Mrs Bianchi put her head around the door and asked her husband if everything was OK.

"I am fine now. I think you should come back in."

Nicholas asked both of them whether they had heard anything from Alessandra since he last spoke to them. "No," they said together. "We keep on trying her phone but it does not seem to be working."

"You have received something from her though haven't you? She sent a package to you by registered mail, just before she disappeared. Do you remember that?"

Mr Bianchi looked puzzled and looked to his wife for confirmation. She replied: "Yes, I think I know what you are referring to. Alessandra sent it to herself here. We have it somewhere in the study. I had almost forgotten about it. It was sent well before Alessandra went missing and we assumed it had no relevance to her disappearance. It hasn't been opened and I am not sure where it is, exactly. Let me go and look for it." She left the room, coming back after a few minutes with a yellow packet. "Here we are. It was sent from Rhodes back in September. We kept it for Alessandra. See, it is addressed to her, care of us, here."

She passed it to Nicholas. On the front, printed in red, he read: "Under no circumstances to be opened, except by addressee."

"Would you allow me to take this with me?" asked Nicholas. "It might provide a clue as to where Alessandra is being held. I quite understand why you would not wish to go to the police. I'll look at the contents and return it to you resealed. That way you won't compromise your position. Hopefully, the only person who will ask for it will be your daughter. In any event, if someone else asks you, you can truthfully say that you have nothing."

Mrs Bianchi asked her husband whether he was comfortable with the idea. "I don't think we have a choice, particularly if there is a chance to learn where Alessandra is. I just do not want to put her at any further risk," he said. "Take it Nicholas. Just return it to us, and please take care".

"Thank you," said Nicholas. "I understand the almost impossible position you are both in. I've decided to continue my search and try to find and help Alessandra. I think that I'm the best person to do it, at this moment. I'll do my utmost to ensure nothing happens to your daughter. You have my word."

Chapter Nineteen

An island in the Dodecanese

Alessandra remembered little of the journey. It had been a rough trip. The Lady Gabrielle made its way slowly through the heavy swell up the west coast of Rhodes towards Turkey. She had slept for most of the journey. She was not sure how long she had been at sea: it could have been four hours or it could equally have been twenty-four hours. She continued to feel unwell, possibly due to the drug she had been given. Her throat was dry, her face still ached from the violence of the blow. She knew the Lady Gabrielle well. Before she had stayed in the stateroom with Andriy. When she regained full consciousness, she realised she was in one of the smaller cabins. The door was locked. Luckily, the cabin had its own toilet. The handcuffs had been removed and she was free to move around.

Alessandra did not know where she was being taken, although she had an idea. She did not know what would happen to her.

She was frightened. She had always felt Andriy was capable of considerable violence. This was the first time she had experienced it directly. When Andriy had hit her she had been shocked and afraid.

She needed to remain strong. She had to show him she was not scared of him – it was her only chance. She tried to go back to sleep. There was nothing she could do at the moment and she needed to be as fresh as possible. Some opportunity to escape would occur at some stage, she had no doubt.

She dozed fitfully until it became obvious they were arriving at their destination. The sea had become calmer. They were entering somewhere sheltered – perhaps a port. Alessandra looked out of the porthole and saw pale grey limestone cliffs. She thought she knew where she was and was not surprised. She lay back on the bed and waited. It was not long before she heard the door being unlocked.

Andriy entered. "I see you are finally awake. We have arrived. You will wait here for a while until we take you to the house."

Ten minutes later the door opened again and Vitaly entered. "Get up," he commanded. She stood, slightly unsteadily, and Vitaly roughly ushered her out of the cabin by her arm. They went up on deck and Alessandra could see that it was still dawn. She knew exactly where she was. She knew the bay from previous visits. The boat was moored alongside a stone jetty. After the small cabin, the sea air and pine forest in the valley beyond smelled fresh and wonderful. The crew were unloading a couple of boxes into a black four-wheel drive Nissan that had been driven onto the shingle of the beach. Vitaly escorted Alessandra off the Lady Gabrielle and into the back seat of the vehicle, beside Helena. Vitaly returned to the boat. She recognised the driver next to Andriy, who was sitting in the front passenger seat.

Once the boxes had been loaded, they set off slowly on the narrow dirt track, skirting the beach and winding through the trees and into the valley between towering hills. As the vehicle slowly climbed, Alessandra knew where they were heading. Engine whining, the vehicle bumped and swayed its way up the pitted track towards the farmhouse. Alessandra had stayed there once before, when she and Andriy had visited the island to dive around the coast. Arriving at the farmhouse, the driver got out and unlocked the front gates. The two dogs were running free, jumping and barking excitedly around the vehicle as it drove up to the house.

Alessandra was ushered into the building and taken through the kitchen into a dark room, part of an annexe to the main house. Inside the room was a metal bed, with a small table beside it. She was pushed inside and her bag was thrown onto the bed. The door was locked behind her. She turned on the light and surveyed her accommodation. The room was square and a reasonable size. High up there was a small window that was barred on the outside. By reaching up she could just get a purchase to open the window and let in some air. She could now at least hear the sounds of the morning starting, the cicadas and the birdcalls. The dogs were barking.

She sat on the bed. It was firm and had sheets and a thin duvet. Looking through her bag, she found a paperback she had been reading. She took it out and lay down. There was the sound of a key turning in the lock and Helena entered, carrying a bottle of water and a bag containing basic toiletries.

"I'm afraid the accommodation will be quite different from when you last stayed," Helena said. "I'll bring some magazines and find you another blanket. The nights are starting to get cold."

"Thank you," said Alessandra. "How long am I to be kept here?"

"I don't know. You will have to ask Andriy. Alessandra, please just cooperate with him. The sooner you do it the quicker you can get away from here and go home." Alessandra just shook her head. "I wish you would listen to reason. We may no longer be friends, but I do not want you hurt or even to be kept captive here. Andriy won't change his mind. He will force you eventually to tell him what he needs. Please don't push him to this.

"Do you need to use the bathroom, perhaps have a bath?"

"Thank you. Yes, I will."

"I am afraid it is my job to look after you while you are here," Helena told her.

"You mean you will be my jailor."

"I am so sorry. Come with me. I am going to have to lock you in the bathroom. I will wait outside. Just take your time. Knock when you want me to unlock the door and bring you back here."

The water was hot. Alessandra lay in the bath for a long time, feeling her muscles starting to relax. Things had moved so swiftly. Less than two days ago, she had stepped off the ferry in Halki. Then, she carried the hope that she could put a stop to Andriy and his threats and attempts to scare her. She found it hard to believe that a kidnapping like hers could still occur. She was now brutally aware of what Andriy was capable of, and she knew how serious her position was, but she could only hope that reason would prevail. She doubted anyone would look for her for a while. Hopefully, during this time, Andriy and his criminal colleagues would see some sense. If not, she had to believe that there would be some opportunity to escape. These thoughts kept her positive. She would be strong.

She was in the bathroom for so long that Helena had to knock to ask if she was alright. When Alessandra was ready, she called to Helena to let her out. Helena escorted her back to the room. She said she would bring her something to eat shortly.

It must have been around midday when Helena arrived with yoghurt and some fruit. Before she left, she said Andriy had agreed that Alessandra would be able to exercise in the courtyard for an hour each day. He was back at the boat, but would be back in the afternoon.

The afternoon passed slowly. The sun was starting to go down when Andriy unlocked the door and came into the bedroom. "Come with me," he said. "We will let you out into the courtyard each day. You will be watched, so there is no point trying to escape." He led her roughly out into the open. Alessandra sat at the bench in front of the fountain. The sun warmed her face. "I have your maps. Tomorrow we are going to visit some of the dive sites that you so kindly marked for us. Hopefully, this will jog your memory. We have diving equipment on board."

"I won't do anything for you."

"We will see. Do not underestimate me. If you do not help me tomorrow, then you will just be kept here longer. Eventually, you will crack." Alessandra said nothing. "I am only here for two days. After that I have to make a delivery to Turkey, so I will be away for three or four days. It is almost November. Soon the weather will make diving impossible until the spring. Surely you will not wish to spend the next four months here, away from your friends and family, at this remote farmhouse?"

She smiled. "Please understand me, Andriy. As you have said I can be quite stubborn. Time will make no difference. I am not going to help you now, or tomorrow, or even in four months."

Andriy sighed. "Very well, you are leaving me little alternative. I will see you tomorrow. Enjoy your evening." He turned and left the courtyard. Alessandra sat calmly and waited for someone to come and collect her.

The next morning she was woken early. Helena came into the bedroom to bring her something to eat and to allow her to go to the bathroom. "I have brought you some of my clothes," she said. "I know I am a bit bigger than you, but they will have to do until I can buy you some more." She placed the clothes at the foot of the bed. Alessandra forced herself to eat something and then was escorted to the bathroom. She took the clothes together with the meagre toiletries: she was going to miss her blue nail polish she thought, ruefully. She selected a pair of shorts and a T-shirt. They were an approximate fit. She shouted for Helena to unlock the door and return her to her room. Once back, she finished the rest of her breakfast.

The barking dogs signaled the arrival of someone outside. Alessandra heard voices and soon Andriy opened the door. "It is a good day for diving," he announced and indicated that she should follow him. The black vehicle was standing ready on the driveway and Andriy took the wheel. Helena got in beside him in the front and Alessandra heard the click of the central door lock. Fifteen minutes later they passed through the grove of tamarisk trees and arrived at the beach. The Lady Gabrielle was now moored out in the bay. They waited until a dinghy arrived to transport them.

Vitaly stepped on to the beach and indicated to Alessandra that she was to get on board. Andriy followed and the small boat headed towards the Lady Gabrielle. Helena stayed behind to drive the vehicle back to the farmhouse. Once on board the yacht, they began to glide out of the bay, towards the open sea. Alessandra enjoyed the sea breeze and the warmth. It felt wonderful, compared to her captivity. She vowed to enjoy these precious moments of freedom. Andriy had taken out a large maritime map of the area. He also had Alessandra's marked charts of the coastline with him. "As you know, we did a lot of research on the old trading routes in this part of the Mediterranean. We managed to show that a lot of the shipping in the early centuries passed this island. Normally, it was en route to Turkey, but sometimes they went from there through the Bosphorous and on to the Black Sea ports," he reminded Alessandra. "Often this route was also used to sail from Rhodes through to Cyprus and beyond that to Syria."

"Of course I know that," responded Alessandra. "That is why there are such strict laws on sports diving," she said, indicating the pile of scuba gear in the stern. "I have only ever used snorkeling gear here. You know better than anyone that the government is trying to protect the many archaeological treasures that lie off this coast."

"Of course," Andriy laughed. "Naturally, you and I will only use a snorkel." However, I have an expert diver with me who will be going down. He will not be noticed. There is no one out on the water now. Vitaly is staying on the boat and will have binoculars. He will alert us if he sees anything suspicious. Now you just need to show us where to go."

"I will not change my mind. You will have to locate the wreck yourself."

"Eventually, you will help. You will get tired of playing this game."

Andriy showed Alessandra her own maps. He pointed to the islet, separated from the north-west tip of the island by a shallow straight. Alessandra had identified with asterisks two small bays on the west coast. Andriy pulled out another of Alessandra's maps, on which she had marked two sites on the east coast.

"We are going to start with this one," said Andriy. "I know you spent more time exploring around here than around the islet, so I have a hunch that you had a particular interest in these two locations. We will leave the islet for another day." He indicated to the captain the way they needed to be heading. The boat swung east and they sailed out to sea. Past the headland, they turned south, keeping the cliffs to their right. Presently, they came across Agios Georgios Bay, a site Alessandra knew well. She had first investigated it more than a year ago. More recently, she had snorkeled around this bay to divert Andriy, after she became worried that he was following her. It was no surprise, then, that he chose these sites on the east coast first.

Agios Georgios Bay had always delivered a feeling of anticipation whenever she had visited it. It had a dramatic rock face of more than three hundred metres, plunging vertically into the sea. It looked mysterious and was a likely shipwreck site. Between the cliffs was a narrow strip of shingle and pebble beach. It could be reached only by boat and today, as usual, it was deserted. The Lady Gabrielle anchored fifty metres from the shore. The diver began to put on his wetsuit. Meanwhile, Andriy selected a snorkel and mask for himself. Alessandra used the one that had been returned to her. She welcomed the idea of getting back into the water. It felt familiar, like an old friend she could rely on. She had a passing thought of escape, but the precipitous cliffs made success unlikely. She knew she would not get far trying to scramble up the narrow, jagged path that climbed steeply away from the narrow beach. She would never be able to overpower Andriy, even in the water. Besides, his diver would no doubt keep watch.

She had no choice but to don the swimsuit she had brought with her from Rhodes and dive into the water. Although November was in sight, the water was still pleasantly warm and she luxuriated in its feel for some moments. She could feel the sting of the salt water on her lip and the inside of her nose where Andriy's blow had caused her to bleed. The salt water would help to accelerate the healing process.

"You marked the right side of the cliffs over there on your map," Andriy reminded her. He had brought an underwater camera with him. "Let's start there, by seeing what it looks like underwater. Your map indicated that the depth was up to twenty metres along the cliff edge, so my diver will be below us, checking on anything interesting." Alessandra followed him, swimming comfortably in the huge shadow cast by the towering cliff. The shadow made the water look almost black. She was familiar with the rocks and crevices of this bay. She donned her mask and snorkel and tried to enjoy the excitement she always felt from being underwater. Despite the shadow, the visibility was still good. As she swam small silvery fish surrounded her. She thought she could make out a dogfish in front of her and then a large grouper swimming idly below.

As she neared the rocks an orange starfish clung to the cliff face and a small octopus slid quietly back into a narrow crevice. The sides of the cliff above and below the surface of the water were covered with dark sea urchins. She could almost forget the difficult circumstances she found herself in.

Despite the visibility, there was a sea swell and she had to use her hands to keep her body from being thrown against the sharp rocks. She was careful to keep them away from the spines of the sea urchins. Below her Andriy's diver explored the rocky sea floor, shining his light into any openings in the rocks he came across. He trailed a mesh bag, in case he came across anything. She knew he would find nothing that was relevant.

Andriy indicated to Alessandra that she should swim over to him. "Are we in the right vicinity?" he asked. Alessandra just smiled and carried on swimming. After another half an hour, Andriy told Alessandra to get back on board the boat. He discussed something with his diver and gave him the camera. The diver continued the search. Andriy came back to the boat. "We are going to check out each of your locations thoroughly. We will analyse all the photographs as well. We are going to find it with or without your help," he said grimly. "The outcome will be the same. The only difference will be that we will have to hold you for a lot longer."

Alessandra just shrugged. "You will not get away with this."

The diver returned to the boat an hour later. He gave the camera and mesh bag to Andriy. He took out some small artifacts. Alessandra saw a piece of pottery and what looked like an encrusted piece of metal. Andriy scraped away some of the corrosion with his thumb nail. "We will have this analysed," he grunted. Soon after, the yacht's engines started up and they continued slowly. They passed the bay with its closed-up beachside taverna and apartments for rent where, a life-time ago, she and Andriy had spent a carefree weekend. She pushed the memory out of her mind.

The Lady Gabrielle sailed smoothly past the bay and ahead they saw the cape. Andriy gestured to his captain to bring the boat closer to the ragged cliffs. They anchored as close to the rocks as it was safe to do. The sea here was rougher and there was a significant swell. Alessandra had snorkeled at the base of these cliffs, examining unusual cave formations below the water line, but the sea had been more benign then. She was not sure that it was safe going into these waters. Andriy was consulting Alessandra's maps and charts and discussing options with the diver. This time, the diver took the underwater flashlight and camera with him and slipped off the stern into the rough waters. He beckoned Alessandra to follow him in. She said she did not feel that it was safe.

"OK, you stay onboard," Andriy ordered. "You will be watched at all times by the crew." He attached his mask and slipped over the side. Alessandra was curious to see what the pair might find. She had always thought this was an interesting location, from a marine archaeological viewpoint. There were rocks protruding above sea level and it was not an easily navigable part of the coast, particularly in a storm. There was also a strong current and she could imagine boats running aground on the rocks. The combination of the sea swell and the power of the waves breaking over the rocks would soon break up any unfortunate boat. When she had snorkeled here the water had been too deep and murky to make out much of what was below. She could see Andriy struggling to avoid being washed onto the rocks. He had donned a wetsuit and his gloves were preventing him from scraping the skin off his hands. Despite its anchor, she could feel the engine of the Lady Gabrielle working to keep the boat away from the rocks. She thought the captain would be keen to get away as soon as possible.

Andriy was eventually forced to return. If anything, the sea was getting rougher. The diver returned soon afterwards. "It is too difficult to see anything," Andriy told Alessandra. "We will have to return when it is calmer." He told the captain to head for home. Turning to Alessandra, he said he would be away on business for the next ten days or so. When he returned they would resume the search if the weather held up. She would be held at the farmhouse until he came back. "You will begin to understand the consequences of your failure to cooperate with us," he said, grimly. "Let's see how you enjoy this. Perhaps when I return you will have a change of mind."

Chapter Twenty

ENGLAND

AFTER A FEW RINGS EFFIE ANSWERED HER PHONE. HER VOICE
was cautious. When she found it was Nicholas, her tone became
cool.

"Hi," he said, trying to keep things light. "I was phoning to find
out how the ankle is. And, of course, how you've been keeping."
Nicholas had debated whether he should phone Effie now, or leave
it for a while longer. He needed to maintain a distance for her
sake, but he also wanted a reassurance that she was alright.

"I am fine, thank you," her formal tone wounded him, though
he didn't blame her. "The ankle is healing nicely and I can put
some weight on it. I still use the crutches, but I have become quite
used to them – even up and down stairs. My mother has been
wonderful, helping me around the apartment with the cleaning
and cooking. I went back to work yesterday, which was good for
my morale. A friend gave me a lift to and from work, which helped
a lot. I needed to get out and get back to normal life."

Nicholas knew she was referring to more than just her ankle. "That all sounds good. Your recovery seems to be going well."

"I think it is. At the end of next week I am due to have the cast off and the doctors will then decide whether I need any physio on the ankle. And how are you? Are you very busy back at work?"

"It is pretty frantic, at the moment." He hated lying. "I am having to spend a lot of time with a difficult customer. We have been having a lot of supply problems. Trying to resolve it is taking me all around the country."

Effie's cool tone seemed to warm. "I am sorry you are having all these issues, and on top of the stress of your search for Alessandra. I have missed you. And of course I was hurt when you had to rush back to the UK without even saying goodbye."

"I am really sorry, too," he said. "I don't think I behaved well. It was all very sudden and came out of the blue." This much was at least accurate.

"Does this mean that you have dropped your search for Alessandra?" she asked.

Nicholas found it hard to maintain the pretence, even on the phone. "I am afraid I have had to. I have to put work first now, particularly since I have been away for so long. The problems that we are having here are going to mean that I will not be able to get away from the UK, certainly not for the foreseeable future. I am sorry. But in any event, I was starting to feel that I was not really making much progress in finding her. Now might be a good time to leave the search to others."

Effie said she was surprised to hear that. "I thought, particularly on Halki, that we were starting to make progress."

"No, I don't really think so. I have spoken to Alessandra's parents. I have already told them that I am going to have to give up on the search. I also let them know that I was back at work and heavily involved there. That has to be my priority. They understood and were OK with it. They still believe Alessandra is fine. That she is off travelling and will be back in touch, eventually. Apparently, she has done this before, when she took off for South-East Asia a few years ago."

Effie did not sound convinced, but Nicholas felt the need to persist with the story. "Effie, can I ask that you also do the same as Alessandra's parents; you have to believe that, in all likelihood, she is fine somewhere. I am sure that she will surface when she is good and ready. Her parents know her best and, I think, in the absence of any other evidence, we should trust their intuition."

Effie didn't reply immediately. She seemed puzzled by this abrupt change and needed some time to think. Eventually, after a long silence, she conceded that she would trust him. She would put thoughts of continuing to look for Alessandra on hold. "I will concentrate on my recovery and, like you, focus on getting back into work," she said.

"One thing I forgot to tell you earlier. It is obviously less relevant now. Michael Kamides phoned me a few days ago. He heard about my accident, somehow, and called to find out how I was. He also asked after you. I told him that you had to return to the UK because of work.

"He asked what progress you had made in looking for Alessandra. I said that you had gone to Halki to look for Helena Milonas, but had not managed to find her."

"Effie, when you speak to him again, can you tell him that I am working flat-out here and have no opportunity to continue with the search. Please thank him from me for his interest and help. It might also be a good idea to let him know that you also have come around to her parents' thinking."

They spoke for a while longer. Nicholas told Effie he would phone her the following week. He felt bad about deceiving her, but he had to, for her safety. He wondered about Kamides. Was there any connection to Andriy? Nicholas did not know whom he could trust on Rhodes – and whom he could not. Was the seemingly innocuous enquiry from Kamides perhaps intended to confirm that he had returned to the UK?

Nicholas turned to the unopened yellow package that was sitting on his coffee table. He suspected that its contents would determine what he did next. Over a boiling kettle, he carefully steamed open the package, scalding his fingers. "Damn," he said, wringing his hand and dropping the packet. Retrieving it from the floor, he opened it and tipped out the contents onto the table.

Out fell the handwritten notes that he recognised as being those torn from Alessandra's notebook. Together with a couple of photocopied documents, he also extracted some maps of Halki and Symi. Among the maps were some photographs. They appeared to show a sequence of barren, grey-white cliffs. Some showed gaping fissures in the cliff walls, others a series of cave openings. Two photographs, taken from a boat, provided a closer view of what seemed to be a partly submerged cave entrance, other pictures were taken by an underwater camera. The water was murky, so they lacked definition. Nicholas held the pictures under a table lamp. They showed underwater objects. There were two photos – taken from different positions – of a large, irregular, dark stone object. It was half-buried in the silt and had a series of long white stains running down it. There were photos of smaller objects as well, some heavily pitted and encrusted with algae and other marine organisms. He turned the photographs over. In small print they showed that the images had been taken on two consecutive dates in August the previous year.

Nicholas turned to the plastic maps. They were maritime maps of the coastal areas around the islands showing sea depths and tides. Both were marked with what he assumed were dive sites; the markings presumably made by Alessandra. There were two on Halki and three on Symi – two on the east coast and one just off what looked like a small island to the north. The Halki map showed strong currents around the two dive sites on the island. This must be the reason for the poor visibility and quality of the underwater images. The documents and notes would help to make sense of the images and maps. He picked up a lengthy in-depth article detailing historical Russian involvement in Syria.

He had a lot of reading to do. He studied Alessandra's handwritten notes, going through them slowly. He read through them again to make sure he had not misunderstood. So this was what Andriy was so desperate to get his hands on. Nicholas was filled with awe, but also a deep dread. He understood now how much danger they were all in. He needed to act quickly. It was not safe to keep the papers with him. He needed to find somewhere secure. It would be catastrophic if Andriy got his hands on these. He left the unread documents on one side – they were just journal articles – and put the notes, maps and photographs back into the yellow envelope. He could not risk returning them to the Bianchis. They might let slip to Andriy that they had received something from her, particularly if they were threatened. Keeping the information safe might provide some guarantee that Alessandra would be kept alive and unhurt.

Not for the first time did he wonder at the bizarre twist of events that had led him to this moment. He phoned Josh Bingham, his lawyer, who had become a good friend over the years. Josh agreed to store the package in the firm's safe. Nicholas drove there and deposited the envelope, now encased in a larger, sealed package, addressed to him.

Back home and sitting at his laptop he searched for records of the Lady Gabrielle. Eventually he came across a vessel-finder site providing real-time tracking. Entering the name Lady Gabrielle and its port of registration, he found that the boat was moored in Mandraki Harbour in Rhodes. So Andriy, or at least his boat, was still in Rhodes. Unfortunately, the site could only provide current positions of vessels. What he really needed was an historical record of ports the Lady Gabrielle had used in the past six months. Nicholas assumed that Andriy, rather than his father, was using the boat; a record of its movements would show exactly where he had been. Nicholas knew little about boats, and even less about the logistics of mooring in ports. He assumed that boats could not just moor wherever there was a vacant space, particularly one the size of the Lady Gabrielle. He guessed that a berth had to be booked in advance. He remembered that Adam, a friend from his past life, when Lynda was still alive, was into sailing. It had been a few years since they last spoke. Had Adam come to the funeral? Nicholas struggled to remember. He tried calling him. The phone rang then went to voicemail. Nicholas left a message, apologising for not contacting his friend. He asked Adam to phone him.

Nicholas hung up. The house suddenly felt empty and cold. Outside, the evening still demanded a coat. He closed his front door, the unread journal articles in his hand, and walked briskly to the Kings Arms. It was his nearest pub, but he knew no one there. However, it was welcoming and warm, and he took his beer and a menu to a table. He ordered the spicy Chicken Diavolo from the "home-cooked specials" and unfolded the first document. It was an article on Russian involvement in the Syrian civil war, with comments and notations made by Alessandra. Nicholas wondered what her interest was. Why was this document so important that she had taken the precaution to send it to herself? Nicholas knew of the support Russia had provided in propping up Bashar al-Assad's government, at great cost to the people of Syria. What he now read was fascinating. A strong political bond had grown between the two nations as far back as the start of the Cold War. The Suez War increased the ties that were further strengthened by Soviet support during the 1966 Syrian Revolution. Five years later, it acquired a stable presence in the Middle East under an agreement with the Ba'athist government's President Hafez al-Assad that allowed it to open a naval military base in Tartus. In 1980, Syria and the Soviet Union signed a twenty-year Treaty of Friendship and Cooperation. As a consequence, thousands of Syrian military officers and educated professionals went to study in Russia over the next thirty years. Nicholas assumed that it was a reciprocal arrangement that had allowed Andriy to similarly study in Syria. After the Arab Spring nationwide protests against Assad's government began. Nicholas was aware of most of this. Violent crackdowns had followed, leading to the emergence of militant opposition movements and large-scale defections from the army, transforming a civil uprising into a fully-fledged armed rebellion. Two years later, the Arab League helped to arm the Syrian rebels. Subsequently, it recognised the National Coalition for Syrian Revolutionary and Opposition Forces as the legitimate representative of the Syrian people.

Nicholas' food arrived and he read while he ate. Russia had supported the Syrian government since the beginning of the conflict. It provided military aid – and, since 2015, direct military involvement. It was the first time since the end of the Cold War that Russia had entered an armed conflict outside the borders of the former Soviet Union. In early 2012, Russia's arms contracts with Syria were estimated to be worth $1.5 billion, ten percent of Russia's global arms sales. A Reuters report revealed that Russian forces were playing a more significant role in ground combat by employing contractors recruited through private agencies registered in foreign jurisdictions. Military advisers were teaching Syrians how to use Russian weapons.

Nicholas flicked through the rest of the document and, after ordering coffee, turned to the second. This dealt with the thriving business in artifacts stolen from Syria during the conflict. The past decade had seen an increase in the illicit trafficking of cultural objects from Middle Eastern countries, particularly those that had been affected by armed conflict. The market for stolen objects had become as lucrative as that for drugs, weapons and counterfeit goods. A separate article detailed a United Nations Security Council-approved resolution that called for countries to take steps to prevent the trade in stolen Iraqi and Syrian cultural property. Alessandra had underlined sections of the resolution. Last came an article from Interpol stating that the illicit trade should be seen as a transnational crime. This phrase was heavily underscored. The trade had been sustained by a voracious demand from the arts market. The opening of borders, the improvement in transport systems and an increase in political instability had all encouraged it. Examples were provided: between 2013 and 2014, about 500 invaluable cultural objects had been stolen from the Raqqa Museum in Syria. The following year, 22 bas-relief sculptures disappeared from the Artaban tomb in Palmyra.

It was closing time and Nicholas gathered up the papers, paid for his meal and left the pub. He would continue his reading in the morning.

Chapter Twenty-One

LONDON

ADAM PHONED NICHOLAS THE NEXT MORNING. HE WAS delighted to hear from his old friend and was happy to help. He said it was possible to track a ship's movements and took Nicholas through the process. His first option was to try the Port Authority for the area that he was interested in. Vessels relied on the internet for most of their services. The authorities should be able to provide a historical record of boats using port facilities around Rhodes and that area of the Eastern Mediterranean. Nicholas thanked his friend for his help. They agreed to meet up in the near future.

Nicholas returned to his search for the Lady Gabrielle. Eventually he was directed to the Central Port Authority of Rhodes, which was also the supervising authority for the islands around Rhodes, including Halki and Symi. The site listed vessels currently in each port, as well as their originating port or authority. An archive of moorings went back a few years. It revealed where a particular boat was on any particular date. It was going to be a time-consuming exercise to build a picture of all the movements of the Lady Gabrielle, but he had the time. He settled down for a long stretch in front of his computer. Working backwards from today's date he noted that the Lady Gabrielle had been in Mandraki for only three days. The record showed that she had sailed from the Syrian port of Latakia to Rhodes. He saw that the yacht had been back in Rhodes over the period that Effie had been hit by a car. She was still there when Andriy had threatened Nicholas in his hotel room. She had remained in the harbour for the next three days, presumably then departing for Syria. Nicholas delved further back. Just before the Lady Gabrielle had moored in Rhodes she had been in Symi for ten days. Before that the yacht had been back to Latakia, as well as making a brief stay in the Syrian port of Tartous. He fetched an atlas from his bookshelf and found Latakia was close to the border with Turkey. Tartous was further along the coast, being the nearest port to Homs.

Returning to the Port Authority records he began to detect a pattern. There was a triangulation of the boat's main movements between Rhodes, Symi and the Syrian ports. Occasionally, she also docked in Antalya, one of Turkey's main ports. The Lady Gabrielle seemed to spend as much time in Symi as it did in Rhodes. From the arrivals logs the boat did not spend much time moored around either Syria or Turkey. But these destinations were obviously very much part of Andriy's business activities. He made a note of all of them.

Nicholas studied the records back to early October, when he had first visited Halki. Sure enough, the Lady Gabrielle was recorded as mooring in Emborio between the third and twelfth of October. He searched the records for where the boat might have sailed on to. She duly turned up back in Symi. All of this tied in with what he had learnt on Halki. Soon after Alessandra disappeared, Andriy's boat had left Halki and headed for Symi. The Lady Gabrielle had arrived there the next day, October 13. Rather than dock in the main port, she was recorded as mooring in a nearby bay. She remained in Symi for three days, before departing for Antalya where the boat stayed for ten days.

If Alessandra had been on board the Lady Gabrielle when she left Halki, then it was likely that she had remained on Symi for at least the next two weeks. Was this where she was being held? Nicholas had already established that it would have been difficult to hold Alessandra on Halki. But why Symi? Was it that much larger or was the island the base for Andriy's business operations? Or, was it because Andriy believed that what he was searching for would be found there?

Nicholas needed some exercise after sitting for so long. He had always been a keen tennis player, but had rarely been to his club over the past year. As he was thinking of getting changed he looked out into the rectangular garden, enclosed on all three sides by a brick wall, and realised how much he had neglected things. Leaves and broken branches left over from the winter were scattered about and the lawn needed attention. It looked disheveled, as if it were down on its luck. Feeling guilty, he went outside. Four hours later, he put the lawnmower away and surveyed his work. He was not a gardener, but the physical activity had left him feeling good and he was pleased with how the garden looked now. He remembered a time when he took a pride in things. That feeling was slowly returning.

For now, he still had the remaining journal articles to read, so he made a pot of tea and settled down in the living room. He found a series of articles on the illicit antiquities trade. One covered the smuggling of plundered antiquities in Syria and Iraq. Another detailed the increasing evidence of the involvement of organised criminal gangs – including the Russian mafia – in the smuggling and sale of looted artifacts. There was a further Interpol document that outlined how the organisation sought to work with governments to raise awareness and improve the policing of the trafficking of national cultural property. Interpol had established a database of stolen works of art and looted cultural objects. The trade had become a highly sophisticated and lucrative business, not only for the looters but also for the collectors, professional dealers and middlemen. It would not be so lucrative for the locals in the countries ravaged by economic hardship, conflict and political instability, Nicholas thought sadly.

One article contained a further report from Reuters, detailing the strategic involvement of Islamic State militants in the trade of antiques and archeological treasures. Another covered the smuggling of stolen treasures to Western and Far East markets. The Reuters report estimated that the annual profit derived by Islamists from the trade was in excess of $150 million per annum. Almost unbelievably, Islamic State had actually established an antiquities division to organise the smuggling of artifacts. In 2014, the United Nations had used satellite imagery to assess the damage to cultural heritage sites in Syria. It showed looting across most of its sites. Turkey was accused of being a main centre for the smuggling. Stolen goods were sold at illegal auctions and then on through a network of antique shops as well as local markets. It was also claimed that jewellery, coins and other looted items were brought to the Turkish cities of Izmir, Mersin and Antalya, where criminal groups would produce false documentation about their origin. The antiquities were then offered to collectors from various countries, generally through internet auction sites, specialised online stores and elsewhere on the dark web.

A later report described how looted items often remained in storage until they could be smuggled to art markets around the world. Investigators in Spain, Italy and the US had begun cracking down on the looters. A huge cache of many thousands of artifacts had recently been discovered in Italy. It included 118 ancient Egyptian items enclosed in a diplomatic container. IS members and mafia groups exchanged looted artifacts for weapons that came from Moldova and Ukraine, through the Russian mafia.

Where was Alessandra's research leading? The size and complexity of this lucrative trade meant it was likely that criminal gangs played a significant role in its growth. Was Alessandra suggesting that Russia, or at least well-connected Russian individuals, had exploited their position in Syria to loot and smuggle artifacts? Was she also hinting that Andriy could be caught up in this trade?

The next day Nicholas took the mid-morning train from Windsor and Eton station. At Waterloo he caught a Northern Line Tube to Tottenham Court Road and exited into a busy New Oxford Street. He walked eastwards away from the bustling crowds of London's main shopping street into Museum Street and on towards Great Russell Street, in Bloomsbury. He wanted to see, close up, the image of the Colossus that had cropped up repeatedly in his research on Rhodes. The Colossus Solis dated from 1660 and was housed at the British Museum. He found it displayed in one of the halls.

The engraving depicted the medieval view he was now so familiar with. The Colossus, a huge man holding a flaming torch in one hand, a sceptre in the other, straddled the entrance to Rhodes harbour, a ship under full sail passing through its legs. On his head was a large spiked crown. In the foreground men were busy carving a huge head and a foot. To the right of them stood a group of men pointing at the statue. Judging by the size of the men doing the carving, Nicholas estimated that the head was the height of a man. The image of the crown showed about twenty spikes around the circumference and Nicholas guessed their length at about one-and-a-half metres.

He had also made an appointment the day before to visit the Study Room, which formed part of the archives of the Department of Ancient Greece and Rome. He had said he was researching the construction of the Colossus of Rhodes. He walked up the stairs to the Upper Floor and through the gallery housing artifacts of everyday Greek and Roman life. He was early, so he meandered among some of the exhibits. He loved the British Museum. Nicholas understood Alessandra's love and fascination for antiquities. Without hard evidence of our pre-history, we would be different. We needed these artifacts to understand who we were now.

He found the study room at the end of the gallery and gave the administrator his name. "Ah yes. You are interested in the Colossus of Rhodes. Please come this way." Nicholas was shown to the section of the archives he needed and took a seat at a long table. "Not surprisingly, there are few authenticated records. I made some copies of documents that you would be interested in. They have been translated," the administrator said. "We also have some further electronic records." He pointed to the computer screen.

Nicholas started to read. Much of the detail covered what he already knew. He had become conscious of how little was really known of what was the last and best known of the wonders of the ancient world. The 226BC earthquake had caused the statue to break off at the knees and topple over into pieces. It lay untouched for more than 800 years. It was said that thousands came from all over to marvel at the sight. Nicholas came across a description of the ruins attributed to Pliny. "Even as it lies it excites our wonder and admiration. Few men can clasp the thumb in their arms and its fingers are larger than most statues. Where the limbs are broken asunder, vast caverns are seen yawning in the interior."

The documents did not add much to his knowledge of the events at that time, until he came across an unattributed description of the engineering and planning of the project by Charos of Lindos. The account described the final phase of the construction, that of the crown circling the head of the statue. It stated that the spikes adorning the crown were made from both bronze and silver.

Third-party accounts of the eventual sale of the fragments revealed that a trader had bought what remained of the toppled statue for its metal content. After the earthquake, the head had been transported for safe storage in Rhodes Town in the belief that the statue would eventually be rebuilt, but 800 years later, the head, including the crown, was included as part of the sale and the eventual removal.

Nicholas shut down the computer. He had enough information. He knew what he needed to do. What he needed now was some luck. He left the study room, thanking the administrator for his assistance.

"Did you find what you were looking for?"

"Possibly. Time is going to tell."

Nicholas left the museum.

Chapter Twenty-Two

An island in the Dodecanese

THE WEATHER DETERIORATED STEADILY AS WINTER PROGRESSED. They made one further attempt to return to the cape, after Andriy returned from Turkey. The sea conditions had made it too dangerous for even the professional diver to go down. Andriy made his irritation at the delay evident and had little to do with Alessandra. She was left to her own devices, communicating mainly with Helena. Helena had bought her a selection of clothes from Rhodes, including a couple of warm sweaters and some socks. There was no heating in the room in which Alessandra was held and it was starting to get cold at night.

Alessandra wondered if her parents had alerted the police on Rhodes that she was missing. She was starting to feel very isolated. She thought about her friends, particularly Eleni and Effie. They knew her. Surely they would not believe the text messages sent from her phone by Helena and Andriy? They must realise she would not just leave her work. They must know that she would not take off on a whim with someone she had only recently met. Surely, someone would look for her?

The days started to drag, particularly when she was confined to the farmhouse. She read as much as she could. Helena had kept her supplied with books. She had even brought some books on Greek history and archaeology over from Rhodes Town.

At night, Alessandra tried to read by the light of her little bedside lamp. Sometimes geckos scurried along the ceiling. Where did they go during the daytime, she wondered, idly. One was missing part of its tail. She had become fond of it. It had a favorite corner and appeared every second or third day. Alessandra thought of naming him – in her mind, the gecko was definitely a male. She had considered various names, but had still to find the right one. She looked forward to the times when she was allowed out into the courtyard. Often, she was left on her own, particularly when Andriy was away on business. She was watchful for any possible escape route.

She tried to keep healthy by exercising. An unused exercise bicycle had been kept in the corner of one of the recreation rooms. Alessandra had talked her captors into allowing her to use it on the covered verandah, surrounding the courtyard. During the rainy days of winter it proved invaluable as she cycled away, with the rain cascading off the corrugated roof above. She had also found a mat and practised yoga and pilates, preferably out in the sun, when the weather allowed. Her relaxation exercises blended well with the gentle flow of the fountain. During these times, with Andriy away, Helena often allowed her into the courtyard twice a day, once in the morning and then in the early evening. Once a day, she was able to have a bath, and was allowed to spend as much time as she needed. It was her one solace. Luxuriating in the heat of the water, her mind could drift and she could almost imagine normality. She tried to stretch the time out. She missed the little everyday comforts that had made her feel feminine, though, particularly her nail varnish and lipstick.

She spent the rest of the hours locked in her room. It was there that time stalled and she felt very much the prisoner. Her watch had been taken from her, but she was able to tell the approximate time of the day from the passage of the sun across the corner of her window. With the passing of time, the days and weeks started to meld into each other. Gradually she was losing hope that she would be freed.

Christmas passed and she thought she could just make out the distant sound of the fireworks floating from across the hills in Pedi and Emborio to celebrate the start of the new year. Andriy was absent for longer and longer periods. Helena was also away for some weeks, presumably to spend the holidays with Andriy. During these times, the farmhouse staff was reinforced with a Russian crew member from the boat.

From her room Alessandra loved hearing the sound of the goats and their bells. They were often in the fields at the back of the house. Their simple bleating reminded her of the normality of life that carried on around her. She missed her friends and her work. She had loved her job and tried to maintain a distant hope that she would be able to resume her career.

She wondered how her precious dogs at the sanctuary were doing. She smiled as she remembered all the Sundays that she had spent with the mistreated or abandoned dogs that were housed there. She hoped that someone else was providing the love that they deserved. Every little bit of attention they received was important for them. She had often felt at her most content on those Sundays. She reflected on how full her life had been, but she knew she had to try to keep positive and believe that Andriy could not keep her much longer. Over time, she would become an increasing liability to his operation.

Alessandra also thought of the man on the ferry, which seemed strange since they had met only the once. She had felt he was a kindred spirit, somehow. She couldn't remember being able to talk so easily to a man before. She remembered his name: Nicholas, Nicholas Adams, and his smile. He seemed such a genuine person. It helped that he was also attractive and well dressed. She remembered the hint of sadness in his deep blue eyes. She could imagine herself with him. She was sorry she had not been able to meet up with him and wondered what he had thought of her failing to make the return ferry trip. They had even agreed a time to meet up at the museum and go for a drink, she remembered. She was going to show him around some of the historic areas of the Old Town. He probably thought she had stood him up. No doubt, he had forgotten her. Of course, he would hardly recognise her now.

Andriy had almost given up trying to convince her to cooperate. He had not hit her again, although she sensed that he would not hesitate to if the need arose. Alessandra knew he could switch off his emotions and would treat people contemptuously, as if they barely existed. He hardly spoke to her now. He was used to getting his own way. She had seen him bully people, and not just his staff. He would even bully those whom he considered to be his friends if it served his needs. She knew Andriy realised that would not work with her. She could only suppose that he was waiting for her resolve to crumble.

The storms and high winds of the past months had made further exploration of the dive sites impossible. During January, persistent heavy rain had made the dirt track up to the farmhouse impassable.

There was a routine to the early months of the year. She slept a great deal, when she was not reading in her room. She was struggling to stay positive and felt some shame that she occasionally cried to herself, late at night. She had become physically weaker, thanks to the lack of good food and the imprisonment. It was becoming increasingly difficult to not become overwhelmed by feelings of isolation and despair. When Helena and Andriy were absent, she would often not speak to anyone during the day. Alessandra had always regarded herself as resilient. She was good at making the most of things. She desperately tried to maintain hope. Increasingly, she wondered what might change to secure her release. She fought this sense of powerlessness; she needed to do something before it was too late. Clearly, neither the police, nor anyone else, were still looking for her. She felt sure that Andriy or Helena would have said something to her if that were the case.

In an attempt to keep both her body and mind as fit as possible she had taken to spending the early afternoon doing yoga and meditation in a corner of the room. This made her feel better on those days when she couldn't go outside to the courtyard. The meditation helped to counter the feelings of anxiety and helplessness that came with the captivity.

The weather improved gradually from late February. The storms had subsided, to be replaced by intermittent rain. It was becoming warmer. While the sea temperature would still be cold, Alessandra imagined that the sea swells along the coast would be subsiding and water visibility improving. It would not be long before Andriy resumed his search. She was right. A week later, on one of his visits, Andriy asked mockingly whether she had changed her mind. Would she now cooperate?

"There's nothing I can tell you. But even if there were I would not do so."

He now treated her with open dislike, as if she were a troublesome employee. "You are being very reckless. I have been patient up to now. That will not last," he warned.

"Why not just let me go? If I'm not going to help you it will not affect your search. You have all my maps. There's nothing else that's hidden from you. Surely you'll be better off without me here." Andriy did not answer. "If you let me go, I give you my word I'll tell no one what has happened to me."

He laughed. "That is not what I am concerned about, Alessandra."

She tried one last time. "If you're concerned that I will inform the authorities of your so-called business activities, then I'll also give you my word on that, too. If you let me go and leave me alone, I promise I'll keep quiet about you and your business colleagues. I just want to leave here."

"I do not believe you any more. Besides, you already know too much. Think about this very carefully." His face had taken on a menacing expression. "My business partners already think you are too much of a liability. You can work out for yourself what that might mean." Andriy left, slamming and locking the door behind him.

A week later they resumed the search. This time Alessandra made sure that she was wearing a wetsuit. The Lady Gabrielle headed down the east coast again, towards the cape. The sea was fairly calm. The boat anchored away from the cliffs and the diver disappeared over the side of the boat.

"Make this simple for yourself," Andriy said. He signaled for Alessandra to follow him into the water and they swam towards the cliffs. The water was cold, particularly on her exposed face. It was a far cry from the balmy temperatures of September and October.

Putting on her mask, Alessandra saw a school of barracuda eying them with suspicion from a distance. Inserting her snorkel, she dived below the waves to get a better view. She had thought carefully about this trip. She knew that just around the bluff was a beach. It was accessible only by water taxi. There were no roads or even dirt tracks that connected the beach to anywhere on the island. Despite its isolation, it was scenic and the bay provided occasional shelter to pleasure boats and yachts. She was steadily running out of options. During the times she was imprisoned in her room, she had thought of trying to swim to the cliff point, if currents allowed. If Andriy was not watching her closely, she might be able to swim around the bluff to the other side. If there was anyone on the beach, or if there was a boat anchored in the bay, there might be a slim opportunity to escape by trying to attract their attention. She realised she would need to get out of the water as soon as was possible. Otherwise, the dinghy from the Lady Gabrielle would pick her up quickly.

There might be an opportunity to hide among the rocks. She might even try to scale part of the cliff face. Any success would depend on the initial surprise. She would just need a period of time where she was out of their sight. Slowly, Alessandra edged closer to the cliff point. She tried to give the impression that she was studying the rock formations underwater. She could not see Andriy's diver below her. Andriy was twenty metres behind her.

She took her time. She did not want to alert either of them to what she was doing. She dived down as deep as she could go and looked around. The cliff below sea level was pitted with caves and crevices. Not for the first time did she think to herself how difficult such a search was. It would be near on impossible if you did not know the precise location. Even if you did, you would still then need sufficient visibility to be able to spot anything. Alessandra needed to surface briefly for more air. As she did, she looked around to position herself. She was still about thirty metres from the corner. Seeing no one near her she dived again. She needed to spend as much time underwater as her breath would allow while letting the current sweep her to the point.

From time to time, the waves brought her up against the sharp rocks and she was glad of her protective gloves. She could sense that she was nearing the point, as the swell and the current increased. Despite being a strong swimmer, Alessandra was conscious of the power of the sea and how easily it could overcome you. She was nervous of the danger she was placing herself in. All of a sudden, the current and direction of the waves changed and she was dragged around the corner of the cliff.

Immediately, she started to swim as frantically as she could in the direction of the beach. Pausing to catch her breath and look up out of the water, she saw with dismay that the bay was deserted. There were no boats and there was no sign of anyone on the beach.

Alessandra realised with a sinking heart that it was still too early in the season for the water taxis to be operating to this remote part of the coast. Tears of frustration welled inside her mask. She looked at the jagged rocks protruding at sea level in front of her and up at the steep cliff. She drifted aimlessly and waited for the inevitable. Sure enough, she heard the roar of an outboard, as the dinghy loomed above her in the water. Andriy and Vitaly were looking down at her.

"Get in," ordered Andriy, as he pulled her roughly out of the water.

"Thank you," said Alessandra. "I got swept around the point. I was getting a bit scared for a moment" she replied, honestly.

"I don't think I believe you," Andriy replied. "Did you think you might manage to make it all the way to the beach without us noticing?"

"I completely underestimated the currents. They suddenly changed and took me by surprise. I was starting to panic."

"I think you are lying, Alessandra. You are too experienced a diver to be caught out by something like that. Anyway, as you can see, any attempt to escape is completely futile. Did you not think we were watching you? We are finished here, anyway. There is nothing to see on the seabed. There is not even any pottery. The currents are too strong here to find anything. Any shipwreck and its contents would have been washed further out to sea, certainly well past the point."

The dinghy returned to the yacht. Once back on board, they made their way back to the bay, where the black four-wheel drive was, as ever, waiting for them. Driving slowly past the taverna, Andriy exchanged shouted greetings with the owner. Back at the farmhouse Alessandra felt chilled, partly from the time spent immersed in the cold water, but also by the deep disappointment she felt. She had been unlucky. She was allowed a hot bath to warm herself. Lying in the tub she told herself that she had tried. She had done something positive and, while she had failed this time, there would be another opportunity. She had to believe that.

That opportunity came three weeks later. By now it was late-April and the weather was turning from warm to hot. Any night-time chill had disappeared from Alessandra's room and been replaced by the incessant high-pitched hum of mosquitos. According to Helena, Andriy had spent the time in Syria taking on a delivery of goods and then had to return to Rhodes to deal with an issue that had arisen unexpectedly. Despite being pressed, Helena would not divulge any more. However, Alessandra had the impression that "the issue" was somehow related to her disappearance.

This feeling was reinforced when Andriy arrived back at the farmhouse. Alessandra heard the excited barking of the dogs. The sound of voices grew louder in the annexe and, though she did not understand much Russian, she could tell that Andriy and his men were moving heavy or fragile items into the storage room next door. There was much grunting and swearing. The sounds eventually died down and she then heard the key being turned in her door. Andriy entered. He looked impassive. He stared down at Alessandra. "I have told the crew that tomorrow we are going to head for the west coast of the islet. This is the last of the sites around the island that you marked on your maps. We will try to do both the bays you marked in one day, but, if not, we will anchor off the coast there and resume our search the following day.

"OK, I will check my diary to see if I can make it," Alessandra managed to joke.

"Alessandra this will be pretty much your final chance to cooperate with us. I have had meetings with my business associates and they are now not happy with me."

"What is it you are trying to say?" she asked.

"They see you as a loose end, as a significant threat to our business. They are putting pressure on me to resolve this. There is a deadline. Their prospective purchaser is getting impatient. And believe me, so am I.

"I have just come from Rhodes where I have had to deal with someone who had been asking too many questions about you. He will not worry us further."

Alessandra wondered whom that might be, but thought better of asking. She could only assume that, like most of those he dealt with, he had paid off someone in the local police who might still be asking questions. She did not wish to raise any hope that someone could still be looking for her.

"I can't put off my partners any more. You do not understand just how much is at stake," Andriy continued.

"You're right, Andriy. I probably don't have a full understanding of the extent of the vile business that you've chosen. What I do know, however, is that you and your partners are all morally bankrupt," she replied.

"Let me repeat for you," Andriy's voice was rising. "You have no more chances. There is a deadline. If you have failed to cooperate with us by that time, I have had to agree to hand you over to my associates. I will have nothing more to do with you."

He looked around the small room. "People disappear all the time. My associates can guarantee that those that disappear are never found. They are, however, hard men without any mercy, unlike me. Knowing them, they will have some fun with you before you disappear. You are an attractive woman, Alessandra." Andriy reached out to touch her hair. She recoiled. "You are just not my type ... now," Andriy sneered. "Just think carefully on this."

Alessandra shivered. She had heard Andriy describing the brutality of his partners before. She had even met some of them. Rape was not uncommon among such men used to atrocity. She had no doubt as to what would happen to her before she was disposed of. She was silent. There was no more to be said.

The next morning, earlier than usual, she was woken by Helena with a simple breakfast. It was still quite dark. "Andriy wants to make an early start this morning" Helena said.

"All right." Alessandra's tone was emotionless. She had not slept. She had replayed Andriy's awful words all night. She might never escape this nightmare. She felt defeated. She had her breakfast and dressed quietly. While lying awake, she had realised that the coming days would represent her last chance to get away, perhaps even to stay alive. Rational thought was becoming difficult. Physically, she was getting weaker by the day. She needed some strength for one last effort. It was a daunting thought. She had hoped for more time.

The Lady Gabrielle was moored alongside the dock. Alessandra assumed this was because of the shipment that was offloaded the previous day. It was going to be a hot day. Despite the hour, the sun was already radiating heat from a cloudless sky. To most, a day such as this on the island would seem idyllic. For her, it was bleak.

Alessandra took a seat under the awning on the rear deck. She was dressed in a T-shirt and red shorts. It was too hot to put on the wet suit: she would wait until they reached the dive sites. She watched the retreating beach scene, loungers already positioned invitingly for any early sun seekers, making their journey from nearby Pedi along the cliff path. Heralding the onset of the tourist season, there were already two other large yachts moored out in the bay.

This time, the Lady Gabrielle headed north. They passed small fishing boats returning to port after a night at sea. Andriy was discussing the route with the captain. The narrow strait, separating the islet from the body of the island, was too shallow to allow the Lady Gabrielle to pass through safely. The boat turned north and followed the east coast of the small island until they rounded the cape. They were now within touching distance of the Turkish coastline.

Andriy was consulting Alessandra's maps and again talking animatedly to the captain. They were pointing towards a series of small jagged bays on the west coast. Alessandra had snorkeled around these bays, a couple of which had narrow strips of beaches. The whole island was uninhabited and the bays were rarely visited, even in the height of the tourist season. She had chosen them to explore, as this part of the island was close to the ancient trade routes. The desolate area was surrounded by other small islands and rocky outcrops. In a storm they would have proved fatal to the wooden vessels of antiquity. Andriy knew these coasts well and would have a similar understanding. She could not count on there being any other visitors. The only way for her to escape would be to slip away and hide in the mountainous interior of the small barren island. She also knew that there was no food or water on the islet and she would have to reach the main island as soon as possible.

The Lady Gabrielle slowed and anchored about forty metres from the grey, limestone cliffs. Alessandra and Andriy put on their wetsuits. This time Andriy ordered Alessandra to join Vitaly in the dinghy attached to the stern. He debated possible sites with the diver, who then slipped over the side. Andriy got into the dinghy and they pulled away from the yacht. They headed towards one of the inlets in an unnamed bay that Alessandra had marked. Vitaly guided the craft to within twenty metres of the rocks. The sea was rougher on this more exposed west coast of the islet. Before they entered the water, Andriy said to Alessandra: "Vitaly will be watching you and following you closely. We do not want you trying something again. And you know this island is completely uninhabited."

Alessandra and Andriy jumped into the water and put on their masks and snorkels. With the exposed coastline here, the visibility was less clear than it had been off the main island. The seabed was some thirty metres below. With today's visibility, it was hard to make out any objects on the sea floor. The currents in the bay were also stronger. Her heart had sunk when she had heard that Vitaly would be shadowing her. She dived below the surface and noticed a large school of sardines alongside the rocks.

She surfaced and saw the dinghy close behind her. She examined the rocks and cliff face. Alessandra felt the surface of the rocks at sea level. They had been worn smooth by the incessant action of the waves on this part of the coast and felt slippery to the touch. She dived and tried another section about twenty metres further along. It was the same. The sea swell was washing her against the rocks. She felt desperate. She tried again and could not get a proper grip to raise herself. Diving again, she tried another part of the cliff further on, towards the shore. The force of the waves, together with the smoothness of the rock face, would make escaping this way impossible.

Despair set in. The last faint hope had ebbed away with the motion of the sea. There was nothing left. She was at the mercy of Andriy and his associates and knew what to expect. There was nothing she could do. Tears were flowing freely, making seeing almost impossible. She took off her mask to try to clear it, then looked up at the sky. She felt small, lonely and terribly frightened. Her life seemed to be ebbing away.

After a while, she composed herself. Killing herself was the only option left. It was the one action still within her power. She glanced over her shoulder at Vitaly in the dinghy. He had been distracted by Andriy calling out to him. She put on her mask. How might she drown herself? After all, there were worse places in the world to end your life. With a sudden resolve, she thought she might be able to dive down to the sea floor. If she made it all the way down, she could make sure she would not have enough air to make it safely back to the surface. Perhaps she might also have the courage and strength to remove the snorkel from her mouth and breathe in enough seawater to fill her lungs.

Alessandra was not given to prayer, but she took a quick moment. She looked up at the vast and distant sky and felt how insignificant she was. She had to be brave. She could only hope that her body would be washed away to sea by the strong current below and would not be recovered by the two Russians. Vitaly was still not looking at her. She took a breath and dived under the water. She reached halfway to the bottom and felt herself panic. She surfaced choking and coughing. She needed to remain as calm and committed as possible. Letting all thought go, she took a deep breath and dived down into the unknown with as much strength as she could find. As the darkness welcomed her, she was suddenly no longer scared. She felt warm and, finally, at peace.

Chapter Twenty-Three

SYMI

SYMI WAS LESS THAN A TWO-HOUR FERRY CROSSING FROM Rhodes. Nicholas had flown in the previous evening. At Diagoras Airport he had hailed a taxi to take him to one of the huge, impersonal tourist hotels on the beach at Paradisi. As it was only the start of the holiday season, there were plenty of rooms available. Early the next morning he caught a taxi to Mandraki Harbour. The Dodekanisos Seaways catamaran was fast, modern and comfortable. It was half-full. Most of the passengers were tourists on a day-trip to the island. Even though it was mid-April, the air conditioning was welcome. Nicholas settled back in the comfortable seat to mull over what he was about to do.

On its approach to Symi, the ferry rounded Cape Koutsoumpos. His first sight of Gialos harbour reminded him of the approach to Halki. Gialos was, however, on an altogether larger scale. As the ferry glided towards the port, ahead stood a bronze statue of a boy, seemingly beckoning boats into the harbour. Surrounding the port were tiers of Italianate houses, painted in ochre, indigo and terracotta. Most had balconies and iron railings facing the sea. Small fishing boats bobbed at anchor in the clear blue waters and the ferry slid by two large yachts before mooring along the dock. Nicholas was relieved to see that neither belonged to Andriy. He had checked the Port Authority records the day before. The Lady Gabrielle had left Symi two days earlier and had not entered any ports on Rhodes or Halki. Nicholas guessed that, based on its previous pattern of activity, it was bound for Turkey or Syria. This would give him a few days at least to investigate the island.

Emerging from the ferry he looked around. Like Emborio, the town of Gialos tumbled down steep hills to the blue of the port. Similarly many of the buildings were pastel-painted neoclassical villas, but unlike the less-sophisticated Halki, there was a sense of old-world glamour and elegance about the place. It was far more than a working fishing town.

Nicholas had chosen a small hotel in the old town, well away from the main tourist areas. He wandered through the maze of narrow streets, with their shops and tavernas angling away from the port, in search of the way up to the old town, perched high above the port. After getting lost in the tangle of back streets, he asked directions from a friendly supermarket owner, who directed him to the Kali Strata – the broad set of stone stairs that linked the alleyways behind the harbour to the hilltop village of Horio.

Arriving at the top twenty minutes later, he paused to catch his breath. He had climbed hundreds of steps and was glad of the shade provided by overhanging trees. Lavish villas and small boutiques lay ahead in what had once clearly been a wealthy part of Symi. His more modest hotel, a small family-run business, with a dozen or so rooms, was at the edge of town. He checked in, leaving his passport at the desk, and was shown up to his room, where he opened the white-shuttered windows. The views were spectacular, stretching across the harbour all the way to the sea. He could see the quayside and the clutch of superyachts that dominated the port. During the height of the tourist season Symi attracted the world's glitterati. This room was perfect. It would provide the ideal vantage point to see the Lady Gabrielle if she entered the harbour.

Nicholas unpacked carefully. He had no reason to think that anyone would know he was on Symi, but after the break-in on Rhodes, he now positioned his unpacked items in a particular way so that he would know if they were disturbed. Leaving the hotel, he walked back through the cobbled streets of the old town and back down the oleander-lined Kali Strata, through the winding alleyways towards the port. At a small waterfront café he ordered a coffee and a glass of cold water. It was midday and it was already starting to get hot.

The waiter spoke good English, so he asked for directions to the tourist office to find accommodation. Nicholas was directed to the Symi Visitor Agency, on the southern side of the port. The agency was on the corner of a narrow street, next to a pottery shop selling hand-painted ceramics. Mauve bougainvillea trailed over its arched entrance. Inside, it was small and quiet, with one other customer – an elderly English woman enquiring about bed and breakfast. Only one of the two desks was occupied, so Nicholas waited on the empty seat by the desk. The woman eventually left and Nicholas sat down in front of the blonde, slightly overweight assistant.

With a welcoming smile she asked: "And how can I help you?"

"I am making an enquiry on behalf of a friend who is planning to come to Symi for the whole of the summer – perhaps for four or five months," Nicholas said. "He has a grown-up family and is coming with some friends. He probably needs a house, perhaps slightly outside of the main town. Is that possible here?"

"Of course," she replied, in her accented English. "Most things are possible on Symi. Down here in Gialo most of the properties are B&Bs and shorter-term rentals. But in the old town above the port – Horio – we have a number of old sea captains' houses and villas that have been fully restored. Some have their own swimming pools. Most are quite large, with six or seven bedrooms."

The assistant adjusted her tortoise-shell glasses on her nose and consulted her computer screen. After a pause, she continued: "Horio is the old town of Symi and has many wonderful old tavernas and bars and narrow, winding streets. It is very atmospheric. Not as touristy as down here at the port. And, of course, most houses still have amazing views across the harbour."

"Are any of these properties rented out for longer periods?"

"That is what I am just checking."

Nicholas noticed that she had a small tattoo of a butterfly on her upper arm. He looked around the office and saw a board displaying properties for sale across the island.

"Here we go. At present there is only one property big enough for the needs of your friend that is still available in Horio. Symi is a very popular island for holidays. The demand is not just from Greeks. People come from all over the world. We get a lot from the United States, but also from England and Australia. If you want a house, it is normally advisable to make a booking the previous year."

"Do you get a lot of Russians coming, as well?"

"Yes we do. It is very popular with Russians. Why do you ask?"

"My friend is actually Russian. I would guess that he would be more comfortable renting somewhere where other Russians traditionally go."

"Well, Russians have been coming to Symi for many years now. From my experience, they prefer the noise and the excitement around the harbour. Although some do also rent the larger villas in the old town," she added, hastily. "If your friend wants something in Horio, we have this place," she said, showing Nicholas the details of a villa on her screen. "My advice always on Symi would be to make the booking as soon as possible or else there will be nothing available."

"And what about elsewhere, outside of the port area and Horio?"

She spread out a map of the island. "Have you been to Symi before?"

"No, this is my first visit."

"Well, as you can see, there are not many roads on the island. It is very mountainous and not many parts are readily accessible. This long road here," she indicated with her finger, "goes all the way through the mountains to the south of the island. It goes up to the monastery at Panormitis. This route is very difficult and remote. Apart from the mountains it is heavily forested and, aside from some old farmhouses, there are not many properties this way. I have never known of a property available to rent up there. There is nothing really to do up that way. Aside from the monastery there is a small museum and bakery and a basic taverna."

"What about this way?" Nicholas pointed to a road leading away from Gialos and Horio eastwards to Pedi on the coast.

"Yes, I think other than Horio, this is your only option. It is less than three kilometres from here and there are a couple of beaches, at Pedi and a bit further on a smaller one at Agios Nikolaos or St Nicholas Bay."

"Can you tell me about these areas?" asked Nicholas.

"Well, Pedi is about twenty minutes' walk from the old town above. Or else there is a regular bus service from here. It is a seaside village with a couple of tavernas looking out over the bay, some small shops and a supermarket. It is quiet, compared with Gialos. It's really a working harbour for our local fishermen. There is a small marina there as well. There are some properties there for rent, as well as a hotel."

"Do you rent any properties there for longer periods?"

"Yes we do sometimes. It is particularly popular with the sailing crowd as they can moor their boats there."

"You also mentioned somewhere else?"

"Yes, St Nicholas Bay. It's a bit further on – about a kilometer along a dirt track. There is a natural harbour there with a jetty and a beach. It is east of Pedi and, if you are going on foot, you can reach it along a cliff-top path."

"And are there any properties around there for rental?"

"There are a few properties dotted around the hillside. But, it is quite remote. There are not really any proper roads around there – the tarred road ends at Pedi. The bay is also enclosed on both sides by rocky cliffs. There is a dirt track that winds past the cliffs and does go to some of the remoter properties, but you would need a four-wheel drive to get to most of them."

"That sounds interesting. How would I find out about properties in that area?"

"I have no record of any properties for rental in that area. They will typically be older, more traditional: some of them are just farms. There is a small legal office and estate agency in Pedi. My suggestion would be that you speak to them. You will find it easily in the main road through the village. Sorry that I can't be of more help."

Nicholas assured her that she had been very helpful and left. It was too late to go to Pedi, so he decided to explore the upper town of Horio. Walking slowly up the steps again, he felt that Alessandra was not far away. He was getting closer. He thought about the other bays on the island and wondered whether they were sufficiently deep to take a boat the size of the Lady Gabrielle. If so, Pedi and the next bay further on with its jetty might be natural places for it to come and go, particularly if Alessandra was being held nearby. He found a lively taverna in the central square and ordered a drink. It was warm enough to sit outside – and to bring out the mosquitos. He swatted one away from his head. Tonight he needed the sound of people around him. He watched the steady ebb and flow, and listened to the excited chatter against the background of bouzouki music. He felt content. He was doing the right thing.

Later he wandered the narrow lanes of the old town, happy to be left to his thoughts as he meandered slowly through the small squares and streets. He stopped for an ouzo at a quiet local bar before making his way slowly back to his hotel.

The next morning, he found the road down from the old town that would take him to Pedi. He had opted not to take the bus; he wanted to get a feel for the surrounding countryside. At the top of the hill, approaching Pedi, the valley, dotted with olive and fruit trees, opened before him. This was the agricultural heartland of the island. The bay's turquoise water and the village lay ahead. The houses and apartments he passed were built close to the road and none looked discreet enough to provide a hideaway. Cresting the hill, he saw some villas set among trees and scrub further up the valley, away from the village. These looked more likely places to hide someone. Some were behind walls, one or two had gates and fencing.

There was a warm sea breeze. The cicadas had started their noisy chatter. Approaching the village, he came to a fork in the road and saw the sign for the Pedi Beach Hotel. He continued on and the houses grew older, more like the neoclassical villas in Gialos. The village was quiet. There was a small supermarket and, down the street, Nicholas found the small estate agency. Inside was a small, untidy office where a man and a woman sat at desks.

"Kalimera," he said. He apologised for his lack of Greek.

The man replied: "That is OK. A lot of my customers only speak English. How can I help you?" He had an extravagant brown bushy moustache covering most of his mouth.

"I am staying in Horio. I am looking for an old friend. She told me she was staying on Symi, in this area, and asked me to come and visit her if I was ever here. She said she was staying in a house away from the main areas. She works as a housekeeper for some Russians who were renting a property."

The estate agent smiled, and the moustache twitched momentarily. "Pedi and the surrounding area is popular with some Russians. But you have not given me a lot to go on."

"I am sorry," said Nicholas. "I did have the name of the house and her phone number, but I seem to have lost them. She will be upset if she knew I was here and did not contact her. All I know is that the house would have been rented for at least the last six months, if not longer. The name of the person who rents the property is called Andriy Solokov, I believe. Does that name ring any bells?"

The estate agent said: "Please wait a moment while I discuss this with my colleague."

He consulted the woman in Greek. They conversed for a while. The colleague checked her computer and Nicholas heard the name Solokov mentioned.

After a bit the estate agent, said. "I am sorry. We are not able to help you."

Nicholas was not giving up. "What if the Russian actually owned the property? Would you know which properties were foreign owned?"

"Of course, but sadly only those that have been bought in the last few years."

The female colleague intervened. "There are Russian buyers. Most buy in Gialos and Horio, usually big expensive properties. There are a couple of properties owned by Russians here in Pedi. None are owned by this Solokov. His name is not known to us."

The man said: "There is a problem establishing ownership on Symi. Many Russians buy property through an independent company. Also, if the property has been owned for some time, we will have no records. You will find it very difficult to find this out on Symi."

Nicholas produced the photograph of Alessandra with Andriy and her friends that he had taken from her apartment. "Can I ask if you recognise any of these people in the photograph?

"This is my friend," he said, indicating Alessandra, "and this is the Russian who has the property."

The estate agent took the photograph and showed it to his colleague. "I am very sorry. We do not recognise anyone in this photograph. We are sure they have not come to us to rent any property."

"That's all right," Nicholas replied, his spirits sinking. "I appreciate your time."

The estate agent's colleague said something to him in Greek. "There is one last thing you could try," he said. "If they have been living here for some time, they would have had to buy food. You could try the supermarket here. They might recognise your friend. The owner speaks English. He might be able to help you."

Nicholas said "Efharisto" and left the agency. The supermarket was small: there were just two aisles. There was no one at the front counter, but he found what looked like the owner restocking a shelf with tinned goods to the rear.

"Kalimera. May I speak English?" he asked.

"You can," the owner said. "How can I help you?" The careworn man seemed to be the only one working in the store. "Oopa" the man exclaimed as he tried in vain with his elbow to stop a tin from rolling off the shelf. Nicholas waited before repeating that he was trying to track down an old friend, working for a Russian family. He asked if this was the only supermarket in Pedi. If so, he assumed they would have used his shop from time to time. He produced the photograph and showed it to the owner, who took it to the front of the shop, where there was more light.

"Yes," he said, tapping the photograph. "Here, I recognise this one. He has been in here a few times." He was not pointing to Andriy, but the man next to him. It was Vitaly, Caroline's ex-boyfriend. "He is Russian," he added. "Yes, definitely a Russian."

"Thank you. Do you recognise these two people?" Nicholas pointed at Alessandra and Andriy.

The supermarket owner took the photograph again and had another look at it. "No, they have not been in. I have a good memory for faces, yes. However, this man," he pointed to Vitaly, "he come in a couple of times with a Greek woman. She spoke to me, asking me about something." He went on to describe Helena.

"Can you remember when was the last time either of them came into your store?"

"Two weeks ago I think. Maybe a bit more. They bought canned food, meat, some oranges, melons, vegetables and of course ouzo and vodka. They bought a lot, so there must be people staying with them."

"Did they say where they might be living by any chance?"

"No they didn't. But, it must be somewhere near here. Probably one of the big farmhouses. There must be a lot of people staying and they have dogs. Quite a lot of dogs, judging by the amount of dog food they bought. They drove here. I helped take some of the food they bought out to their car. It was a big, four-wheel drive car."

Nicholas took the photograph back. "That has been very helpful. Efharisto. Could you show me the way to get to St Nicholas Bay – Agios Nikolaos? I am walking there."

Nicholas walked down to the waterfront and came to a small jetty. A water taxi was moored alongside. Fishing boats were anchored in the shallows. Further out were the larger boats. To the right, on the curve of the bay, was the narrow, pebbly beach, a whitewashed church with its blue dome and window frames in the background. Most of the sun beds and umbrellas had already been taken in the early season sunshine. He continued on along the waterfront, past blue-shuttered doors of what looked like holiday rentals, until he came to the rocky stone pathway leading up and along the hillside.

Chapter Twenty-Four

SYMI

THE CLIFFSIDE PATH SOON BECAME STEEP. NICHOLAS HAD TO step carefully as it narrowed and became uneven. He disliked heights and became nervous as the path climbed and skirted the edge of the cliffs. Below lay sharp black rocks and the dark water. A black plastic pipe had followed the contours of the path, presumably providing a supply of fresh water to the next bay. He felt the breeze strengthen as he ascended. Eventually, the gradient lessened and then leveled out as the path neared the cliff top. The tinkle of bells revealed the presence of grazing goats, as he made his way around the headland. Nicholas's phone rang. It was Effie. He couldn't speak to her at the moment. He was not up to further deception. Besides, she would hear the buffeting wind and wonder where he was. The phone rang for what seemed like an eternity and then fell silent. He looked back, the view reached across the bay and all the way through the valley and up to Horio in the distance. His phone rang again. This time he was tempted to answer. Perhaps Effie really needed to speak to him. He resisted, again letting it ring out. He did not want Effie to know where he was or what he was about to do. He particularly did not want her to try to talk him out of it.

He had a good view to his right of the hills behind what must be St Nicholas Bay. The hills were partially covered by shrubs and thickets of trees. Elsewhere, barren rock and scrub dominated. He could just make out the faint outline of a dirt road snaking through the valley from the bay. At the cliff edge he saw below the basin of St Nicholas Bay, surrounded by high, grey, jagged cliffs. Below was a small, shingle and sand beach, fringed with tamarisk trees, with a small taverna on the near side. From the cliff summit he approached the steep stairs down with caution. Far below, he could see part of a stone jetty at the base of the cliff. A large boat, not unlike the Lady Gabrielle, was anchored out in the middle of the crystal-clear water.

He took his time descending. Half-way down he passed a goat, clinging to the cliff edge in an attempt to reach the furthest leaves of a scrubby myrtle bush. He was relieved to see that the boat was not the Lady Gabrielle. Eventually reaching the safety of the beach, he walked across to the taverna and sat at an outside table, ordering a fresh orange juice and a coffee. Terracotta pots of geraniums and daisies separated the taverna from the beach. It was half-full with customers having an early-afternoon lunch. A jeep and a motorbike were parked to the side of the building, beyond which was the dirt track that he had seen from the cliff. He saw goats seeking food and shade from the nearby trees. On the other side of the beach was the whitewashed chapel from which the bay took its name.

Nicholas's drinks arrived and he sat for a while enjoying the sunshine. Customers began to return to their sun loungers and the owner began clearing the tables. Once he had finished, Nicholas took out his picture of the Lady Gabrielle and showed it to him. Nikos was in his thirties and had the lean and weathered look of a fisherman. He had a ready smile and, whenever he did, he exposed a gold tooth at the front. Nicholas asked him whether he had seen the boat in the bay. Nikos recognised it. It visited the bay two or three times a year, he thought, and had been doing so for at least the last three years. "We only open for seven months of the year so it is hard to tell" he shrugged apologetically. Most times it moored out in the bay, but occasionally it came to the jetty, when the crew often came to eat in the taverna. Nicholas asked when the Lady Gabrielle had last visited.

"I think it was about three weeks ago, maybe a bit longer," Nikos replied. "It normally only stays for a few days and then leaves. Sometimes, it only moves around the headland to Gialos. I know, because I have seen it there quite often. The crew prefer that because there is more to do in the main port."

"Do you ever speak to the crew?"

"Yes. But they don't speak Greek and only a bit of English, so conversation tends to be limited to what they wish to order from me. They are not very kind people – they can be arrogant and impatient. Can I ask why you are interested?"

"Yes, of course. A friend of mine from Rhodes – a woman – came over recently with the boat. I was wondering whether she was still here on Symi." He showed Nikos the picture of Alessandra with Andriy.

"I have never seen her here, but the other one – I think he is the boss, the owner of the boat. I recognise him. The crew talk about him, and not always in a good way. I think they are scared of him."

"This one – the boss – do you know whether he has a house here on Symi?"

"I think he must have. I don't think he stays on the boat when it is here. When the boat moors at the jetty over there, the crew sometimes offload things. Things that we do not ask about. They have someone waiting with a truck. They load it up and drive off up the track there," he said, pointing behind the taverna.

"Normally most of the crew stay on board the boat. One of the crew told me once they have a farmhouse in the hills behind here. It is surrounded by a high fence and they have dogs."

"That does sound like the property I'm looking for. And how would I find it if I wanted to visit this friend of mine?"

"Well if it is the house I am thinking of, it will take you more than an hour if you are walking. Maybe one-and-a-half hours from Pedi. It is hard going. The road is not good and it is steep. The dirt track goes all the way past it, but it is very hilly all the way there. If you are driving, you will need a four-wheel drive vehicle for sure. Then it will still take at least fifteen minutes, depending on whether it has rained. It is very rough, with lots of rocks in the road."

"Thanks, Nikos. I will think about it. Can I buy you a drink?"

Nikos said he would have one later, when he had finished tidying up.

"Could I ask a favour of you? I am not even sure that I will go there, but can I ask you not to mention that anyone was asking about the place, particularly to any of the crew. My friend said that the owners are very sensitive about their privacy."

Nikos looked enquiringly at Nicholas, but was happy to agree. He did not seem to have much time for the crew of the Lady Gabrielle. Nicholas ordered the red snapper, which Nikos assured him was freshly caught from the bay that day.

"Excellent choice," he confirmed, and went to the kitchen to prepare it, while Nicholas sat back and looked out to sea. He needed to plan his next steps carefully.

Leaving the taverna and thanking his new friend, he headed back up the steep steps of the cliff. It took him the best part of half-an-hour to get back to the bus stop in Pedi. By that time it was late afternoon and the sun was starting to set over the horizon. He would catch the bus back to Gialos.

At the port he went in search of a flashlight and found one that was not too bulky. He had brought binoculars with him.

Before he ascended all those steps to the old town and his hotel, he decided to spend some time in the port. He found a pleasant bar with cushioned seats and ordered a drink. Looking out across the port, he saw no sign of the Lady Gabrielle. Before he left the next day he would check again.

It was early evening and the lights began to come on around the port. He sat enjoying the view and planning. He would not hire a vehicle for the next day. The remoteness of the place would mean that an approaching car would be heard and seen. Particularly, if the track was as bad as he had been told it was. He needed the advantage of surprise – it was probably the only advantage he would have. He would leave later the next day. By delaying to mid-afternoon, the light should be fading as he neared the farmhouse. Nicholas was nervous, but he was resolute. It had taken too long to reach this point.

Back at his hotel he got out his laptop and found a Google Earth satellite image of Symi. He scrolled the image to follow the coastline to Pedi, then retraced the path, which he could just make out, up the steep cliff and over the top to St Nicholas Bay. The beach was clearly visible, as was the taverna. He could even make out the trees lining the beach. The image showed the small chapel on the opposite side of the beach. Interestingly, the wider image of the bay showed a large boat moored some distance from the beach. It was impossible to see whether it was the Lady Gabrielle.

He zoomed in and located the narrow track that disappeared through the trees at the back of the taverna. When it reappeared, he could follow its snaking progress through the valley behind. It climbed and then joined another track coming from the direction of the village at Pedi. The grey satellite images showed the terrain become increasingly barren and rugged as the track climbed steeply inland. On either side were what looked like low stone walls, presumably built originally to retain livestock. The track continued through thickets, emerging into the open, across the arid, uneven ground. He saw a couple of small buildings, which could be outbuildings or farm sheds. The track then wound its way up and down gulleys, past another couple of small dwellings and, after a while, a more substantial building appeared on the image. It seemed to have another smaller building to one side, which could be an outbuilding or a large garage. The larger of the buildings had a sizeable central courtyard, enclosed on all sides. Leading up to the property and extending to one side was what seemed to be a tarmac or paved driveway. This must be the place. It looked too substantial to be a mere farmhouse and it was surely too far from the coast and village to be a holiday property.

Beyond the perimeter, and to one side, there was a small grove of trees. That might help him to get closer to the house without being seen. He continued to study the satellite images. Zooming in again, he could make out, on the other side of the house, near to the external fence, a small garden shed, possibly housing garden equipment or perhaps, he thought, a generator. This far from the nearest village they would need their own power supply. That was probably good news, as the fence – if it was a chain-linked wire fence – was unlikely to be electrified. It was hard to tell, precisely, from the satellite imagery, what the terrain was like around the farmhouse. It looked as though it occupied a flat piece of ground, but it was difficult to say whether it was overlooked. He would only know when he got there.

Nicholas scrolled over the satellite image and traced the dirt path as it continued on past the farmhouse. It wended its way further inland into a valley, deep in the interior of the island. Every so often he saw what looked like either buildings or ruins. It was certainly isolated. He retraced his way back, past the farmhouse and towards the coast, trying to imprint as much of the route in his mind as he could. On a piece of paper he drew a rough map of it, noting particular topography and buildings on which he might orientate himself. He came to the intersection. He drew the route back to St Nicholas Bay and then followed the track as it wound its way around what look like a craggy outcrop and up a rough incline. After a kilometer or so, he started seeing the outlying houses of Pedi village. The track forked once more, one track leading up through what appeared to be orchards and fields. The other soon became what looked like a tarred village street leading down between houses to the little harbour. Nicholas closed his laptop. He saw he had another missed call from Effie. He had switched his phone to silent.

That night he tried to sleep, but it proved elusive. In the dark his mind turned over his options for the next day. After breakfast in the hotel and a walk around the quaint old town, he returned to the hotel in the early afternoon and packed all he would need in his black rucksack. He was as prepared as he could be and felt a confidence that had not been there before. As he walked the now-familiar route to Pedi his senses felt heightened. The colours of the sky and the fields, with their pine and olive trees, appeared more vibrant. He felt good, empowered.

At the supermarket, Nicholas stopped to buy some bottled water and an energy bar. He exchanged greetings with the owner, who remembered him from the previous day. Instead of walking to the waterfront, he turned right and walked down the street lined with the square houses that he had viewed on the satellite image. It took him to the edge of the village. At the end of the road, he picked up the track that led further inland. Beyond the village, the track began its steady climb up the hill. At the top, the pathway turned left and entered a small, shaded clearing, where brown pine needles blanketed the ground. They gave off a warm, sweet, slightly horsey smell, reminding him of Mediterranean holidays when he was much younger. Emerging from the trees, the track resumed its meandering climb up and over another hill. The ground was becoming more dusty and strewn with boulders, the countryside more barren. The going became progressively harder. He had to be careful to avoid turning an ankle. He started noticing the low dry-stone walls that he had seen on Google Earth. They looked old and unkempt. Nicholas consulted the rough map he had drawn. He estimated that he was almost halfway. He probably had another thirty or forty minutes' walking before he came to the farmhouse. It was still some time until dusk, so he found a shaded spot to sit and rest. He drank some of his water while he waited.

Resuming his walk, he needed to be careful from here on. There was no recent evidence of tyre tracks in the dust, but he did not want to be caught out in the open. It would be hard to explain what he was doing here, in the middle of nowhere, at this time of day. After a while, he was on the lookout for the copse he had spotted on the satellite image. The sun was starting to set over the hills. The path skirted a smaller cliff and, as he rounded the bend, he saw the dim lights of what could only be the farmhouse. The grove of trees was off to one side, just before the entrance to the property. There was no movement at the house. He walked carefully towards the protection of the trees.

Once there he took out his binoculars and trained them on the perimeter. He could not see any dogs. The outbuilding he had seen was clearly used for storage, a four-wheel drive vehicle was parked on the driveway. Three of the house windows were lit.

Darkness had descended very quickly. Nicholas was confident that he could not be seen from the house or grounds now. There was no movement in or around the house, so he settled down to wait. He needed to be able to identify some of the occupants. If he recognised anyone associated with Andriy, he would know he had found the right place. The next step would be to observe the patterns of activity in and around the house. He also needed to establish where the exits were. Then he would wait until everyone had gone to sleep.

Nicholas sat patiently among the trees. He checked his phone to make sure it was switched to silent. He saw, with some surprise, that Effie had tried to phone again. She had not left a message. He wondered why she was being so persistent. Nicholas would phone her the moment this was all over. Mosquitoes buzzed around him and he could feel himself being bitten. He tried to brush them away. After an uncomfortable half-hour, he was rewarded with people entering one of the lit rooms. Through the binoculars he saw a woman, whom he assumed to be Helena. She was talking to a man he had not seen before. They seemed to be arguing.

Some time later, a side door opened and a broad-shouldered man he did recognise emerged. It was Andriy's silent accomplice, the man who had wielded the gun in his hotel room in Rhodes. He was carrying two bowls and he called out into the darkness. Two German shepherds raced from the shadows, as the man put the bowls down. Nicholas noticed both dogs were attached to their kennel by long chains. At this distance he couldn't see how long the chains were, but assumed they would not extend to cover the whole property. Clearly, the farmhouse's occupants were feeling complacent; expecting little threat. He was buoyed by this realisation. He knew he could scale the fence somewhere, away from the dogs. As he settled down for a long wait, bats swooped around the branches overhead. It was after midnight when all the lights finally went out. It was getting cold and Nicholas was glad that he had packed a sweater. It would also help with the mosquitoes. Nicholas leant his head against a tree trunk and fell into a light sleep.

Chapter Twenty-Five

SYMI

AN OWL SCREECHED IN THE TREES. WAKING WITH A START, Nicholas looked at his watch. It was just before two. The bats had disappeared. All the lights in the farmhouse were off and he assumed its occupants were fast asleep. He had a drink of water and ate his energy bar. Getting up cautiously, he began moving slowly away from the trees. The ground was littered with rocks and branches, making progress difficult. There was moonlight and shadow and he made his way carefully around the fence and away from the front gate. The dogs seemed to be asleep in their kennel.

Occasionally, he dislodged a small stone and stopped in his tracks, half expecting the dogs to start barking. It took him twenty minutes to negotiate his way carefully to the rear of the property, away from them. The lights were all off. Nicholas could see four windows, two were slightly ajar to let in the breeze. All the windows at the rear had metal bars set into the stone. He supposed that was why the dogs were required to patrol only the front of the farmhouse. Further along, in what looked an annexe to the rear of the original building, was another window, also with bars. The room was separated from the rest. Was this where Alessandra was being held?

He examined the fence. It was about three metres high. Standing on his toes he could reach to just below the top. Luckily, there was no razor wire. He took out padded gloves from his backpack and put them on. Reaching up, he tried to get a purchase with his foot in the chain link. He slowly raised himself but slipped back. He tried again. This time he managed to insert the toe of his boot into a link and get a foothold. Gradually, by pulling himself up, he worked his way to the top. He paused to get his breath. His arms ached from the effort. There could be no return now.

Slowly, Nicholas worked his leg over the top and clambered down the other side. On reaching the ground, he heard nothing. No dogs appeared around the corner. No lights went on. He took out his torch and crept towards the window furthest from the main house. It was closed, its curtain drawn. He thought of tapping on the window, but decided against it. He could not take the risk that it was not Alessandra inside.

He moved carefully to an open window. The gentle rhythm of snoring came from the inside. The snoring sounded deep and male and he moved stealthily away from the window. He crept past another window that was also slightly ajar and looked in. It was too dark to see anything. Nicholas remembered from the satellite imagery that the farmhouse had what looked like a flat roof. He retraced his steps back to the annexe, examining the rough stone walls as he went along. At one corner the wall was lower; the annexe was probably an extension. Nearby was a metal rubbish bin. He quietly picked it up and brought it over to the wall. By climbing onto it he could get a good grip on the top of the wall and pull himself up. Standing on the corner of the roof, he felt safe from the dogs. He made his way gingerly across the roof, until he came to the edge of the enclosed courtyard and peered over. It was quiet. No lights were on inside.

He suddenly had a powerful feeling that he was close to Alessandra. He knew instinctively that this was where she was imprisoned. Somehow, he also knew that she was in imminent danger. Nicholas's original plan had been to obtain proof that Alessandra was being held against her will and then contact the Rhodes police. A photograph of Alessandra being held captive might be sufficient proof. He had planned to send it to the police from his phone for verification. They would then be forced to act. Now, he was not so sure. He was not certain whom he could trust. He was not even sure whether the police would take it seriously. Increasingly he felt that he was on his own and that Alessandra's fate lay in his hands.

Looking across the brick-paved courtyard he saw it was surrounded by an open walkway. He carefully let himself to the ground. The clouds had disappeared and the weak moonlight provided sufficient light for him to see around the courtyard. Two large terracotta pots contained what looked like bougainvillea trailing up the stone pillars. To one side was a wooden bench in front of a fountain. Water splashed softly into a lily-covered ornamental stone pond. Of the windows into the farmhouse, most were open or ajar, allowing a breeze into the interior. There was a set of French doors to one side. Nicholas peered into the darker recesses. To one corner was an open passageway that led, he presumed, into the farmhouse. Nicholas oriented himself. The barred window in the annexe was towards one corner, beyond the passageway. Cautiously, he made his way across the courtyard towards it.

It was much darker in the shadows. He could barely make out the walls. At one stage he stumbled against a box of what looked like canned provisions lying on the floor. He could not risk using the flashlight. He felt his way along, until the passageway opened into a kitchen. Moonlight filtered through the window and he was able to make out a cooker, with a fridge in one corner. Finding a set of drawers near the stone sink he slid them open gingerly. Using his flashlight he searched the contents and selected a sturdy-looking knife. He was not sure whether he could actually use a knife on another human, so he also took a wooden mallet from the bottom drawer. He would know whether he could use either only when the necessity arose. If Alessandra was there, he hoped to find her and escape, without disturbing her captors.

Nicholas shone the light quickly along each of the walls to establish where the light switches were. He looked for keys hanging from the coat rack or on the counter tops. Suddenly, he heard a door opening along the main hallway. He turned off his flashlight and retreated to the dark safety of the passageway.

Helena, stretching her arms sleepily above her head, came into the kitchen. She was dressed in a white T-shirt and was taller than she had looked in the photographs. She turned on the main light in the kitchen and opened the fridge, rummaging inside for a carton of milk. Taking a glass from a cupboard, she sat down at the table. Nicholas remained motionless in the shadows. Helena lit a cigarette from a packet lying on the table. She idly leafed through a magazine while she smoked. Eventually, she finished the milk, stubbed out the cigarette and put the glass in the sink. She sat for a moment, lost in her thoughts, then stood, turned off the light and left the kitchen. Nicholas made it to the corner of the kitchen in time to see her return to her bedroom. It was the second door on the left of the hallway.

He crossed the kitchen again and silently moved down another, narrower, passageway leading from the kitchen to where he thought Alessandra's room was in the annexe. At the end of the passage he found the door on the right. He shone his light on it. Slowly, he tried the door handle. It was locked. He could hear no movement inside. He looked around in the hope that the key was hanging nearby. It was not and he had to creep back to the kitchen. He turned on his flashlight and searched the walls and counter tops again. He could see nothing. He returned to the passageway from the courtyard hoping that keys to the rooms might be hanging there. His search was fruitless.

Back in the kitchen he found a couple of towels hanging near the sink. He had packed strong tape. Putting the towels in his pocket, he crept down the hallway towards Helena's bedroom. He hoped she was sleeping alone. He assumed so, with Andriy away on the Lady Gabrielle. Slowly opening the door, he saw a double bed on the left. A ray of moonlight falling across it revealed a single sleeping shape. She was lying with one leg on top of the duvet. Nicholas closed the door softly and edged across the room. Taking out the knife, he put the towel over Helena's mouth and held the knife above her so that she would see it.

"Keep quiet," he whispered. "Keep quiet and nothing will happen to you." Helena woke with a start, eyes wide. She looked as though she was about to scream and Nicholas held the knife against her throat, keeping the towel pressed to her mouth. "Nod your head if you understand," he whispered, his mouth close to her ear.

Helena nodded. "Who are you?" she gasped.

Nicholas ignored her. "I am going to tape your wrists together. Nod if you understand." Helena nodded again.

"What are you going to do to me?" she whispered. "Are you going to hurt me?"

"Turn over in the bed and put your arms behind you." She struggled onto her front and placed her arms behind her. Nicholas tied the towel over her mouth and then taped her wrists together behind her. "Turn to your side." She did so, eyes still wide. "I am going to ask you some questions. Nod, or whisper your answer, very softly." He kept the knife close to her throat and loosened the towel. He brought his head close to hers. "Is Alessandra here in this farmhouse?" She nodded.

Her eyes widened. "You are English. I think I know who you are. You're the guy from the ferry. Nicholas? Is that right?

Alessandra told me about you. But, what are you doing here?" she looked perplexed.

Nicholas continued to ignore her questions. "Where is she? Is her room the one in the annexe; at the end on the right?" She nodded again, starting to cry. "Where are the keys to her room?"

Helena whispered: "In my bag on the chair over there."

Nicholas retied the towel and went across to her bag. He extracted a set of keys, then went back to the bed and said: "Show me which one it is." He held each key up in front of her until she nodded. He removed the key. "And which one is yours?" He removed this as well. "The man sleeping in the room next to you, which is his key?"

"Is there anyone else here in the property? he asked. She shook her head.

Nicholas looked at the rest of the keys left on the key ring. He loosened the towel again. "What about this large one? What is this for?" he asked.

"No, you can't take that one."

"What is it the key to?"

"It's for the storeroom in the annexe. I am not meant to let it out of my sight. Andriy would be furious. I am the only one who is allowed access." She was still sobbing softly.

He looked at her and put the key in his pocket. He tightened the gag again, then, leaving the rest of the keys on the floor in the corner, he made to go. Nicholas stopped and turned back to Helena. He knelt close to her again, loosening the gag again. "Tell me why you would do this to your oldest friend? Help me to understand what would make you do this."

Helena continued to cry quietly. Eventually, she calmed and said: "Andriy made me do this. He is offering me a lot of money to look after Alessandra and I need it. I have not hurt her."

"So you have placed money above loyalty to your long-standing friend?" he asked.

She started sobbing again. "I'm sorry," she said, lamely.

It was Nicholas' turn to shake his head. "I don't understand you. Do you think Alessandra would ever have done this to you?"

Helena shook her head, miserably. "No," she said.

"I'm not going to hurt you, Helena, although I think you are contemptible. I just want to get Alessandra out of here safely. You will be fine if you keep quiet and allow me to do this." She nodded, looking up at him. "I am going to go now," Nicholas said. "I am going to lock your door and I need you to keep completely quiet."

Nicholas carefully let go of Helena and retied the towel around her mouth. He went out, locking her door quietly. He put the key in his other pocket and listened. He could hear faint muffled sobs.

Moving to the next door he found the correct key and silently inserted it into the lock. He turned the key, then listened. He could still hear the slow, rumbling snoring from inside. Placing the key with the one from Helena's room, he moved silently through the kitchen and into the annexe. He passed the door on his right and felt for the key in the lock. He assumed it opened to the back of the property. He moved on towards Alessandra's door. Nicholas was careful not to use his flashlight. To its left was another with a more substantial lock. He needed to check it out before opening Alessandra's door. He turned his flashlight on. Above the lock was a red sign, printed in Russian, saying what he presumed was "No entry" or "Stay out". He inserted the large key and unlocked the door. From inside came a muted hum. It opened to reveal a large storeroom with shelving lining two walls.

In spite of the air conditioning there was a musty smell. He could see a thermostat on the wall. On each shelf was an array of boxes. Alongside the boxes were objects wrapped in clear plastic, each one labelled. They took up most of the shelf space. He went to one of the shelves and shone his light on the items. One was marked "Marble bust, unattributed, Syria 1ˢᵗ C", another "Silver bowl, Palmyra, 2ⁿᵈ C", and another "Marble frieze, 1ˢᵗ C, Iraq". He saw icons and frescoes from Northern Cyprus and what was described as a "gold/lapis bowl" from Baghdad. There was a box marked "Jewelry, various, Greece", containing numerous wrapped items, and another with "Figurines, Turkey, 1-2 C BC". Nicholas played the light along the shelves. He was amazed at the sheer scale of the operation. On the floor, in a corner, was a large crate. Inside was a statue of a horse. The labelling indicated that it came from Libya. The value of all the items must be incalculable. He understood now that the dogs were at the front to protect the treasure in the storeroom. He hurriedly completed his survey of the room. Playing the light on one of the shelves he took a couple of pictures with his phone. Turning off the light, he turned and closed the door on the looted treasure. He needed to get to Alessandra.

Nicholas selected the key for her room and inserted it in the lock. He turned it slowly. Too late, he heard a sound behind him. He tried to turn, raising an arm in self-defence. A blow came from the side and then everything exploded into blackness.

Chapter Twenty-Six

SYMI

NICHOLAS FELT GROGGY. HIS HEAD WAS POUNDING. HE FELT the area around him and found he was lying on a concrete floor.

"Who is there?" came a hesitant voice from across the room.

He tried to talk. His voice came out as a whisper. "Is that Alessandra?" he said. His mouth was dry and he could taste blood.

"Who are you?" came the woman's voice again. She sounded scared.

"It's Nicholas, Nicholas Adams, from the ferry to Halki," he croaked. "You might ... You probably don't remember me."

She was quiet for a long time. He thought he could hear crying coming softly from the corner opposite. He couldn't see anything and he wasn't sure that he could stand or even sit up. He heard a muffled voice say: "This is not happening. This isn't true. It's a cruel trick."

It was still so dark. He could not see a thing. He felt the rough wall and tried to pull himself into a sitting position. His legs felt rubbery and his head hurt with every movement. Eventually, he was sitting up. He felt nauseous and immediately threw up.

"Are you all right?" came the hesitant voice.

"I will be," he said, eventually, wiping his mouth with his arm. "I recognise your voice, Alessandra. Are you OK?"

"Nicholas. I just can't believe it. What on earth are you doing here?"

"It's a very long story, but I have been looking for you." There was another long silence. He heard the whine of mosquitoes circling the room.

"Just stay there," she said softly. "I'll come over to you." She turned on a dim lamp at her bedside. Nicholas heard movement, as she made her way over to him in the shadows. She gently felt his face and then sat down beside him and held his hand.

"I remember you really well," she said, after a while. "I have thought of you often." She had to stop momentarily to cough. "I am so sorry that I did not meet up with you again that day." She was crying again.

"That is all right. I understand now what happened."

After some minutes she moved away and returned with a bottle of lukewarm water and a cloth. Nicholas drank thirstily. When he had finished, she took what was left in the bottle and gently cleaned away the blood from the wound above his left ear. Then she held him tenderly for a long time. Nicholas drifted back into unconsciousness. When he awoke, dawn was starting to break. He could see the red-streaked sky from the small, barred window opposite. In the corner was a small, metal-framed bed with a blanket on top. Beside him Alessandra was asleep, still holding him. Her long dark hair fell across his shoulder. He couldn't help noticing that her nails were bare. Gone was the dark blue nail varnish. Nicholas's leg was becoming numb. He moved it, trying not to disturb Alessandra. The pain in his head had subsided to a steady throbbing. He checked his pockets. They were empty. His wallet and his phone had been taken, along with his backpack.

Gradually, the light improved as the morning progressed. He looked at Alessandra next to him. She looked thinner and much paler than when he had last seen her. Beside the bed he could see a small table with books piled on top. From where he sat, they looked like a mix of paperback novels and more academic works. There was the small lamp. It seemed that this was where Alessandra had been held for some time.

She murmured in her sleep, and Nicholas could feel her slowly awaken next to him. "I thought I had dreamt it," she said, when she became fully awake. "You are here and you have been looking for me? Why?"

"That's a question I have asked myself many times. To start with, I thought you had stood me up in Rhodes and I was very disappointed. I first heard that you had gone missing when I got back to England, last year. It was on television in the UK ... on the local news. I realised that I was one of the last people to have seen you before you disappeared. Also, when we met I felt strongly drawn to you. I could not get you out of my mind." Nicholas felt sheepish admitting this.

"Then something changed for me – a decision I made about what I needed to do for myself. I knew then that I had to look for you – and I had to try to find you no matter what.

"It has not been easy, but I think I have managed to piece together most of the clues you provided along the way. Somehow, it just feels right that we will now both face the same fate, whatever that will be. You are not on your own any more." He tried to sound reassuring and more confident than he felt.

Alessandra's eyes misted and a tear slowly tracked down her face. She brushed it away with the back of her hand. "My very own Saint Nicholas," she murmured. She was silent for some time and then said: "We have an hour or so before they normally come in. Please tell me what has been happening since I was kidnapped."

Nicholas took Alessandra through everything he knew, from when he first heard of her disappearance and making the decision to become involved by contacting her parents. He tried to include everything he remembered, including his return to Halki and his meeting with Andriy. Alessandra listened intently, frowning occasionally, but she did not interrupt him. She continued to hold on to his arm as if for support. Nicholas told her about meeting Kamides and Eleni and Effie and even Catherine on Halki. He told her he had tracked down the dive operator on Rhodes and that Spiros had shown him the places on Halki and Alimia where Alessandra had been diving.

"At the moment the police have you listed as a missing person, which means that they have stopped actively looking for you. We are going to have to sort this out ourselves." For Alessandra's sake, he tried to sound positive.

She was no longer the vibrant woman he had first met. It was as if her spirit had been crushed. Nicholas asked her if she had been harmed.

"Andriy promised me, and he promised your parents, that he would not hurt you."

"Well, I have not exactly been treated well. He hit me hard once, when I was first kidnapped on Halki. After that, he has largely ignored me. Most days, particularly when Andriy is away, I spend my time alone in this room. I am let out for an hour or so, but only in the courtyard where I can exercise and get a bit of sun."

She looked fragile and defeated, as though all hope had been taken from her. "Andriy has now finally realised that I will never show him what he has been searching for, so he intends to dispose of me. I have become too much of a threat to him and his business associates."

"What does that mean?"

"I think it means that his business associates will take me somewhere. They will probably hurt me – they are exactly that type – and then they will kill me. There can now be no advantage to them in keeping me alive," she said, her voice low.

Nicholas felt chilled by the brutal logic of Alessandra's words and wanted to change the direction their talk was taking. "Have you been held here for the last six months?" he asked.

"The only times that I have been out of this damned house have been when I have been on the boat, supposedly trying to help locate the site of the shipwreck. I led Andriy to believe that I was close to discovering what he has been desperately seeking for a long time. For him, it is just business. He does not care about the artifacts for themselves or about our cultural heritage. He says he already has a buyer lined up who would pay an astronomical amount".

Alessandra went silent while she decided how much she should tell Nicholas. "He still believes the ship was making for Turkey and went down just off the coast here. He didn't make me dive over the winter, but when the weather got better, he resumed his search. Now, he's lost all patience with me and the searches have stopped." She hesitated, then had a sip of water. "This is very difficult for me to talk about, but I need to tell you."

"Go ahead," said Nicholas, gently.

"A week ago, I tried to kill myself," she said, starting to sob quietly again. "I had come to the end. I was sure there was no one still looking for me. I had no hope left."

Nicholas put his arm around her shoulders and held her. "Please go on."

"I'd got to the stage where I knew I had to do something positive. No matter what, I had to try to escape. It was impossible here at the farmhouse, where I'm watched all the time. I knew my only opportunities would be when we were out on the water. The first time I tried there was no one to help me and Andriy soon realised what I was trying to do. The second time was when we visited a bay on a small island next to Symi. I knew the bay we would be diving in well and the only hope left for me was to somehow try to climb the rocks and hide somewhere on the island. Everything just went against me." She started coughing uncontrollably.

Nicholas waited until her coughing fit subsided. "Go on," he said, gently.

"It was my last hope. Andriy had made it clear that if I didn't cooperate it had been agreed that he would turn me over to his business associates. I was too much of a liability to their whole operation to be allowed to go free. I knew what that meant. I would just disappear – forever.

"I really tried to escape. When I found that I couldn't get sufficient grip on the rocks to get out and hide, I knew that was it. There was no hope left. But I was determined that, no matter what, my fate would not be in Andriy's hands – or his vile business partners. All I wanted was for my body to be washed out to sea," she said slowly, trembling.

Nicholas held her close, while she gathered herself. "The first time I tried to dive as deeply as I could, I panicked and came back up to the surface. I tried to be as calm as possible. I took a huge breath and dived down as far as I could go. I don't remember anything else. Everything just went black. The next thing I knew was that I was lying on the deck of the Lady Gabrielle – that's Andriy's boat."

"I know," said Nicholas. "I tracked its movements." He swatted away a mosquito that was attracted to the dried blood on the side of his head.

"I just remember coming around on the deck, coughing and retching. I felt like I couldn't breathe. It was a terrible feeling. I was told by Andriy, sometime later, that they saw me drifting under the water and managed to pull me out. I was probably semi-conscious, but I don't remember much. According to Andriy, I had ripped the snorkel away from the mask."

Alessandra's voice was almost inaudible now. "I don't know whether they knew I was trying to kill myself. Perhaps they think I just got into difficulties with the currents. But Andriy has now said that he's given up on the search, so I'm just waiting to be turned over to his associates."

"I'm so sorry, Alessandra." Nicholas didn't know what else to say.

"It's OK. I know I swallowed a lot of water and I'm still coughing a lot. I could hardly walk for the first few days after I was brought back. I felt so confused and have just slept most of the time since then. Now I just feel weak. I have no resistance left. At least Andriy knows he hasn't won."

"It might not be much consolation, but I'm here with you now. You're not alone."

"You cannot imagine how good that feels. I've felt alone for such a long time. I am sorry, though, that you're involved in this mess."

"It feels as though I was destined to be here with you. One way or another, our fate is now bound together. I'll try to provide the strength for you. There still has to be hope."

They lapsed into silence. A while later they heard the key turn in the lock. Helena walked in, carrying a pitcher of fresh water and bread. Behind her stood the man Nicholas had met before, holding a gun by his side. Helena said nothing and left. The man by the door indicated that Nicholas should move to the far wall. He asked Alessandra if she wanted to use the bathroom. She stood up, uncertainly. The man followed her out, locking the door behind him.

Nicholas leant against the wall. He did not feel well, but he could just about stand. He made his way slowly across to the water pitcher. A small jar of jam had also been provided. Half an hour later Alessandra came back. The door was locked behind her. She looked brighter and there was a slight colour to her cheeks. She sat next to him on the bed and he poured her a glass of the water. "How are you doing?" she asked Nicholas.

"I still have a throbbing headache, which is not surprising. God knows what I was hit with. But I feel better after the water. Here, have something to eat."

Alessandra helped herself to some bread and jam. "I'm sure they'll let you clean yourself up in the bathroom. You have a nice bruise on the side of your face, though." Sure enough, the door was unlocked again shortly afterwards and Helena told Nicholas he could use the bathroom. The man with the gun escorted him out. When he returned to the room, Helena told them that Andriy should be back the next day. He was arranging for his business associates to take over custody of Alessandra. He had been told about Nicholas and would no doubt have plans for him, too. They were to be kept locked in the room until he arrived.

Nicholas had managed to clean himself up in the bathroom. His pale blue shirt still had traces of blood over the shoulder and the collar, but he had removed some of the dried blood from his face. The wound had stopped bleeding. He and Alessandra lay down on the narrow bed. Alessandra turned to her side and put her arm around Nicholas, holding him closely. He was not sure whether this was for her comfort, or for him. They slept intermittently through the afternoon. Nicholas felt himself wake, as she stirred and coughed next to him. Once she murmured his name. He lay listening to her shallow breathing and wondered whether the seawater had caused any lasting damage to her lungs.

Nighttime arrived and they were woken by Helena bringing more food and water. She said Andriy was expected around lunchtime the next day and his colleagues would arrive later. "You will both be leaving here tomorrow," she said, as she left.

Alessandra and Nicholas talked for some time. Alessandra told him about her life on Rhodes and her friends. Her eyes shone when she spoke about her Sundays at the dog sanctuary. Nicholas explained about Lynda and their child and the circumstances that led to his decision to spend some time on Rhodes. It was Alessandra's turn to whisper how sorry she was. They fell asleep on their sides – the only comfortable position on the narrow bed. Alessandra snuggled into Nicholas's back, with her arm around him.

After Helena brought them a bowl of overripe red grapes and two oranges for breakfast the next morning she allowed them to use the bathroom. It was going to be a long and difficult day. The sky had darkened and it had started to rain. Alessandra and Nicholas spoke little and dozed fitfully through the rest of the morning.

It was starting to get lighter as the rain stopped. The barking of the dogs woke them. They heard voices – all of them Russian. There were greetings being exchanged, raised voices and laughter. The voices died down as the newcomers went into a room on the far side of the farmhouse. The sound of a door slamming echoed through to the annexe. Alessandra sat up to cough. When her coughing subsided, she gathered her energy to try to explain what had happened to her on Halki. She revealed the duplicity of her old friend Helena and her surprise and concern when she saw Andriy again.

"I understand Andriy's motives, as he's driven only by money, but how can Helena treat you this way?" Nicholas said.

"Andriy is a very domineering character. He tends to get whatever he wants. I'm sure that's the case with Helena. She's useful to him at the moment. Helena is quite weak. She's always been reliant on others. In some ways I feel very sorry for her. Though she has carried out all of Andriy's commands, she's not been unkind to me. When it was getting colder, she found me some warmer clothes. She also brought me books to read, which kept me going."

Nicholas shook his head. "You're an amazing woman. After all she's done to you, you're still able to find compassion for her."

"I do feel for her. When she's no longer useful to Andriy, he will finish with her."

They heard voices approaching. One belonged to Andriy. The door opened and he entered, with a smaller, wiry, middle-aged man, with coarse dark hair. "Well, hello again, Nicholas," Andriy said. "I really did not expect to see you again. You clearly cannot keep away."

"The pleasure must be yours. It certainly is not mine," said Nicholas. "You need to let both of us go as soon as possible. This is meant to be a civilised world."

"You are a funny man," laughed Andriy. "And a man who is very stupid. I thought I had explained to you very clearly the risks you were taking. You will learn that when I told you what the consequences of your foolish behavior would be, I never make idle threats. I hope you believe Alessandra was worth your stupid attempt to rescue her."

"You know you won't get away with this." Nicholas replied, with a calmness he did not feel.

"We will see. We will see. And how are you, Alessandra? Are you feeling any better after your diving mishap?" Alessandra looked away. Andriy turned to the man next to him. "The last time we went out she had an unfortunate accident. We found her floating, almost unconscious, and had to pull her out. Perhaps we should have just left her."

"I am sorry," Andriy turned to Nicholas and Alessandra. "I should have introduced you all. This is Pavel. He is one of my close associates." Pavel's smile revealed matching gold teeth. "I am afraid Pavel speaks very little English. He will be looking after both of you from now on. He and his men will be taking you with them later when they leave Symi. Unfortunately, Pavel's boat will not be as comfortable as mine," he laughed. Pavel seemed to understand and share the joke.

"Where are we to be taken?" Alessandra asked.

Andriy translated for Pavel. Pavel nodded and grinned. "You do not need to know. It will be very secure, however. Pavel and I need to have a business meeting, but they will take you later and before it gets dark. Unfortunately, we are going to have to sedate both of you. We do not want you to be causing any problems while we transfer you to Pavel's boat."

"You're never going to release us are you?" said Alessandra. "We're going to be killed and our bodies will be dumped overboard somewhere."

"Alessandra, you always had a vivid imagination. Anyway, it is now completely out of my hands. Both of you get some sleep. You will need it for later." Andriy ushered Pavel, who was still grinning, out of the room. The door was locked behind them.

Nicholas went to the bed where Alessandra was sitting, sat next to her and put his arm around her. "You've been unbelievably strong over these past months. I don't know how you have done that, but you need to remain strong for a bit longer. We'll get out of this somehow." He had no idea how he would fulfill that promise.

She smiled up at him. "I'm just so grateful you are here. Thank you for all you have done for me." There seemed little more to say. They sat with their own thoughts and waited quietly.

As the sun started to go down, they were both thinking it couldn't be long now. They could hear the sounds of the goats in the fields. The door opened. Helena came in, accompanied by someone they had not seen before. An automatic weapon was slung over his shoulder. Helena was carrying a dish containing two syringes. The gunman gestured to Alessandra and Nicholas to sit up. "I believe Andriy explained what we need to do." Helena advanced on them as they sat on the bed. "I will do you first," she said to Nicholas. "Roll up your ..."

Suddenly, a loud thumping noise from outside startled them. They heard shouting. There was the sound of running and then they heard gunfire. An explosion shook the farmhouse.

Chapter Twenty-Seven

SYMI

"WHAT THE HELL?" NICHOLAS STARTED. THE GUNMAN disappeared, leaving Helena standing, perplexed, a syringe in her hand. A muffled voice boomed from a loudhailer above the farmhouse. They heard the command to lie down and then something was shouted in Greek. "They are telling them to throw their guns down," said Alessandra, in amazement. They could hear the dogs barking frantically. The sound of automatic gunfire and shouting reverberated through the farmhouse, followed by screaming, then more firing. The air smelled acrid. In the confusion, Nicholas lunged at Helena. The dish and syringes flew across the room. Helena's head slammed against the doorframe and she crumpled. "Come," he said to Alessandra, holding out his hand, "We should get out of here."

"I don't think I can run. I don't have the strength," she said. "Please save yourself, Nicholas. Leave me here."

"I'm not going to do that. We're going to leave this place together. Here, let me help you." Helena was still lying across the doorway. Nicholas half-lifted Alessandra over the prone body and helped her out of the room. Emerging from the annexe they were met with a chaotic scene. One of Andriy's men was lying dead on the kitchen floor, blood pooling under him. Nicholas recognised him with a start as Vitaly. Another was prone in the passageway to the courtyard. There was a haze of smoke drifting through the house and the overwhelming stench of gunfire. Someone with an automatic weapon was shooting out of the farmhouse from one of the windows at the front.

Nicholas had his arm around Alessandra, who had started choking and coughing. He was worried that both of them were now exposed to the crossfire within the farmhouse. Through the smoke haze, he saw the door that led to the back yard, opened it to a rush of fresh air and helped Alessandra outside.

There was no shooting on this side of the house. Supporting Alessandra, he made his slow way as far from the house and the shooting as possible. A scattering of palm trees provided some screening. To one side, they found the concrete structure that Nicholas had assumed housed the generator and unlatched the door. The generator was still running and Nicholas helped Alessandra to sit in a cavity behind the noisy motor. She was coughing, trying to get her breath, but managed to smile her thanks. "This should be safe for a while. I'm just going to see what's going on. I'll be back."

"All right. Please just be careful."

"I will. I'll see you soon. I'll close the door to keep out the smoke." He latched the door behind him and crept back through the palms to the corner of the farmhouse. He was stunned by what he saw. Nearby were the burnt-out remains of the Nissan. The interior was still smouldering, spewing acrid black smoke across the drive and the front of the farmhouse. Beyond it, about thirty metres away, was a helicopter, its rotor blades turning slowly. Outside the perimeter fence, near where he had hidden among the trees, he saw a second blue helicopter landing in an open scrubby area. It bore the insignia of the Greek military. Armed men in camouflage emerged. Gunfire was still coming from the farmhouse, directed towards the far side of the property. Sporadic firing was also coming from the roof. Beyond the driveway, the gates were hanging open.

Nicholas hung back. He saw Pavel emerge with one of his men, firing wildly towards the helicopter. As they neared their target a volley of gunfire rang out and Nicholas saw the smaller man stagger and collapse onto one knee. He was still firing as his head exploded in a red mist. He sat there, headless, for a moment, and then toppled forwards. Nicholas felt ill. The gunfire gradually became more intermittent. Three men in camouflage emerged from the trees. Two others, automatic rifles held in front of them, made their way carefully along the dirt track towards the open gates. From where he was crouched, Nicholas saw a movement to his right. His eyes were drawn to the corner of the garage. Through the smoke he could just make out a group of people sheltering behind a pillar. Two were armed. They looked like soldiers or police. The third was tall and slight and there was something familiar about the figure that grabbed his attention. All three emerged cautiously from the shadows and Nicholas was astonished to see Effie in the rear. He tried to call out to her, but his voice wouldn't work. He took a deep breath and tried again. Effie, dressed in camouflage gear saw him and ran across. They embraced hurriedly. "What on earth are you doing here? Do you know what's going on?" Nicholas said.

"The cavalry have arrived," she said. "We have come to get you out of here. Are you OK?"

"I'm fine. So is Alessandra."

"Where is she?"

"I'll take you to her. She's quite weak. Follow me."

Effie told her colleagues she was going with Nicholas. They skirted the farmhouse to reach the back and Nicholas led Effie to the generator house. Effie leant down beside Alessandra. "Effie, what are you doing here?" Alessandra exclaimed as they hugged each other.

"I am here with the police and the military. We have come to get you, both of you."

"But why are you here?" asked Nicholas. "How are you involved?"

"I have held something back from both of you. Actually, quite a lot," she confessed. "But now is not the time to go through that. I promise I will explain everything when we are out of here safely. I need to let people know you are both here and are safe. I will be needed inside the building when it is secured. They will come and get you when things are stabilised. Please just remain here."

Effie stood up to leave. As she was about to open the door it was wrenched open and Andriy stood there wielding a semi-automatic. Pointing the gun at them he surveyed the scene inside.

"I saw you coming in. I am tempted to shoot all of you, but I need to get out of here. Come," he grabbed Effie, who was nearest, and dragged her out. "You two stay here or I swear I will shoot you." Andriy held Effie roughly in front of him and pressed the gun into her back. They made their way through the trees and along the fence towards the front of the house.

Nicholas told Alessandra to stay where she was. "You'll be safe now. I have to go after Effie. I have to help her." Alessandra nodded.

Outside the shed, he could just make out movement and then saw Effie, Andriy behind her, moving slowly through the trees to the side of the farmhouse. This side was sheltered from the gunfire, although Nicholas could still hear shouting in Greek and Russian, and screaming. Andriy was using Effie as a shield. Nicholas tracked them. Luckily, Andriy, concentrating on what might be ahead, did not hear Nicholas approach from the rear. Nicholas moved slightly to the side as he came close. "Andriy," he shouted and, as the gunman turned, Nicholas leapt forward and grabbed the muzzle of the gun. He managed to wrench the weapon away from Andriy, as they fell to the ground, wrestling. Effie twisted out of Andriy's grip.

"Get help," Nicholas shouted at her.

As the men grappled, Nicholas kept a firm grip on Andriy's weapon, despite taking several blows from the heavier man. "You are not getting away from here," he grunted. Andriy tried to wrestle the weapon from Nicholas. Nicholas felt his strength ebbing, as Andriy punched him in the chest and face. Somehow he managed to hold on to the gun and direct it away from his body. Suddenly, he was free. He was lying on the ground, winded and groggy, but still with a firm grip on the gun. He looked up and caught a quick glimpse of Andriy heading cautiously out of the front gates.

Nicholas looked behind him. Effie was nowhere to be seen. He got to his feet and steadied himself, then threw the gun to one side. It would only hamper him and he might be mistaken for one of the Russians. He followed Andriy out of the property. Outside the gates and lying across the dirt track was a man in camouflage. Nicholas could not see whether or not he was alive. His gun was lying under him. Nicholas did not have time to check on him. It was suddenly very important to stop Andriy.

Ahead of him he saw that Andriy had crossed the track and was heading across country, parallel to the path. He was making for the coast. Despite the time of day, the heat was oppressive. Nicholas heard gunfire from behind and did not know if it was directed towards them or elsewhere. He was about seventy metres behind Andriy. The low afternoon sun, the rough terrain and scrub bush were making it difficult to keep him in sight. The shouting and sporadic gunfire drifted across from the farmhouse. In spite of the noise, Nicholas tried to move quietly. It was difficult to know whether Andriy knew he was being followed.

Andriy was running, crouched, wherever the ground allowed. Nicholas believed he was making for his boat in St Nicholas Bay, a few kilometres away. The Russian crested a rise and disappeared over the side into a gulley. Nicholas momentarily took his eyes away from the ground and stumbled over a rock. Picking himself up, he decided to track Andriy from the side by following along the path. He was careful not to silhouette himself against the setting sun at the top of the ridge. He soon saw Andriy emerge from the other side of the gulley and resume running. He did not look behind him. Nicholas could afford to be more cautious, as long as he kept Andriy in view. He came to a rocky outcrop and the track bent sharply to follow the contour. He remembered this outcrop from two days before, a lifetime ago.

The going got tougher as the incline increased on the approach to the cliffs. Andriy was making for the eastern side of the bay. He was going to have to climb the steep cliff on that side before heading back down to the beach. Nicholas still felt ill from the blow to the head he had received the previous day. Andriy disappeared into a grove of trees and Nicholas lost sight of him. He crossed the dirt track and followed a narrow goat path into the pine trees. The mosquitoes were out in force in the shade. A cloud of the insects surrounded Nicholas's face and he tried to brush them away. It was darker among the trees and, as he peered ahead, he saw a flash of Andriy's shirt and followed, trying to stay hidden behind the trees.

The narrow path undulated through the grove, following a small gorge before the steep climb up the cliffs. Nicholas emerged into the open, to see Andriy scrabbling up the rocky path at the base of the incline. He held back, catching his breath at the same time, until the Russian disappeared around a corner and then set off again in pursuit. He knew he had to catch him before he reached the beach. He could not let him get to his boat. The climb was treacherous. The footpath was not much more than a goat track and was slippery after the rain. It clung to the cliff face as it followed the contours of the headland, snaking between boulders and brush as it climbed. He felt exposed up here. The uneven surface was littered with loose pebbles and larger rocks. Occasionally, Nicholas had to use his hands as he scrambled upwards.

The path finally emerged around the headland and Nicholas had his first view of the bay. Dusk was now well advanced and the outline of the path was blurred. He had to watch his footing. Below him was the vertiginous grey cliff, ending in jagged rocks protruding from the sea some fifty metres below. A warm breeze had picked up across the bay, causing a ripple of waves. Nicholas could see the beach at the end, plastic loungers still scattered haphazardly across the sand. One or two people were still sitting outside the taverna, waiting for the sunset. He made out the dark colours of the Lady Gabrielle docked alongside the jetty. No one was on deck. Alongside the yacht, a smaller, white and silver cabin cruiser was moored. He assumed it was Pavel's boat. He could make out a crewmember standing at the stern. Ahead, Andriy was suddenly framed against the evening sky. The Russian was much closer now, less than thirty metres away, making his way cautiously along the path. The muscled figure disappeared around a bend and was momentarily lost from view. Nicholas's opportunity to catch Andriy was disappearing.

Directly below the cliffs another moored yacht came into view. People were sitting on a deck at the rear, enjoying the sunset. The path narrowed as it followed a corner. Nicholas had to tread carefully, to avoid slipping on the loose gravel. Ahead, a juniper bush protruded into the path and, as he approached it cautiously, Andriy stepped out holding a small gun.

Nicholas came to a stop. Both men were exhausted. Andriy's clothes were spattered with blood and his white shirt was ripped down one side. "What do you want from me?" Andriy panted.

There was a grim determination about Nicholas. "I want you to face justice for everything you've done."

Andriy managed a sneer. "That is not going to happen. Let me get to my boat and I will make you very wealthy. There will be enough for Alessandra and for your girlfriend, if you wish. Just let me get away from this island."

Despite his bravado he looked defeated. His business empire was disintegrating. The gun wavered in his hand. Nicholas shook his head. "No. One way or another, this ends now. Give me the gun. You know you're finished." He took a step forward and held his hand out.

Nicholas felt a jolt and knew immediately he had been shot. It was as though he had been punched. He was warm and sticky, and blood spread slowly down his side. He staggered into Andriy and they teetered in an ungainly dance on the edge of the narrow path. Nicholas's feet slid from under him on the gravel and, as he slid towards the edge of the cliff, he grabbed hold of Andriy to try to stop his fall. Locked together, they plummeted over the side.

He was falling. He had somehow come untangled from Andriy, who had disappeared from view. His shoulder crashed into a protruding rock with a sickening thud. For a moment his descent slowed, but then he continued his slide over the loose rocks and pebbles. Nicholas dropped over the sheer cliff face down to the sea, twenty metres below. He was unconscious before his body smashed into the surface and disappeared into the depths.

Chapter Twenty-Eight

RHODES TOWN

ALESSANDRA FELT FRAGILE, DRESSED IN HER HOSPITAL-ISSUE pyjamas, and started in her chair in the intensive care unit's waiting room, when Effie came in. "Sorry, I'm still quite jumpy," she said.

"How is he doing? asked Effie.

"So-so I think. He had the surgery this morning and is still very groggy. The nurse said that he shouldn't have any visitors for a couple of hours. I was just sitting here."

"Do you know how the surgery went?"

"It was pretty major surgery. The bullet shattered two of his ribs and punctured a lung. They have done their best to repair those. The shoulder is more problematic. The fall shattered the ball and socket in the shoulder and a pin has been inserted. The problem now is more to do with the damage to the cartilage."

"Oh no," replied Effie. "Poor Nicholas."

"The surgeon said that Nicholas is young and fit and hopefully should pull through. They need to monitor him to see how the lung is responding. When he came in he was put on a ventilator. At the moment, as you'll see, he is now receiving oxygen only through a nasal tube. He also had a head injury. I think that was from the blow he received when he was captured at the farmhouse."

"I did notice that there was a swelling on the side of his head when I saw him," said Effie.

"The doctor accompanying the surgeon said Nicholas had had an X-ray and there is no significant damage. He will need further surgery to replace the damaged cartilage in the shoulder."

"Alessandra you look exhausted. Shouldn't you be back in your room, in bed?"

"I've been in bed for the last two days. I was just waiting for Nicholas to come out of surgery and to hear how it had gone."

"Well, while we wait, why don't you come with me for a tea or coffee? We can walk slowly."

"I should be fine, if we take it easy," Alessandra struggled out of the chair.

They walked slowly down the corridor, the taller woman supporting Alessandra, and caught the lift to the ground floor. Effie told Alessandra to sit and went to get their drinks. When she returned she asked Alessandra how she was feeling.

"My lungs were damaged in a diving accident I had on Symi. The doctors thought I might have something called ARDS – Acute Respiratory Distress Syndrome. After they examined me, they immediately gave me an oxygen mask. I managed to convince them this morning that I was feeling better and that a bit of exercise would do me good. I came here to wait for Nicholas."

Alessandra sensed her friend didn't believe she was feeling as well as she pretended. "The doctors have me on antibiotics. I am sure I'll start to improve. They are going to assess my lungs again at the end of the course. I still feel quite weak and, naturally, I won't be able to go diving for a while. Apart from that, they told me I was malnourished as a consequence of the imprisonment."

Alessandra smiled at Effie. "Of course, my mother is going to make sure that there will be food always available when I get back to the apartment. When I spoke to her on the phone she said she's already enjoying the thought of looking after me. I think I'm going to be spoilt. She is flying over tomorrow."

"You deserve to be pampered for a while. And your dad?"

"Unfortunately, he can't come. I spoke to him. He told me he cannot get away from his teaching duties at the moment. He feels so bad about what happened. I think he's too embarrassed to see me. Even my mother didn't know the full extent of his indebtedness to Andriy and his father."

"Don't worry Alessandra. He will get over that in time. Just wait and see." Effie gave Alessandra a quick hug.

"Thank you. You have been a good friend. So tell me how you managed to track us down on Symi and how come you were there. I knew that you had some involvement with Interpol. I remember you telling me once that part of your job was to report any artifacts that you thought might be stolen or looted."

"Are you up to sitting here for a bit?" asked Effie.

"Let's go back to my room and we can catch up there. We still have a wait before we can see Nicholas," Alessandra said.

Back in her room, she sat up in bed. Effie took the chair beside her. "It's a long story," she said. "You are right about my job. It has been an important part of my work for some time. Stolen items have been surfacing in increasing numbers on Rhodes. It's a large problem, made worse by the high values the items command. There are also more cash buyers, often in the Far East. It means the items do not necessarily go through the auction process, where there are some controls.

"As you know, organised crime dominates the trade – particularly mafia groups in Russia and Italy. And, of course, you realised Andriy was heavily involved. Many of his business associates also have strong mafia links."

Alessandra sighed and nodded. "I did know, not at first. I

thought he was just a knowledgeable academic, with a rich father. I believed, or wanted to believe, that he had a fascination for archaeology and our history. That is why we initially got on. He was very believable ..." Her voice tailed off.

"I know. I thought the same when I first met him," Effie said.

"I started to become suspicious because of his secrecy about his business," Alessandra told Effie. "I couldn't understand it. I wondered what type of work would take him away so often, to places like Syria and Turkey. I feared it might be drugs. He assured me that what he was involved in was all above board."

Effie poured her friend a glass of water. Alessandra took a sip and resumed. "And then there were his friends and other business associates – they were all Russian. But they didn't seem like normal business people. They were hard men, secretive. I was aware of the illegal antiquities trade, and things slowly began to make sense. It all tied in with Andriy's area of expertise. He really knew a lot. I challenged him several times. Each time he denied it. I had stayed at the farmhouse on Symi before and had been there when goods were unloaded. It didn't look like drugs that were being stored."

"He had been on our radar for some time," said Effie. "Like you, we never had any direct proof. That is, until Nicholas inadvertently helped us. I could not say anything directly to you, but, if you remember, I did try to warn you to be careful."

"I do remember," said Alessandra. "I thought you were concerned about his behavior towards me. And I knew you were concerned, quite rightly, about his friends." Alessandra started to cough and she lay back against the pillows until it subsided.

"We can finish this later," her friend suggested.

"No, I should be fine. I just need to get my breath." She replaced the mask over her face. It was a while before she felt she could talk again. Effie sat quietly beside her. Alessandra then continued in a halting voice. "Increasingly, I felt I couldn't trust him, that his interest in our research was becoming purely commercial. When I finally challenged him and said I would no longer help him, he got incredibly angry. I became afraid and it was then that I wondered what I had got myself into."

"It is easier to see with hindsight," said Effie. "He was very believable. And he was an experienced criminal who had been trading on the hardship of others for years."

"I know," said Alessandra, her voice suddenly strengthening again. "The moment I understood what was going on, I broke it off with him. He threatened me and said he knew my father. He also said I had no proof and no one would believe me."

"These people are very good at disguising and protecting their activities. We will probably find that there is a legitimate business that acts as a front for their criminal interests," Effie said.

"I didn't see him after that, but I had a strong feeling he had not lost interest in my research. I felt a number of times that I was being followed. I started to feel nervous when I went out on my own. Then I received a threatening call from him saying that my family would be harmed if I did not tell him everything I knew. He had obviously got desperate. It was then that I thought of Helena. She knew him and she also knew some of his friends. I believed she might be able to help me by talking to Andriy." She sighed. "I didn't realise how wrong I was about her."

"Let me do the talking now. You lie back and take it easy while I try to explain my involvement," Effie said. Alessandra tried to smile and settled back. "We have been working with the police and Interpol for some time trying to track down some of the international criminal networks involved in the illicit trafficking of objects on Rhodes. My job was to liaise with both. Completely independent from your involvement with Andriy, his operation became known to us as a suspect in the trafficking of stolen archaeological treasures. As you know Interpol works with local police, sharing information with member countries. My involvement was with the smuggling of cultural objects. It's part of the new Interpol initiative called Protecting Cultural Heritage."

"How long had you suspected Andriy?"

"I can't tell you everything, but we have been tracking Andriy's activities over the past year. We believed he was a major player in the looting of artifacts and smuggling them to lucrative markets in the east. After you had broken up with him, we obtained a significant lead through an informant. He had worked on Andriy's boat. We have him in protective custody."

Alessandra remembered one of Andriy's crew leaving him after a furious row. She had thought the argument was over money owed by Andriy.

"Through him, we learnt that Andriy had extensive operations across the eastern Mediterranean. We also found out he had storage facilities on one of the islands, as well as in Turkey. Initially, I didn't link your disappearance with Andriy or his business activities. However, with Nicholas's inadvertent help, I began to think there might be a connection. Over time, I became convinced that there was. Then, last week, we were alerted to Nicholas's sudden arrival back in Rhodes. We tracked his movements to Symi and the farmhouse where you were held. At the same time, we received intelligence from our counterparts in Ankara that there was a big meeting arranged on Symi between Andriy's business partners. We knew we had to act."

"Thank God you did. I think the meeting was called to arrange for our disposal. We had both become too much of a threat to them."

"The main objective for the police and the military was to capture Andriy and at least part of his network, but I felt sure we would find you as well. It took a lot of convincing on my part to be allowed to accompany them as a civilian. We knew the Russians would be heavily armed and would defend their operation. I think it was because I said I could identify you that I was allowed finally to join them. I just wanted to be there so much when you were rescued. And of course there was Nicholas, too."

Alessandra looked up, surprised, a question starting to form in her mind. She wondered how well Effie knew Nicholas. She was about to ask, but thought better of it. Instead, she said: "And how is the investigation going into everything that happened at the farmhouse?"

"Well, you know we recovered Andriy's body from the bay. They are carrying out an autopsy, but I think it's clear he died when he hit a rock at the bottom. Nicholas was so lucky to miss the rocks when he fell into the water."

"I know. I can't believe he survived that fall."

"The Lady Gabrielle was taken into custody and it contained a lot of evidence. The other boat managed to get away, but I am sure we will pick it up at some stage."

"How many were left alive? What happened to Helena?" Alessandra felt detached. She struggled to come to terms with her release and felt overwhelmed by the events of the past few days.

"Three Russians who worked for Andriy and his partner are in custody. One was seriously injured and it is not certain whether he will survive. Andriy's business partner was shot dead fairly early on. Four others died in the gunfire. Sadly, we also lost two people, one was a policeman. Helena is alive. We found her cowering in the corner of the room you had been locked up in. She is under arrest."

"Poor Helena. I hope the courts go easy on her," said Alessandra. "She did betray me, but she never really mistreated me. I hope they'll take that into account."

"I am sure they will. They will probably also consider that she was weak and easily dominated by Andriy."

"And the farmhouse? Andriy used it to store a lot of the stolen items."

"We know. It was amazing what we found there. There were millions of euros worth of artifacts and treasures looted from across the whole region. Two people from Interpol are on Symi, cataloguing everything on the site before they transport it, probably to Athens. There is so much, that it will take months before we can get close to a prosecution."

They were silent for some time, reliving the events. Alessandra finally suggested that they go back to see how Nicholas was. Effie helped Alessandra from the bed. At the entrance to Nicholas's ward, a nurse told them he was still asleep.

Effie suddenly said to Alessandra: "I will leave you to wait here. I have so much to do back at the office. I have to go back to Symi the day after tomorrow for a couple of days to help with documenting the objects."

Slightly puzzled by the abrupt change, and the businesslike tone, Alessandra said to her friend: "Thanks so much Effie. I owe you so much."

"Please tell Nicholas when he wakes that I will come in to see him tomorrow, if he is well enough." They embraced and Effie left. Alessandra resumed her wait for Nicholas.

—

Nicholas was awake when Effie arrived the next day, armed with magazines. He smiled at her. "How are you feeling?" she asked. "At least you are now off the ventilator."

"I have felt better." His words came out with a rasp. "I hurt all over, although the pain medication helps." He struggled to sit up and Effie helped him adjust his pillows. "You just missed Alessandra, and her mother who has just arrived."

"You don't need to say much. I just wanted to see you. To see how you are doing. I won't stay long. I don't want to tire you out."

"I am glad you came. And it is good to see you," he added. Effie had to lean in to hear him. "Alessandra told me a bit last night. Perhaps you can fill in some of the pieces."

"I can. I'll do it as quickly as I can. But, first, Nicholas I wanted to say I was sorry for not being entirely honest with you from the start."

Nicholas smiled. "I think I have a similar apology to offer to you. You must have been surprised to find me on Symi. All I can offer in my defence is that I thought that I was trying to protect you." He struggled to speak.

"I now know that. I was very hurt when you left me. And your distance towards me when you first went back to the UK upset me, but I worked it out over time. Try not to speak much. Let me bring you up to date with what has happened over the last few days. That will be enough for today. I'll let you sleep and will come back tomorrow and tell you all I can."

"Thank you. I get exhausted quite quickly. But tell me about Andriy. What happened to him? When he shot me we both went over the cliff together. I remember nothing after that until I woke up here."

"If you feel up to it I will." Her hand rested lightly on Nicholas's arm. When you found Andriy on the cliff above Agios Nikolaos did you notice a yacht anchored in the bay?"

Nicholas's memories of that time were still very hazy. He shook his head. "Well, when you were shot, the people on the yacht heard the gunshot. They saw the two of you on the cliff. According to them, you both toppled over the side together. Andriy plummeted straight down to the water. Your fall was partially stopped by a boulder. You seemed to tumble down. That was probably what caused the injury to your shoulder, but it was also what saved your life."

"Yes," said Nicholas. "The doctor said much the same thing."

"Anyway, when you fell, you somehow missed the rocks at the bottom. Andriy wasn't so lucky. He hit them and that's what killed him."

"That sounds awful, but I'm glad he's dead. He was a monster. He deserved to pay for what he did to Alessandra."

"With him gone, hopefully it will make it easier for us to roll up the rest of his operation. I suspect that some of his business partners will be more willing to cooperate now." Effie poured Nicholas some water. She saw he was getting tired.

"When you both hit the water, you were not too far from the yacht. Two of the boat's passengers dived into the water to see if they could save you both. A member of the crew used the yacht's dinghy to get to you. You were unconscious. Luckily, they managed to pull you out quickly and give you first aid. You started breathing again on the dinghy."

"I need to thank them for saving my life," Nicholas said softly.

"Don't worry. I've done that on your behalf," Effie said. "They got you to the yacht and called the emergency services. A helicopter was dispatched from Rhodes and brought you here. Andriy was also pulled from the water. He was taken on the same helicopter to the hospital morgue."

"I remember none of this. I remember slipping, falling and I remember the intense pain when I crashed into the boulder – and then nothing. Until I woke up here, with Alessandra looking down at me with a worried expression."

"I was also really worried about you," said Effie. "When I went to get help to subdue Andriy, you had disappeared. We found Andriy's gun abandoned and I feared the worst. But one of the team thought they had seen one of you leaving and escaping down the dirt track." Nicholas closed his eyes, trying to remember. He could vaguely recollect some events.

"Once we had captured everyone and taken Alessandra into the farmhouse we scoured the whole property. That's when we realised that you had probably gone off in pursuit of Andriy."

Nicholas tried to smile. "That was probably not the smartest move I have ever made," he said. "Stupidly, it never occurred to me that he might have another weapon on him."

"He is a criminal. They plan for these eventualities. I stayed with Alessandra at the farmhouse. Some of the team had gone to take control of the two Russian boats moored in the bay. While we waited, we got a call from the emergency services on Rhodes to say that another helicopter had been dispatched to a third yacht moored in the bay. The report was that two men had fallen from the cliffs and one was dead. I knew instinctively it was you and Andriy. I was beside myself. I didn't know which one of you was alive. I couldn't bring myself to tell Alessandra." Her eyes were moist. Nicholas squeezed Effie's hand. "I need to finish," Effie said, "and then I will leave you to get some rest."

"Half an hour later we got the full report. They said that the man who was shot was being treated on board the helicopter. They were taking him to the hospital on Rhodes for treatment. The man had dark hair they said. I asked what colour shirt he had on. They said it was pretty blood stained, but it seemed to be a light blue. The shirt of the dead man was torn but was white. I remembered what you were both wearing and knew you were alive. I can't tell you what I felt. I found Alessandra and told her. She just broke down."

Nicholas's eyes were starting to close. He continued to hold her hand.

Chapter Twenty-Nine

RHODES

NICHOLAS WAS FEELING A LOT BETTER. THE BRUISE ON THE side of his face had darkened. His voice was stronger. He was to be moved out of intensive care later on that day. His lung was healing well and the bruising around the shoulder was going down. The doctors hoped to be able to assess the cartilage damage in the next few days and then start some gentle physiotherapy.

Effie had come to see him again. "You sound so much better," she said. She told him she had been back to Symi to oversee the cataloguing of the stolen items. "I saw the room where Alessandra was kept. It made me shudder. I don't know how she managed to keep going all that time."

"Yes, she's amazing," said Nicholas. There was a pause. "You were going to tell me how on earth you managed to find us on Symi."

"I was. I will. I just hope that you will forgive me. Can I have a glass of your water?" Effie helped herself and sat down next to

Nicholas. "As I told you, part of my role at work is liaison with Interpol on items that come to our attention. They are either artifacts that are brought into the museum or are recovered as stolen goods. Sometimes they even appear for sale on the internet. It is a small but important part of my work at the ministry. Naturally, I am not allowed to talk freely about it.

"But, I was not entirely open with you about Andriy and his business empire. We had had our suspicions for some time. Even before Alessandra started going out with him, we believed he was part of a major trafficking cartel, but had no proof. When Alessandra went missing I didn't make the connection with Andriy. It was only when you arrived and started asking questions that I started thinking that there might be something. You were building a case to link the two".

"Go on," said Nicholas.

"Initially, I believed what everyone else believed. I knew that her split with Andriy was difficult and she was worried that he would not leave her alone. I thought that she did need to get away for a bit. I always believed, though, that she would be back at some stage."

Nicholas listened intently. He was starting to wonder what was about to come and how he would feel about it. Effie continued: "If I think back, it was when you received the threat from that woman at your hotel that I began to think there was something more to Alessandra's disappearance. Our trip to Lindos made me think it might well have something to do with her private research. And when I joined you on Halki I became convinced that something had happened to Alessandra and that it might well be linked to Andriy. That was when I first raised it with Interpol and our local police, through the ministry. I was not allowed to discuss it with you. The plan was that we would use your search for Alessandra to move the investigation forward. As a tourist you were the perfect front."

Nicholas was taken aback. "And I was worried about you all the time," he said. "I thought that I was protecting you."

"I am so sorry."

"Did you know Andriy visited me in my hotel room in Rhodes and threatened me at gunpoint?"

"No I didn't. What happened?"

"He barged into my room one night with one of his thugs. They had a gun. They told me they were holding Alessandra. My staying on in Rhodes and, I suppose, my trip to Halki, had convinced them I hadn't taken their earlier threat seriously. Andriy told me they were responsible for your accident. They had knocked you off your bike and put you in hospital. He said if I didn't break it off with you and leave Rhodes immediately, worse would happen to you. I just couldn't let that happen."

Effie was quiet as she tried to absorb all of this. "I knew nothing about this. I did have my own concerns about the accident. The car came from nowhere and I wondered whether I might have been deliberately targeted." She frowned. "The police never managed to track down the vehicle."

Nicholas shook his head. "It doesn't surprise me. With all this I completely forgot to ask you how your ankle is now."

"It is coming along," said Effie. "It just gives me the occasional twinge every so often. Anyway, why don't you get back to the visit from Andriy?"

"Well, he also said he would not guarantee Alessandra's safety if I did not leave Rhodes immediately. He suggested that the police would never believe my story. He led me to believe that she would be released safely, as long as no one interfered. So, that's why I told you I had to return to work in the UK. I had to distance myself from you, for everyone's sake. I felt it was the only thing I could do."

"I was really hurt by your abrupt departure and your coolness towards me. I did not understand at the time. I thought you had decided to get on with your life and that it didn't include me."

"I know and I can quite understand that. I'm sorry, but I really thought that I had no other option."

"The more I thought about it, though, the more it did not add up. I discussed what had happened with my colleagues and we had our suspicions. It just didn't feel right and there was a thought that you might have been threatened. Despite you telling me that you would not be returning, we decided to put your passport details onto a watch list. We were alerted the moment you flew into Rhodes. I am so sorry."

"Go on," said Nicholas softly. "What did you do then?"

"We tracked your movements electronically through your mobile phone. We knew that you stayed in a hotel near the airport. We were surprised when you got on the ferry to Symi, but we knew it had to do with Alessandra's disappearance, and with Andriy. We were on alert to mobilise both the military and the police in case something happened. I tried to phone you several times while you were on Symi, to warn you of the danger you were getting yourself into."

"I know. I didn't want you to know I was back here; I didn't feel up to lying to you again. I was also worried about exposing you to danger. I would have phoned you the moment I had found Alessandra."

"I was not meant to have had any direct contact with you. I was just concerned. I became more suspicious when you did not answer. We traced your phone as you moved around the island. We tracked your movement along what appeared to be a dirt track away from the coast and realised you had probably discovered Andriy's storage facility; that that was where, in all likelihood, Alessandra was being held. We saw that your destination was a smallholding or a farmhouse; the signal remained in position for some hours. When we lost the signal, we realised something had happened to you."

"That was when I tried to break into the farmhouse."

"Soon after your signal died we received intelligence that a meeting with some of Andriy's associates was taking place on Symi. Something had happened that worried them. It gave us the perfect opportunity to roll up a substantial part of the organisation. That was when the military came in. We now knew where Andriy's associates were headed. We waited to hear that another boat had arrived on Symi and then we got the go-ahead to come over by military helicopter. And you pretty much know the rest."

"I'm not sure how I feel about this," admitted Nicholas. "I understand about your job but, even so, I feel deceived by you. I wish you had told me some of this beforehand."

"I am sorry. I wish I could have done more. I really did try to warn you."

"What happens now with whatever remains of Andriy's business network?"

"Well, the stolen or looted objects found at the farmhouse will be taken to Athens. Interpol will then seek to return them to their rightful owners. Normally, that is their country of origin. Andriy's boat has been impounded and brought back here. The team will be going through it forensically.

"We now know he has a warehouse in Antalya and a separate team is raiding that, as we speak. We hope to mop up a significant part of his network – the middlemen, the auction houses involved, possibly even some of the final buyers. It will take time, but it's a major blow to the criminal networks in our part of the world."

"And Helena?"

"She will be charged along with the rest of those taken from the farmhouse. I am not an expert, but I would guess she will be charged as an accessory to the kidnapping and imprisonment. Enough from me. What I really want to know is how you are now feeling. How is your treatment going?"

"I will be going back to the UK as soon as I am fit enough to fly. I need another operation on my shoulder. There is too much damage to the cartilage and I need to have it replaced. Luckily, I have private medical cover through work and I will be able to have the operation as soon as possible."

"And where does this leave us?" asked Effie hesitantly.

Nicholas was quiet for a while. "I just don't know. At the moment it is hard to take all of this in. I think I need some time away and on my own. I do need to get back to work shortly. They have been very patient with me. There is also my mother. My dad needs my help at the moment."

"I might not like it but I understand. I really do."

"I will stay in touch with you. I owe you a lot. Not just for rescuing me at the end. I think you also rescued me much earlier."

Effie seemed to be struggling to keep emotion out of her voice. "I have to go back to Symi to finish off there. I will see you when I get back before you leave for England."

They embraced tenderly and Effie walked briskly away.

Two days later Nicholas was moved into a general ward. He had not seen Effie since his move out of intensive care. He knew that she was due to go back to Symi at some stage. Nicholas's recovery was progressing well. His arm would need to remain in a sling to protect his shoulder, but he was encouraged to get out of bed and walk around the corridors. Alessandra had visited him each day and frequently walked slowly with him as he tried to rebuild his fitness after the damage to his lung. She was calm and gentle as she encouraged him to take the few extra steps he needed as he struggled along. Each day he could see that there was noticeable progress thanks to her patient encouragement.

In turn, Nicholas could see that Alessandra was steadily improving. She was putting on weight and the sparkle was returning to her eyes. He was delighted to see the flash of bright blue again on her fingernails.

One morning, she came in with her mother. Mrs Bianchi had brought a walnut cake she had baked for Nicholas. "Hello Nicholas" she said. "I didn't know what else to bring you to thank you."

"Hello Mrs Bianchi. It is good to see you. I can see that you have been taking good care of Alessandra since you have been here."

"It is the least I could do. But please call me Judy, Nicholas. I feel it is about time." She smiled at him and her face was transformed. "I wanted to see you to thank you for not giving up on my daughter." Nicholas wondered whether this was also a reference to her absent husband.

"I just couldn't. I felt compelled to try my best to find her."

Judy Bianchi smiled. "I understand, and I thank you."

Alessandra said she had not seen much of Effie over the past few days. She knew she was back on Symi, trying to ensure the smooth transfer of the items found at the farmhouse. Effie had told her that the operation was proving to be one of the most significant finds in Greece over the past few years.

Alessandra was sitting on the bed next to Nicholas. She was wearing a simple blue dress and the paleness of her skin stood out. She said she was keen to get back to work as soon as her health allowed. She had been assured that a job would be found for her at the museum. The antibiotics were reducing the infection in her lungs and she hoped to return by the start of the next month.

Judy said she had things to do in the town and would see Alessandra later. They continued to chat. Alessandra radiated happiness as she described how much she was looking forward to returning to her work at the dog shelter the coming Sunday.

Nicholas had been thinking of Alessandra's father. "Perhaps I should visit him again, while he is on his own. I could explain what happened and perhaps I can provide a different perspective," he suggested. She asked if he would try to convince her father he was not to blame. One way or another, Andriy would have managed to prevent anyone from looking too closely into her disappearance. Nicholas said he had booked a flight in five days' time. He had spoken to his manager at work and they were looking forward to having him back within the month.

"I have also made an appointment to see a surgeon when I get back. I am hoping to have the second operation on the shoulder as soon as possible. It would allow a bit of recovery time before I resume work."

"My, you are very organised," Alessandra said, smiling. "It's good, though. It will be good for you to get back to normality. And you have your mother to think of now."

Effie and Alessandra insisted that they both accompany Nicholas to the airport. Nicholas understood that they were trying to reestablish their own friendship. It would help with him being back in the UK. His arm was still in a sling and Alessandra carried his bag from the taxi to the check-in desk. Once he was checked in they walked out of the departures building into the late afternoon sunshine.

"Thank you so much both of you for looking after me these past two weeks. I need to go home but I will be back. I will let you both know when. In the meantime, you also need to get back to your own lives. While I am away I will be thinking of both of you."

He embraced both women and said: "I'll stay in touch. Please look after each other." He turned and made his way up the stairs to the departures gate with mixed emotions.

Chapter Thirty

Halki

Sunset came late in August. The flaming backdrop bathed the harbour of Emborios in a golden light. It framed the tall masts of the holiday yachts dominating the small bay. Along the harbour the fishing boats lining the dock swayed gently in the warm breeze. Stevie Nicks was singing "Rhiannon" in the background. Nicholas savoured his ice-cold Mythos, watching the colours change. He looked at his watch and left the waterside bar, heading away from the rapidly disappearing sun and up through the winding streets. He found the stone-paved road and followed it up and around, past the pink and white oleander spilling over garden walls. Lights were just starting to come on in the houses. A small brown dog lay on top of a low wall enjoying the cool of the stonework. He continued past the school, now quiet. The route felt familiar. He had last walked this way more than four months ago on his way to the abandoned medieval town of Horio. He remembered the precipitous climb up to the castle with its eerie but panoramic views across the Aegean as far as the eye could see.

It was the hottest month of the year on Halki. Even in the early evening the heat was oppressive; well up into the thirties. His linen, open-neck shirt was sticking to his back. He thought back over the past three months as he strolled the route in the evening heat. Leaving Effie and Alessandra behind, he had returned to England deeply conflicted. His thoughts had been diverted by the need to recover fully and resume his career. He had agreed to restart work at the beginning of July.

He had also contacted Alessandra's father. It had been a difficult conversation. Mr Bianchi had said: "Firstly Nicholas I need to add my thanks to those from my wife for your stubborn persistence in finding my daughter. I was not helpful and I will always be in your debt for this." He said he felt ashamed that he had put Alessandra in danger. "I don't think I can ever forgive myself. My failure in business brought all this on. I was weak. I feel I failed my daughter in every way."

"I don't for one moment believe that your daughter feels that way," Nicholas had said. "Nor, from my own experience of her, do I think that Alessandra will judge you. She loves you as a daughter always will. But you need to say these things to her. You need to explain everything that you have just told me. Where do you think Alessandra got her amazing strength from? Even when there was little hope. Please see your daughter and talk to her."

Nicholas had also to work out his confused feelings towards Effie and Alessandra and he had felt that there was only one place that might give him an answer. Windsor cemetery had been bathed in bright sunshine, the occasional high cloud drifting across the sky. It was an almost perfect summer day. Nicholas had put fresh flowers on the graves of Lynda and his daughter and sat on the bench beside Lynda, allowing all his memories of her to flood back: her convictions and her sheer vitality. She had always been brave. Whether it was her willingness to challenge ideas and views, or the cruel news of her illness, she had displayed the same single-mindedness and tenacity. He smiled as he sat there. He had not needed to say to her that they would always be his family. He had sat there for hours in the warmth of the sun, letting the afternoon gently slide away. When he left he had felt a contentment he had long forgotten.

A week later he had been back at work. He had been warmly welcomed back by his colleagues and, before long, he returned to the normal rhythm of business life, with a renewed enthusiasm. He had made a special request that he be allowed a week off in August and, in spite of his long absence, it was granted. In the meantime he had thrown himself into the launch of the new product and had been enjoying the challenge of managing a new team.

Nicholas had spoken to Effie and Alessandra regularly. Effie's contribution towards dismantling Andriy's network had been recognised at work and she had been promoted to lead the repatriation process of the artifacts. The date for a trial had been set for later in the year. Alessandra was back at work and was spending some of her time assisting at a new dig that was due to start at a site adjacent to Ancient Kamiros. Her father had phoned to ask if he could visit her. Helena had been released on bail. It was likely she would receive a short custodial sentence. Both Alessandra and Effie had said that they missed Nicholas. Nicholas had missed them, too, and had needed to see them. What he had to say could not be done over the phone

Nicholas had arrived on Rhodes two days earlier. It was the height of the tourist season and every taverna in the old town was overflowing with customers. The streets were crowded with holidaymakers. Passing the artists at their easels sketching the portraits of expectant customers, he had walked out through St Andrews Gate and across the medieval battlements of the Old Town to the ring road, towards Effie's apartment. She was expecting him. It was a long walk through the dusty streets and he was not used to the stifling August heat, nor the excited shouting and the blaring of horns of the slow-moving traffic circling the town walls. However, he needed the time to get his thoughts in order. Effie met him at the top of the stairs. They embraced warmly and she led him into the apartment. She was still dressed in her work clothes and looked as efficient and businesslike as ever. She offered Nicholas a cold beer.

"You look well," Effie started. "How is your shoulder?"

"It is fine now. The operation went well and gradually the movement has returned. I still feel a twinge now and again but I am now able to carry my own luggage."

"I am so glad. You know, you look better than when I first met you. You seem less haunted, more positive. I think I know why you have come today."

"I am sorry," replied Nicholas. "I owe you so much, not least to be as honest as possible with you." They talked for a long time. Effie told Nicholas she had always felt he was holding something back from her. She had thought that he was still not ready for any commitment after the death of his wife. Nicholas said that was partially true, particularly early on. But Effie had taught him to trust again. "You helped me to recover a sense of what I was, what I am. You brought me back to life."

"I suppose I am glad that I managed to help you. At least something came out of this," she said, sounding doubtful. "I have to say, that I did feel something might have happened between you and Alessandra, perhaps even from when you both first met. Initially, I thought that I was being paranoid, but now I am not so sure."

"Perhaps it had," admitted Nicholas. "I was just not able to properly trust or understand it."

When Nicholas left he said: "I hope we can remain friends. If not for my sake, then for Alessandra's."

"I will try, Nicholas. I really will," said Effie carefully as she closed her front door.

Alessandra's apartment was a short walk from Effie's. She had invited Nicholas to dinner. "Please do not expect anything fancy," she laughed. "My cooking skills are limited to three or four dishes. But I can at least guarantee the quality of the wine."

Despite his nervousness, Nicholas suddenly felt buoyant. He had no idea whether his feelings for Alessandra were reciprocated. All he knew was that he could not wait to see her.

Alessandra was dressed in a pale green skirt and a simple cotton top that contrasted with her tumbling dark hair. Her tan had returned and, to Nicholas, she looked utterly gorgeous. She explained that she had gone back to open-air swimming to rebuild her strength and exercise her lungs. Her greeting when Nicholas arrived reinforced his confidence. She had thrown herself into his arms and they hugged for a long time. Laughing, she finally invited him in.

"After a lot of debate I finally settled on a simple pasta dish and salad. I felt that I could manage that without creating a culinary disaster" she told him. "Anyway, please sit down."

Nicholas looked around the now familiar apartment. He noticed she had rearranged it, it looked more homely, less utilitarian, but still with her own colourful touches. He assumed some of this would be down to her mother's influence. Alessandra had tidied away all the papers, the mail and documents that had previously littered the table top. He still had some of her documents and photographs, he remembered.

Alessandra brought out a bottle of cold, local white wine and two glasses and sat down next to Nicholas. She smelt fresh and wonderful. He was happy to see that her natural vibrancy had returned. He needed to tell her about Effie. He explained that it had been important that he have a face-to-face conversation with Effie before he saw Alessandra.

Alessandra listened quietly as Nicholas told her what he had just told Effie. He said that in many ways he owed a lot to her. She had given him a confidence to look forward, and not backwards as he had been doing. He told her that Effie had sensed that something had happened between Alessandra and himself.

Nicholas had felt this from the first time he had set eyes on her on the ferry. That moment had profoundly changed his life, although he did not realise it at the time.

When he had finally found her many months later and she had laid her head against his shoulder and slept, he realised that he had fallen in love with her. She made him happy. He knew he could not be without her. Nicholas paused. He wondered whether he had said too much. Holding her gaze, he asked: "Is it at all possible that you feel the same way about me?"

Alessandra said, simply: "Yes."

Later he said "There is something that I need to tell you. You do not need to make any decision now."

"OK."

"I've been offered a great opportunity to move to a new job as country marketing director. It's a promotion, but the important thing is that the country is Greece. It will be based in Athens. So my question to you really is – could you see yourself spending your life with me?"

"You are not only my personal saint, but you are also my hero," said Alessandra. "You risked your life. I still find it hard to comprehend everything that you did for me, and I love you."

Nicholas smiled.

—

Nicholas crested the hill and was greeted by a view of moonlight glistening across the crescent-shaped Pondamos Bay. Up ahead and to his right, the grey forbidding peaks had lost none of their menace in the disappearing light. He passed the small church and then saw the lights of the waterside taverna ahead. Despite the heat he quickened his pace. The sound of laughter and conversation drifted up the hill.

Most of the tables were full. Greek music played softly in the background. Through the crowded restaurant he searched for a glimpse of a yellow dress. He saw her, her dark hair cascading down her shoulders. Approaching the table he caught the flash of the blue nails, as she held up her phone to take a photograph of the moonlight over the water. In that moment she saw him and flung her arms around him in greeting.

Alessandra and Nicholas had arrived on the morning ferry, much as they had done so long ago. This time they were staying for three days. Alessandra had contacted Catherine, who had managed to find them a small guesthouse with vacant rooms, looking out over the bay. The guesthouse was in half of a restored villa. Their bedroom had a small balcony that looked across the bay towards Rhodes. It would be perfect.

Chapter Thirty-One

ALIMIA

Spiros Pakourianos got up early that hot August morning. He needed to clean the inside of his boat thoroughly. He was very proud of it. It was a ten-year-old, thirty-two foot XTrim, with two powerful Nanni outboard diesel engines he had bought three years ago. A Greek flag flew proudly above it. Despite it being his busiest period, he had only two customers for the day, but he was looking forward to it. He knew both of them. He considered himself a bit of a ladies' man and he liked the pretty English lady from Rhodes. He had seen her rescue on television a few months ago. He also knew Nicholas and liked him as well. He had been delighted when Alessandra had made the booking three days ago. She had said that there would be no need for oxygen or scuba gear. All they needed were the fins; they had their own snorkels and masks. She would also need a good underwater light. She told him that she would let him know where they were going on the day. Spiros was particularly heartened when Alessandra said she would bring all the food and water and perhaps even a bottle of wine for the day. He just needed to bring the ice.

Nicholas and Alessandra woke to the sound of a donkey braying nearby. Nicholas reluctantly moved his arm from around her. They looked out from their bed through the open window and onto the blue of the Aegean beyond.

"Good morning," he said and kissed her.

"I slept so well," said Alessandra, kissing him back.

"So did I," said Nicholas, stretching.

"Come," she said, leaping out of bed. "We have a really big day ahead of us." Her eyes were sparkling with anticipation. Nicholas was caught up in her exhilaration and sheer energy.

She packed sandwiches, fruit and yoghurt, together with water, wine and cups, into a sturdy bag. Giving the bag to Nicholas, she retrieved a mesh bag with snorkels, masks and maps.

Walking hand in hand down to the port, they stopped for a coffee at a small bar. "How are you feeling?" asked Alessandra. "You haven't got tired of me yet?"

Nicholas smiled at the thought and gave her a kiss. "I can guarantee that will never happen. I can't tell you how full of joy I feel. Oh, and I forgot to tell you last night. When I heard about the new job opportunity, I also took the liberty of looking into archaeology courses in Athens. There is a good course in marine archaeology at the University of Athens that you can do full-time or even part-time. I remember you telling me on the ferry that that was what you had wanted to do."

They walked towards the end of the harbour wall where Spiros would be waiting. The morning visitors were starting to arrive at the port. Nicholas noticed that most of the fishermen had finished their work and had departed homewards, presumably to their beds. The morning ferry from Skala Kamirou had not yet arrived.

"Spiros, kalimera," Nicholas said, shaking his hand. "It is good to see you my friend."

"Nicholas it is good to see you. And of course Alessandra, you are as beautiful as ever. I am glad to see you back again."

Spiros was sporting a jaunty yellow baseball cap, together with a pair of old sunglasses. Alessandra hugged him and kissed him on the cheek. He blushed.

"Here, Spiros. I brought you something." Nicholas leaned over to look. She gave him a silver Saint Nicholas key ring, wrapped in tissue. "This will always keep you safe when you are out to sea." Spiros was overcome. He immediately attached the boat's ignition key to it.

Once loaded up they headed out into the bay. The sea was glasslike. There was hardly a breath of air. They were glad of the canvas canopy as the sun was already high in the cobalt sky. It was going to be another very hot day. Their mood was buoyant. Spiros grinned at Alessandra. "You have a very persistent boyfriend, you know."

"I am so lucky," she replied, squeezing Nicholas's hand.

"And Nicholas, you are also very lucky, with such a beautiful woman."

"Spiros, don't I know it?" Nicholas gave Alessandra a kiss in confirmation.

Cruising slowly out of the port, Spiros gradually increased the speed. Alessandra stood and chatted to Spiros at the controls in Greek and the speedboat changed direction as it cleared the harbour. It was now heading north, past the small beach and the point. Nicholas knew they were making for Alimia. He had passed the hump-backed island several times on the ferry to and from Halki. He had brought a guidebook with him and, sitting comfortably at the back of the boat, read more about the island. It was uninhabited, but had a long and interesting history. With several safe natural harbours these sheltered bays were used in ancient times as safe anchorage for the Rhodian fleet. At that time a Hellenistic fortress was built on the highest peak of the island to provide protection against pirate invasion. Recent excavations on the island had also uncovered Roman tombs, together with ancient walls and the foundation of an early Christian basilica.

Nicholas's reading was interrupted by a cry from Spiros. "Look," he shouted excitedly. He pointed to the bow, where they saw the flash of two dolphins as they played effortlessly around and under the boat. It felt as though the creatures were there to shepherd them to their destination. As a goodbye, they leapt from the water and disappeared in a sleek arc into the depths. Nicholas resumed his reading. The Knights of St John had conquered Alimia, as they had done Rhodes and Halki. During their occupation they had built a medieval castle on the site of the original fortress.

In more recent times a settlement was built along the largest bay on the island. The Italians used a deep, narrow bay as a submarine base during the Second World War. After the end of the war the settlement was progressively abandoned. Now the island was a protected area. Nicholas closed the guide and looked up. They were more than halfway across to the island. Alessandra brought Nicholas a bottle of cold water and gave him a long kiss. She smiled as she saw what Nicholas had been reading.

"You like to be prepared," she smiled.

"Always. You'll get used to it," he laughed.

"We are going to head around to the west, over there," she pointed. They passed the headland and followed the contours of the coast, past some small barren islands. Alimia was greener than Halki, but still rocky and boulder strewn. A covering of pine and laurel trees, along with smaller bushes, made the island seem less arid. This side of the island looked more hospitable than the other. Nicholas had only ever seen the more barren eastern side from the ferry. The boat passed a sheltered bay and what Nicholas took to be one of the ancient harbours. Up ahead he thought he could see some abandoned stone structures set against the hillside. They continued on, keeping to the shoreline. Alessandra had got up and was consulting Spiros. They talked away happily in Greek, with Spiros nodding his head and pointing ahead. After a while, they rounded a point and Nicholas saw that they were now entering a wide bay. They came alongside some buildings that fringed the waterfront. They passed a small, domed church, with a white stone wall providing protection from the sea. "That is the old Church of Agios Minas," Spiros said.

"I have asked Spiros to pull in over there," said Alessandra indicating a small wood and stone jetty. "We can have an early lunch in the shade of the trees here. You will find the whole area quite atmospheric." Spiros shut the engines down and the boat glided expertly alongside the jetty. The turquoise water was startlingly clear and Nicholas could see shoals of fish and the rocky seabed. Spiros moored the boat to a rusting iron stanchion and helped Alessandra out. They walked down the uneven jetty and onto a ramp that connected with a dirt pathway. Weeds and branches littered what was once the main path through the small settlement, lined with pine trees.

Spiros knew of a good place to have lunch. Nicholas and Alessandra followed, looking at the simple buildings of the settlement collapsing into the parched earth around them. They walked between a couple of long low stone buildings. Spiros said they were the army barracks, left behind by the Italians in the 1940s. He led them through a small square and they found an old stone bench set below the overhanging branches of two trees. In one corner, standing proudly and looking somewhat incongruous, was a tall palm tree guarding a white cottage. The heat was stifling and cicadas continued their serenade. Alessandra and Nicholas ate their lunch in the shade of the branches. Across the dusty square, a small white goat munched berries from a spindly juniper bush, eyeing the intruders with suspicion. They ate in silence on the bench, haunted by the ghosts of those who had been forced to say goodbye forever to their island and their homes. There was tranquility, too, in the still air; a sense also that the place was at rest now it had no need to protect its shores and inhabitants, nor its history and riches.

They sat for a while with their thoughts. Above them a bird of prey wheeled in the blue-white sky. Packing up, they thanked Spiros for showing them the old settlement. Nicholas could sense anticipation building in Alessandra. He squeezed her hand.

Back on the boat Spiros set a course across the wide bay, away from the abandoned village. The swell increased and the light breeze that had sprung up took the edge off the oppressive heat. Ahead, grey cliffs rose, waves breaking against jagged rocks at their feet. Spiros slowed the boat and pointed towards a large crack running down the cliff walls. Alessandra had taken out her map. She pointed ahead.

Nicholas looked around. They were now about fifty metres from the cliffs. The powerful diesel engines were working hard to keep the boat away from the sharp rocks guarding the cliff edge. The limestone cliffs here had little vegetation, what scrub there was sought protection in the crevices of the steep rock face. There was no obvious place to get ashore. Alessandra was peering over the side. The sea was clear and the underwater rock formations were clearly visible from the boat. She seemed to be trying to take a fix on a deep fissure in the cliff face, lining it up with a rock formation below the surface. Eventually, she shouted an order to Spiros and the anchor disappeared over the side. Spiros went to the stern, threw another anchor overboard and the craft settled, gently rocking from side to side. It was about thirty metres from the rocks.

"This is the place," said Alessandra. "Nicholas and I are going to do some exploring. We will probably need a couple of hours."

"No problem," Spiros replied. "Take your time. I will wait here for you. I might do some fishing. It seems a good place."

There appeared to be a large gap in the rock shelf. At this point the shelf was smooth, about three metres below the surface. It was about ten metres wide, allowing divers to swim between the rocks towards the cliff wall. Alessandra told Nicholas that this must have been near the spot where a shipwreck occurred thirteen hundred years ago. "This area of the Aegean was well known for the Meltemi. The ship was probably seeking shelter in the bay." She pointed towards the jagged rocks just protruding at the base of the cliff. "The ship was driven over to this side of the bay by the winds and foundered on these rocks. They are so sharp that the ship would have broken up rapidly."

She told Nicholas to follow her. They would only be diving in about four-and-a-half metres of water. He reminded her that she was a more proficient diver than he was. She reassured him that they would take their time. Between the rocks and the cliff face there was not much current and the visibility looked good.

Saying goodbye to Spiros they put on their flippers and jumped overboard. The cool of the sea was blissful. Alessandra held the underwater torch. "I need to show you this," she said. Putting on their masks and snorkels they swam across to the rocks, Nicholas following Alessandra. Nicholas saw a shoal of sardines and, as they neared the rock shelf, a sharp-toothed barracuda guarding the rocks. Limpets and sea anemone clung to the black rock face.

They passed through the passageway and Nicholas saw up ahead the base of the cliffs. They were swimming across to a gap in the rock face. As they reached it Nicholas saw that they were in a cavern, partially exposed above the waterline. An octopus slipped silently into the cave as they approached. The cavern was about ten metres wide, big enough to allow them to sit and rest for a while. Alessandra's eyes were glistening with excitement. They took off their masks and snorkels. "We are going down into the cave below," she said. "There's very little current and the visibility is good. It's ideal. The cave only goes in about six metres and it's about three metres deep. So, take your time with your breathing."

She disappeared under the water and into the cave. Nicholas followed her. It became darker the further in he went until Alessandra turned on her torch. The cavern was speckled with black sea urchins clinging to the sides. Nicholas saw rocks and a large object lying on the cavern floor, before he had to surface.

Alessandra appeared next to him a minute later. "Take your time to acclimatise," she said. It took him several attempts before he became comfortable in the dark cave. Eventually, he could reach the sea floor with ease. Alessandra waited for him to adjust, coming up with him in encouragement.

Gradually, Nicholas was able to spend more and more time in the cave. Alessandra had started to clear away the silt and sand from the objects on the bottom. As the silt settled, some large pieces of pottery and what looked like fragments of calcified wood were revealed. There were also white fragments of what looked like marble. In the corner lay pieces of amphorae, smashed in the wreck. He needed to come up for more air. Next time, Alessandra guided him down to what had looked like a large irregular rock lying on one side of the cave. It was about three metres in circumference. Initially, it had looked like part of the cave formation and was encrusted with molluscs and green algae. Suddenly, he realised what Alessandra had wanted him to see. It did not need any words.

The next time that Nicholas dived into the cave he saw Alessandra had wiped away some of the algae covering the rock. What he had mistaken for stone, he now saw was a dull brown metallic colour. He touched it. It felt like metal. Alessandra trained the torch on an area lower down and he saw the flash of white that he had seen in her photographs. In the torchlight he was startled to see that what he had taken to be white streaks were actually silver. He could make out part of a silver crown, half-buried in the sand. Precious metal spikes about a metre long protruded above the cave floor. Nicholas was shaken to see, trapped in the spikes, the age-whitened bones of sailors who had perished in the ancient shipwreck. Below the spikes he could make out some of the features of the face of the Colossus. The surface was deeply pitted, but he could discern a nose, and, as Alessandra trained the light above, he made out a huge eye, dark and sightless staring out of the cave towards the open ocean. Surrounding the enormous head were other fragments of the shipwreck that had found their last resting place. There were wooden pieces from a hull. In the corner of the cave lay skulls and jumbled bones, bleached white by the sea. He noticed how respectful of the site Alessandra was. Apart from cleaning small parts of the head of the statue for Nicholas's benefit, she made every effort to leave it undisturbed.

The silt was starting to cover the remains on the sea floor like a grey carpet. Nicholas took one last long look and Alessandra turned off her light. Together they left and scrambled up onto the ledge. They took off their masks and snorkels. Sitting on the shelf Nicholas found it hard to formulate any words. He suddenly felt cold despite the air temperature. Alessandra held his hand as they just sat there, looking out over the rocks and the bay.

"I understand exactly how you are feeling," she said softly. "It is very eerie. The image of that face has never left my mind. You understand now why I have brought you here. This will be the last time I ever visit this site. Pretty quickly it will be covered by the silt again. It is right that it remains where it finally came to rest undisturbed, hopefully for ever." Nicholas understood the privilege granted him by Alessandra. He felt humbled by what he had just seen. He could only nod and squeeze her hand. "I just hope that it remains where it is, undiscovered," she continued. "The island is protected and this place is its natural home. You understand that, don't you?" she asked, looking sideways at Nicholas.

Nicholas nodded. "I do. It belongs to Greece. This will only ever be between us," he promised. They sat silently, waist-deep in the water, as the small waves gently washed around them. The sun was starting its slow descent. Nicholas, rousing himself, kissed Alessandra. "Lets get back to the boat" he said gently, taking her hand. They slipped off the ledge and swam for the gap in the rocks, leaving the cave behind.

Spiros set down his fishing rod and helped them clamber aboard the boat. They took off their masks and fins. Alessandra's eyes were shining. They sat recovering in the sun. Nicholas and Alessandra looked at each other and smiled.

"I believe we could do with a drink," he said. He reached into the cool-box for the chilled bottle of wine and poured them all a glass. Looking out to sea they saw the afternoon ferry to Rhodes, leaving Halki behind it.

They sat quietly on the boat. Alessandra reached for Nicholas's hand. As they sat enjoying the cold wine the temperature seemed to drop. Above them the Greek flag had started to flutter. Spiros looked to the cliffs with a frown. A sudden northerly wind had sprung up, briefly ruffling Alessandra's still-damp hair. She brushed a strand away from her eyes then looked up. Nicholas followed her gaze. Out of a clear sky towering dark clouds gathered and swirled around the distant rugged peaks of Halki. "It's time to leave," they said to Spiros.

 Matador

For exclusive discounts on Matador titles,
sign up to our occasional newsletter at
troubador.co.uk/bookshop